I0451427

My Zombie Prince

Russ Crossley

53RD STREET PUBLISHING

Praise for RG Hart's "My Partner the Zombie" in the zombie romance anthology, Hungry For Your Love from St Martin's Press

"Filled with stories from the hilarious to the horrific ... there is something here to tug at the hearts (and brains) of any zombie lover. Highly recommended for anyone's collection." — Monsterlibrarian. com"

"Unrequited love is hard to accept, but Aloha Armstrong knows that she has only herself to blame.

"Being a Zombie is not an easy existence, but Matt Butcher is resigned to making it the best it can be.

Following up on a story of attempted murder puts Matt and Aloha in the path of a madman. They must ferret out the truth before more people are infected with the virus. Aloha wants the man caught, but she is devastated that she could very well lose Matt in the process. There is a great dynamic between Matt and Aloha, and it really makes for some fun reading." http://coffeetimeromance.com/BookReviews/hungryforyourlove.html — Coffee Time Romance — (4 cups)"

"A wonderfully twisted undertaking (pun intended), 'Hungry for Your Love' is a many-faceted feast of love, loss, sex, heartbreak, rotting flesh, and romance from beyond the grave." — Christopher Golden, bestselling author and editor of The New Dead"

Praise for Russ Crossley's Attack of the Lushites

"The first time I read Attack of the Lushites, I was shaking my head by page two and laughing out loud by page five. One of the wildest, craziest, and most entertaining novels I have had the pleasure to read." — Dean Wesley Smith, USA Today bestselling author

"I loved this book. Mr. Crossley has a wonderful way of combining both off-the-wall humor and exciting adventure. I enjoyed all the characters. I thought they were well developed, and even the worst if them had a little bit of saving grace hidden inside. I found myself becoming attached to them and wanting to learn more about them.

The Lushites were my favorites. When I read the description of their leader Jack, I couldn't help but think of Captain Jack Sparrow. Laughing, I could just picture him swaying across the deck.

My favorite character had to be Bud. His interaction with both The Brain and Jal were wonderful. I loved the fact that with all the individuals who held the power and ran the different worlds, it was Bud and Jal who ended up the heroes.

"Underneath all the humor and action ran a thread of warning. A thread
about excess and the consequences of that excess, whether it be overeating, drinking or smoking. All in all a very witty, over-the-top story with a moral warning.

Mr. Crossley's writing reminds me a great deal of the writings of Lionel Fenn, aka Charlie Grant, and like Mr. Fenn, left me smiling and wanting more." — ladybug, Amazon.com

My Zombie Prince

53rd Street Publishing
Copyright © 2013 Russ Crossley
ISBN 978-1-927621-28-8
cover art © Elena Schweitzer | Dreamstime.com
All rights reserved.
Published by:
53rd Street Publishing
Vancouver, B.C. Canada
www.53rdsteetpublishing.com

Cover design and interior layout by R. Edgewood
Book and cover design copyright 2014 by 53rd Street Publishing
This is a work of fiction. Names, characters, places and incidents are a product of the author's imagination. Any resemblance to a person or persons, living or dead, business establishments, events or locales is purely coincidental.

Dedication:
For Mom and Dad. Love you and miss you.

Acknowledgments:

Thank you to my editor, for her patience and expertise. I also wish to thank my wife, Rita for her continuing support, love, and encouragement. A special thanks to my friends at the Greater Vancouver Chapter of the RWA, and my friends at the Oregon Coast Writers Network, in particular Kris and Dean who believed even when I didn't. Cheers, gang.

Introduction

This is a new edition of the first full length book I sold. I decided to create a new cover and title because I thought the previous cover and title no longer work for the story I told. Of course this is all hindsight and may not work to gain new readers but I love the book a lot and think it deserves an audience.

The creation of this story began on the phrase, "Midget Shelby Bass is swept off her tiny feet by zombie, Sir Reginald Kincade." Now the use of the word midget may offend some people but I assure you I mean no offense. The story is about how people are sometimes rejected for who they are, what they believe, or what they look like be it a half-zombie or a midget or a clown. I am personally offended by intolerance and hopefully this story will highlight this important societal issue.

The story is a romance but it is told with humor so hopefully you, the readers, will enjoy the read as much as I enjoyed writing it.

Any errors or mistakes in details are entirely my own no one else.

While I did write acknowledgments I want to highlight my wife, Rita's contribution to this book. She is an awesome friend and my biggest fan. Her support is worth far more than money.

Russ Hart
Vancouver B.C.
2013

One

Shamus MacFee's steady gaze followed King Gustav as he paced back and forth on the thick Oriental rug, his hands behind his back.

His majesty looks more nervous than I've ever seen him.

Shamus suppressed a shiver as a knot of fear formed in his stomach. He shifted in the leather wing chair but the movement didn't ease his discomfort. *If something happens to Reggie, I'll never forgive myself.*

"Thank you for coming so soon, Agent MacFee." With a wave of one hand, the King indicated a man seated in the matching chair next to his. "Meet Mr. X."

Shamus studied the smug face of the dwarf. *Lad's the spitting image of Dr. Evil.* "Yes, Majesty. I had made an early connection at Heathrow. But who is this man?"

"It doesn't matter who I am, MacFee. All you have to know is I'm here to make an offer you can't refuse." The little man's tone and words pegged him as an American. His tiny face wore an arrogant smile that made Shamus' stomach muscles tighten even more, this time in anger. "And time is short for pleasantries."

I'd like ta wipe that smirk off your face, little man. It'll have ta wait until the time is right. At least you're right about time, what little you have left. Shamus' fingers gripped the handle of his teacup tighter. With a barely audible *tink*, a crack appeared on the side of the cup that only he seemed to notice.

1

The King stopped pacing from behind his desk, his swarthy complexion darkened. His eyes shifted to Mr. X, who now kicked his legs back and forth like a child. "Mr. X, this is Shamus MacFee. He's Chief of the Gnotborst Protection Service. GPS' responsibilities include the protection of members of the royal family."

The King's steady grey gaze shifted back to Shamus. MacFee saw the rare but familiar look of failure in the King's eyes. The King had screwed up but Shamus had as well.

Disowning his own son wore on the King. The dark shadows under his eyes told Shamus that his majesty hadn't been sleeping.

The King's guilt at losing Reggie had increased exponentially in the last several weeks. *Angry words bear bitter fruit.*

"Mr. X is going to help us with our problem, Shamus."

This is more serious than I had originally thought. The King has gone outside the royal security for the first time ever. A niggling at the back of his mind itched as he eyed Mr. X. The little man looks looked very familiar.

King Gustav sighed and laid his hands spread-eagled on the surface of the antique desk. "Is everything ready at the location?"

Shamus shifted his attention from the dwarf back to the King, "Yes, Majesty. I checked the location via satellite and everything appears ready."

The polished leather upholstery sighed as Shamus shifted in his chair again.

"Unfortunately, we have no way of knowing exactly where Reginald is in the house." His deadpan gaze fell on the dwarf. "But I'm sure Mr. X knows that already." *I'm sure we've met before. If only I could place where I've seen him.*

According to the report, filed by his field agent, Prince Reggie had left the University for a three-hour cruise with his two roommates. *As far as I can tell those two are lay-a-bouts and not worthy of the prince's friendship.*

After that, the three college seniors disappeared. There were strange reports about zombies but as a professional security agent, Shamus dismissed such nonsense. When he asked the King about it, the King had ignored his question saying only he had disowned Reggie.

Now, two months later, Mr. X appeared saying he had them in a house as part of some reality television show. *I swear, Mr. X, if anything happens ta the heir you're gonna pay.*

The King looked back to X. "Mr. X, our mutual problems will be solved by the end of next week."

"Wonderful news, Highness." His tiny black eyes wrinkled at the corners.

Sooo smug. I know that voice. But from where?

The image of the offices of the Zero Corporation flashed in front of his eyes. GPS had bugged the offices last year for treason against his country, Gnotborst, and he had helped with the Interpol joint surveillance operation. In the lobby on the wall hung a wall-sized portrait of the founder and CEO.

Realization dawned on him that the little man seated next to him was none other than Arnold Zero worldwide industrialist and racketeer. Zero managed to escape last time their paths crossed, when Shamus worked for MI6, but he would ensure Zero didn't escape this time.

Too bad, I can't arrest 'im now. Being in the United States has its limitations. And we might lose leads to finding Reggie if I move too soon. No heir to the throne gets lost on me watch.

Shamus brought the teacup to his lips and sipped the now tepid orange Pekoe. He fixed his gaze on the man who called himself Mr. X. The future of the kingdom was at stake. Failure wasn't an option.

"What do ya *really* want Zero?" blurted Shamus. He knew from the case files Zero never wanted to help others and only wanted something if it benefited him. How did Zero benefit from Reggie's case?

From the corner of his peripheral vision, he saw the King's tanned features whiten to ash-gray. *The King was worried. Why? What isn't he telling me about all of this?*

Zero didn't blink and continued to gaze directly at the King ignoring the Gnotborst security chief. "I'm leaving for Las Vegas immediately." Zero jumped off the chair to land flatfooted with a thud, then waddled toward the office door. *I so want to smack the little guy up the side of his head. Just once.*

"You will of course make sure nothing happens to Reggie?" The King rounded the desk and walked toward the office door.

Zero turned back to face the King, his features free of emotion, his eyes hard.

Shamus' hands balled into fists, and his arm muscles tightened beneath his suit jacket. *Down, boyo.* He crossed his legs to stop himself from leaping out of the chair and tackling the little man. *Now's not the time. First, save the prince, then deal with Zero.*

"Until I have the formula, I guarantee nothing." Zero's cold tone sent shivers down Shamus's spine.

If I know anything, it's Zero wants this formula because it's worth millions or maybe billions. Shamus looked at the King's slack features. His majesty's shoulders were slightly slumped. The normally strong, proud monarch had been cowed. *Tis my duty to restore the King's pride.*

I wonder why this formula is so important to him? Shamus' eyes narrowed as he considered the situation. During his past dealings with Zero, Shamus realized Zero didn't do anything unless there was a lot of money and power at stake. Kidnapping a prince, and threatening his life, meant the stakes were high, very high. *I wish I knew more.*

Shamus uncrossed his long legs then bolted from his chair toward the office door, throwing the cup hard into the fireplace shattering it.

Zero held up a very small hand like a crossing guard and stopped him.

Shamus hesitated.

Zero's gaze flitted to the King. "Call off your dog, Gustav or you'll never see the boy again."

Shamus looked to the King who gazed out the window at the garden for instructions. "Majesty?" He hoped he would have permission to tear Zero apart, but knew what was at stake, Reggie' life and maybe something more. *Zero's hunger for power is legendary.*

Without looking at them, the King waved a hand in Zero's direction and shook his head. "Let him go. We have no choice." His voice was barely above a whisper.

Zero chuckled and his cruel overly thin lips twisted into a grin. "Time Magazine says you are a wise ruler." He sneered. "Glad to see there's still some accuracy in journalism."

The King frowned, then walked back toward the desk and around to his chair. His broad shoulders drew back. He attained his full regal posture as he sat. "Zero, you have my promise that, if at the end of your reality game my son is safe, you'll get what you want. But only if Reggie's unharmed will I give it to you." His gaze narrowed as his dark brown brows pinched together as he glared at the little man poised at the door. "If he's not safe at the end, then there is nowhere you can hide."

The King glanced at Shamus, who gave the King a barely detectable nod. He would do anything for that man.

Zero shook his head and grunted as he turned his back on them and headed through the office door. "I don't respond to idle threats. King or no King, you know I hold all the aces. So don't be making threats you can't deliver on."

He raised himself onto the tips of his Nike's and reached for the doorknob, turned it with both hands, and then swung the door open. He turned to face them. "We'll not see each other again." He grinned. "It's a pleasure doing business with you both." He closed the door behind him with a dull *thump.*

Sure, for you. Not for me.

After what seemed like an eternity, the silence broken only by the crackling of the flames licking at the cedar in the fireplace, Shamus turned to face the king and cleared his throat. "Majesty. Arnold Zero is the worst kind of human, he deals in human trafficking, espionage, illegal arms trading, and a plethora of other nameless things." Shamus snorted in frustration. "If he has your son, then I fear the worst. I hope you don't trust him."

The King rolled the chair forward on its casters and rested his elbows on the desk, his fingers locked together. "Of course not."

The King sighed then leaned back into the chair. It creaked softly. "You'll go to Nevada and ensure my son is kept safe."

My personal honor is at stake. I lost Reggie when he left for the cursed island, and now I have to get him back or die trying. He's my responsibility.

"We could storm the movie studio," suggested Shamus.

The King shook his head. "No. It's too risky. The house is a maze. By the time we found Reggie, Zero would have him killed. In Zero's twisted world Reggie is a pawn to be used so he can gain control of the formula. He's a sick and demented little man. We can't cross him, but we can be prepared." King Gustav shook his head. "No, Shamus, the formula is the only option." Gustav's chin lowered to his chest.

There must be another way.

"Everyone else is expendable," the King's voice dropped to a whisper.

I know. "What about Wills, Highness?"

The King's eyes narrowed and his brow wrinkled. "Wills is in charge of the show. He did the impossible when he infiltrated Zero's organization. Having a double agent on the inside is the only hole card we have. You'll protect him as well."

"Understood, Highness." Shamus stood.

"And, Shamus." He stopped and looked back at King Gustav.

"Yes, Highness?"

The King's eyes drooped at the corners and his shoulders slumped. "You know I love Reggie don't you?"

"Yes, Highness."

With that, Shamus turned away and started for the door. His mouth formed a grim line. *I will not fail.*

Zero and I are in for one hell of a ride. May the best man win.

Two

Dust sucks.

Time was short. Another week, two at the outside, then they were going to be piles of dust. Unless he found a new source of radiation to halt the progress of the decay. *The guys and I are doomed. I'm fresh out of ideas. My medical tech prof used to call me the egghead.* His shoulders slumped. *Some egg head. I'm more like scrambled eggs.*

Reggie shook his head in disgust.

I can't do anything right. But there has to be a way to stop the decay. Science is losing to magic and I can't do anything about it. I've never been so frustrated.

Reggie studied the grey flesh on the back of his hand and sighed. He placed one hand over his eyes as the sunlight streaming in the window facing the street made him wince. *Another sunrise.*

It was early. *Too early.* But it seemed pointless to sleep anymore. Sure, the sunrise chased away the darkness. *But I hate mornings.* Daylight just didn't have the same attraction as it used to. All the sun did was dry you out. Being unable to go outside during the day meant he had to gaze on this sorry excuse for a two-bedroom apartment for hours on end. *It's like waiting for the bus to eternity. I wish I could sleep. Insomnia is the worst side affect of being a zombie.*

The seventies era furniture and forest green shag rug were a far cry from the pristine grounds, oriental silk rugs, and marble floors of the royal palace back home.

My Zombie Prince

Lord Reginald Kincade, Reggie to his friends--no longer crown prince and heir to the throne of the ancient Kingdom of Gnotborst on the Rhine--scooted forward on the cheap leatherette chair with the threadbare cushion.

This chair hurts my butt.

And the itch on my foot is driving me crazy.

Crazy zombie that's me.

He slumped back and crossed his arms over his chest.

If only I hadn't gone along with Matt's stupid idea. For a smart guy, I can be sooo dumb.

Consequences?

We don't need no stinking consequences. Yeah. Right.

A spring break trip with a couple of Phi Beta Kappa chums from Northwestern, what could be more innocent than that? A private island to party? *Sure. Why not?* Three girls. Three guys. *Best odds ever. Now we're zombies. Well, half zombies actually.*

Reggie stood then moved to the sagging brown sofa and plopped himself down with a heavy sigh. Lifting his feet off the floor, he plunked them down on the worn cushions. He scratched his itchy toes through his socks.

I'm shedding like a Golden Retriever in spring. He stood and walked over to the bookshelf and picked up the Northwestern physics department nuclear catalogue. He flipped to the home nuclear reactor section sighed and closed the catalogue. *It's hopeless.* Buying reactor time costs big cash. And they had exactly sixty-two cents to their name. *If only dear old Dad hadn't cut off my allowance after I became a zombie.*

There were only so many pop bottles to return. *If we don't disintegrate, we'll be living in a cardboard box by next month.*

Good thing their landlord Mr. Perkins was a fan of zombie movies or he'd have already kicked us out. Mr. Perkins believed it's bad luck to kick out zombies.

You never know when a good superstition is going to come in handy.

"Zombie's are people, too." Mr. Perkins tone sounded like a rehearsed line.

Reggie knew Mr. Perkins didn't really believe they'd eaten anyone's brain. Nor did their neighbors who barricaded their doors every night. Even the cops visited at least once a week to search for evidence that they'd eaten someone's brain.

As if? Disgusting! How many brains are missing? Is there a missing brain registry?

"Hey, Reg, ya want sum soup?" His thoughts were interrupted when Herbie Holmes entered the living room from the kitchen, a dirty brown apron tied around his waist.

Herbie, used to be a bull necked, dumb linebacker at Northwestern. Now his blue jeans had flesh falling out of the torn out holes and his red sleeveless t-shirt hung loosely off his torso. He was like the Hulk in reverse.

"What kind?" Reggie's attention shifted away from Herbie to concentrate on viciously scratching his foot through his sock.

"Tomato basil."

Ever since he turned zombie, Reggie could hear a pin drop and right now the hand wiping on apron sounded like sandpaper on a two-by-four.

"Yeah. Sure. Is Matt around?" Reggie changed the subject from food he could barely taste. He hated how Matt disappeared for a week at a time, never telling them where he was going or how long he would be gone. This was a risky neighborhood to be a living person, never mind a zombie.

The skin on Herbie's face shook like it would fall off as he wiped his hand across his cheek. A small tear opened on his left cheek. Herbie froze, his eyes wide with fear as his dark brown eyes pleaded with Reggie for help.

These boys have no real idea what's going to happen to them. Denial is a beautiful thing. We're not going to last much longer unless we find a cure. I just don't know how to tell them the end is near.

"Hold it!" Reggie leapt from the worn, scuffed-brown corduroy couch.

Grabbing the sewing kit off the end table, he raced to stand beside Herbie then with his needle and thread he closed the tear quickly with a few deft stitches. *I'm far too good at this body repair thing.*

He smiled reassuringly at Herbie and gently patted his shoulder. Herbie relaxed and smiled in kind at him, "Thank you."

His friends had also suffered prejudice at the hands of classmates, friends, and family. They, too, had become the dispossessed. It really hurt when your family gave up on you. He never thought his mother would ever stop loving him. Apparently, she must have agreed with his Dad. *I'm a worthless son.* Shaking off the memory of his dad telling him he was disowned, he focused on the repair job.

"Look Herbie, the radiation treatment isn't doing what I hoped it would. Don't worry I'll find something else. We'll be okay." *I may be good at sewing, but I'm a piss poor liar. I should be saying were doomed. I'm such a coward.*

Herbie lurched across the living room like Dr. Frankenstein's monster with his arms in front of him, what they called the zombie movie shuffle. He emitted a pitiful moan.

Reggie laughed and sighed. *It's seems like I haven't laughed in years. It feels good.*

Matt Butcher threw the front door open with a bang and yelped with unbridled joy.

Reggie jumped and then winced when his roommate walked into the living room. He sat down next to Herbie on the sofa.

Matt's wrinkled gray features were dotted with thread where Reggie had sewn closed tears. His face split with a wide, cheerful smile.

What the heck has gotten into him anyway?

The former blond captain of the football team with the too white, too perfect smile, and a dimple in his right cheek, was now a gray ghost of his former all-American-boy-next-door glory. Matt should be bedding the head cheerleader right now instead of sharing an apartment with a science geek and a meathead defensive lineman.

Reggie let his head fall back against the couch. He saw the spark of life still in Matt's eyes, his cocked eyebrow, and his silly grin. In a way, Matt's refusal to give into their situation helped Reggie not wallow in misery. He smiled back at his friend.

Matt was up to something. And considering how his last scheme of *party hardy* worked out, his track record wasn't exactly stellar.

Whatever Matt was cooking up, it wouldn't have a happy ending. Some days he would still get mad at Matt for suggesting they go to that island. But Reggie just couldn't stay mad at the guy. *I didn't have to agree to go with him did I?* He'd become a good friend, zombie or not. Like his prof used to say, *Common problems breed common understanding.*

"Hey, guys." Matt planted himself on the matching overstuffed chair across from the couch. The chair erupted with its usual puff of dust into the already stuffy air.

Reggie waved away the cloud of dust that enveloped him. "Okay, Matt, I'll bite. What's up?" Reggie's stomach twisted with anticipation.

Herbie stood and walked into the kitchen he soon returned with his hands hidden by bright florescent pink oven mitts dotted with banana-yellow flowers, carrying a baking sheet covered with warm chocolate chip cookies.

"I have cookies."

Reggie frowned. *Maybe I should get a hobby.* He shook his head forlornly. *Naw. What's the point? We're outta time.*

The remaining taste glands in Reggie's mouth watered profusely at the happy memory triggered by the cookie aroma. He recalled the joys of his childhood when his housekeeper, Olga, would bake sweet treats for him and his two sisters. At least for now, he could still enjoy the taste of food.

"Our problems are solved, boys." To punctuate his point, Matt slapped the arm of the chair.

Herbie jumped at the sound and the cookies bounced on the cookie sheet, but none fell off.

Whew! That's too close. We nearly lost a few.

The look of horror in Herbie's eyes at almost losing some of his precious cookies made Reggie want to laugh.

All the world's a stage.

Herbie sat on the couch after placing the tray on the coffee table.

Reggie looked back at Matt. "Spare us the drama, Matt. What's goin' on? But don't think we're going along on any wild scheme. Your last idea didn't turn out so hot did it?"

Matt's features pinched like he'd sucked on a lemon.

Reggie rolled his eyes. *The prince of drama strikes again.*

"On c'mon, guys you know we're running a little short on time," alleged Matt. "But this time I have a *really* cool idea."

Matt peeled dead skin off the tip of one index finger and dropped it to the worn forest green shag carpet as if to illustrate his point about time being short.

The dead skin drifted to the floor like a leaf in the fall.

"Do you have to do that? Skin is hell to get out of the rug," Herbie shouted.

Ignoring Herbie's domestic princess comment, Matt jumped to his feet. "Listen up, guys. I'm serious. We have an offer we can't refuse." A slow grin spread over his gray face. "It'll mean *a lot* of cash--and maybe a way for us to survive."

Well what do ya know? He's been listening after all. They trust me to get them out of this mess. I'm the science guy after all.

"How much are we talking about?" Reggie's curiosity got the better of him and he cringed.

Isn't this how Matt got us into this mess in the first place?

"No way, man," Reggie shook his head. "This homie doesn't cross your line. Not this time."

Matt ignored him. "More bucks than you can imagine." He rubbed his hands together like a spoiled kid with too many birthday presents.

Reggie snorted. "You have no idea *what* I can imagine."

"How about enough to get us a doctor that will ensure we don't disintegrate before our expiration date?"

"Huh? When's that?" Herbie scooted forward on the couch.

Reggie smirked. "It's an expression, big guy."

Herbie grunted as if he understood, but Reggie doubted the big ox understood much of what Matt was telling them. Being a great football tackle was more his forte. No matter what harebrained scheme Matt conjured up Herbie *always* went along. Regardless if it made sense or not. And now apparently so would Reggie.

Would it be better to steer around this wreck waiting to happen, but what if he's onto something? Reggie sighed inwardly. *What's the use?* In for a penny..."So what's the plan?"

"A reality show. We, my friends, are going to be Team Zombie on the Reality Show Network's newest hit show, Bachelorette: After the Prize!" Matt's eyebrows wiggled comically. "There'll be a girl. And we're the bait."

Three

Shelby Bass, in the rear seat of the 1960 Volkswagen Beetle, stewed over her predicament. *This sucks the big one.* Her two brothers, Clem and Buster, sat in the front bucket seats laughing at their usual bad jokes. *At least they're happy about this gig.*

Seven in the morning and the sun peeked over the low hills surrounding the valley as they headed to the television studio, located in the middle of Nevada's hot, dry foothills fifty miles outside Las Vegas.

Could we be any more remote?

The dry, hot, desert air was like an open oven door. *The next car we get better have air conditioning. Or least be built in the twenty-first century. It must be a hundred and fifty out here.* The oppressive heat added to Shelby's glum mood.

The entrance gate sagged on its hinges and behind them were the massive sound stages made from huge sheets of plywood and oak beams that held the walls up. The wood looked worn and old, the paint peeling, with roofing tiles missing, leaving a patchwork effect. *Great. The studio's a wreck. Dad is sooo gonna pay for signing us to this gig. Getting the diamond back isn't worth the humiliation of being on a reality show.*

If this is reality then I have a big butt, which I most certainly do not.

If the sound stage we're supposed to be on is in as bad shape as the front gate, then this dumps gonna fall on our heads. Shelby sighed. *Better dead than humiliated.*

But if we don't get the diamond back, I'll be a thief until the day I die.

Shelby fumed at her brothers laughing and joking in the front seats. *Morons.*

It's not fair. All I ever wanted to be is a surfer babe in Hawaii. Can that be too much to ask? Bachelorette: After the Prize? Get real. I'm not a prize steer.

Tumble weeds roamed down the dirt street and Cholla cacti took over the entrance to a dilapidated security shack.

Her brothers pointed at the studio and laughed like kids. They looked like two kids who'd just discovered a tree fort in their backyard. *Do boys ever grow up?*

Inside the security office stood a guard wearing a wrinkled, faded blue uniform shirt, holding a wooden clipboard in a withered hand. He shuffled out of the shack moving toward them in that shuffling seniors-retirement-home way.

The guy looked as old as the buildings. *He's probably original issue when the studio was built, which must've been in the nineteen-twenties.*

I hope they have indoor toilets.

The ancient guard tipped his peaked cap in greeting with one gnarled finger. "Hey there, young fella." His voice reminded Shelby of sand paper running over a blackboard.

The slightly dirty and aged white plastic nametag on his shirt read, PAUL.

Great, a prison guard

Only he looks more like a prisoner than a guard. A skinny old guy like him isn't gonna to keep me from going over the wall.

"Hey, yourself." Clem's tone sounded gratingly cheerful.

"Help ya with sumthin'?" The white-haired guard's sleepy gaze dropped to his clipboard.

"Paul, is it?" Clem always refers to people by their first name, something he learned in Marketing 101. *Too bad he never took Marketing 202 or he'd be a more successful thief. Clem is terrible at bartering with fences.*

Paul smiled and nodded. "Names?" He then tapped slowly on the clipboard with the tip of his pen.

Shelby stuck her head between the two front bucket seats and opened her mouth to speak. "We're--"

Clem beat her to it. "We're the Family Bass. You must've heard 'o us?"

A tight, *I'm-so-tolerant* smile crossed the old man's bloodless lips. "Bass...hmmm..." His gaze dropped to the clipboard held in his shaky hand while he thumbed the ballpoint pen's mechanism--*click, click, click*--in rapid succession.

Using the tip of the pen as a pointer, he ran down what must have been a list of names and nodded. "Yup. Got three Bass' here. Shelby, Clem, and Bobby."

Clem chuckled, turned to face Buster and winked.

Buster grunted and his brow wrinkled.

"Nope, my brother's name's Buster, as in Buster Keaton, who I'm sure you knew personally."

Paul chuckled and checked off the names. "Yeah. Good 'ol Buster K. Knew him well." He stepped back and pushed on the counter weight that made the gate go up. "Go ahead."

Clem rolled up the driver's window and stepped on the gas pedal. From the backseat, Shelby glanced at the side mirror as they drove onto the old movie lot and saw the cloud of brown dust left in their wake.

Turning her attention to the front, she caught a movement of bright color out of the corner of her eye. The human shape of the color made an old fear rip through her. Her stomach became queasy. She shook off the nausea. "Naw. Couldn't be." *It can't be a clown. Not here.*

Buster gazed over the back seat. "Somethin' wrong, sis?"

"Nope. Nuthin'. Thought I saw something. But it's impossible."

Clem stopped and parked the car outside the half moon-shaped sound stage.

The massive soundstage towered over the tiny car some forty feet into the blue desert sky. The wall blotted out half the visible horizon with its massive size casting a shadow over them. *How and why would a small television production company build such a monstrous structure?*

Movement out of the corner of her eye again. She swiveled her head sharply to the left. Her jaw dropped and her heart froze in her chest.

A pasty-faced clown had just exited through a door on the side of the otherwise featureless wall of the sound stage.

The world began to spin, the car seat seemed to swell like drifting on the sea. "I don't feel so good." Beads of sweat tickled down her forehead, then her cheeks. She shivered.

I must be coming down with something.

She collapsed onto the seat, and her eyes closed. Her brothers, the car, the studio, and the evil clown disappeared into a haze reminiscent of twilight. As her gaze dropped into darkness, the last thing she remembered hearing was Clem's frantic cry.

Four

A disembodied voice from very far away wedged its way into her mind. The voice gently called her name, "Shelby...Shelby...Shelby..."

Gradually, Shelby opened her heavy eyelids and blinked several times.

Where am I?

She licked her dry lips. *Yuck. Morning mouth.*

Shelby winced and the pain in her forehead increased as she tried to keep her eyes open.

Ohhhh. My head hurts.

Her blurred vision progressively cleared with each passing tick of the imaginary clock in her head until she made out the chipmunk-cheeked face of Clem as he hovered over her.

"What time is it?" Her voice rasped and her dry throat needed moisture.

'Ten minutes since you passed out." Clem hovered over her, kneeling on the back seat by her legs. His dark brown eyebrows were pinched with worry.

She smiled back at him. *How cute.*

The tension in his shoulders relaxed and his creased forehead receded as he sat back on his haunches. "Whew. I thought we weren't gonna be able to do the show."

"You preggers or sumthin?" Buster hung over the passenger seat--he must be on his knees--his round face eager as kid at Christmas. He smelled of bananas.

Shelby frowned. *Wrong. They don't care about me they only care about the show.*

Clem scowled at Buster.

Buster shrugged and flipped around in his seat.

Shelby held the side of her head with one hand, with the other she struggled to sit up. Dizziness overwhelmed her and a nauseous sensation deepened in the pit of her stomach.

"You okay, Sis?" Clem stroked her cheek gently with the back of his hand.

"Whh-ha-happened?" her words were slurred.

"You fainted," Buster snorted from the front seat.

Think it's funny, eh? Try being in my shoes.

Then the image of the clown's green and white stripped baggy suit and purple wig, it's face chalk white and it's lips bright red, flooded back. She shuddered and shook her head to loosen the mental cobwebs. Immediately, she regretted the movement as a sharp pain shot across her forehead. "Owww. Where are the clowns?"

She looked around, dreading she'd see the clown again. A heavy sigh escaped her lips and the knot in her stomach eased. *Nothing. No clowns.*

"The clown went back inside to join the others. His name's Happy." Clem's tone seemed a little subdued. "He seems like a nice--"

Shelby crossed her arms over her chest and glared her brother into silence.

Clem opened and closed his mouth like a trout.

There were clowns here. Right here. Right now. It's like they're following me from the circus. She shuddered.

"We have to leave," she shoved Clem's hands away. "I'm going home."

"We're *not* going anywhere." Buster pushed the car door open with both hands.

Her head had been resting against the VW bug's 'modified for circus use' rear passenger door.

"Besides, where are you gonna go?" His outstretched hand indicated the desert dotted with cacti and tumbleweeds spread out in every direction from the studio to the horizon. "Watch out for rattlers."

I hadn't thought of that. But if I stay here, the clowns are gonna get me. Fear of death by clown or fear of death by rattler. Some choice.

"No! I don't care!"

"Dad said--" Clem moved to stand beside Buster, both outside of her car door. They stood side by side, folding their arms in unison with brows pinched as they silently glared at her.

"No! I will *not* be around clowns. I will *not* work with clowns. I will *not* speak with clowns. You know--"

"Oh, c'mon, Shel, you can't still have that old phobia. Surely you're over it by now." Buster rolled his eyes.

"Don't mock me!" Shelby's anger seemed to boil up from her belly. She crossed her arms and stuck out her lower lip, trying to cover her fear with righteous anger. *I'm afraid. Don't they care at all about me? I thought they loved me?*

Buster glanced at Clem. In unison, they sighed and shook their heads in what must have been wonderment at her behavior.

"Listen, Shel," Clem's tone shifted to soft and soothing.

"We understand how you feel but Dad is depending on us to bring home the pork fat. You know all Mom ever wanted for Dad and us is happiness and a full life." Clem shrugged. "And besides, you wouldn't wanta let Mom's memory down, would ya?"

Shelby's scowled at her brothers. How could they forget Mom died because three clowns didn't hold the net to catch her? *And there is the diamond. We have to find the diamond. I have no choice.*

But I really hate clowns.

As with most clowns, they'd been out partying the night before. Shelby blamed those clowns for her mother's death. After the funeral, she vowed then and there never to forgive those baggy pants-wearing-painted-devils-from-hell ever.

Now I have to be in a reality show with clowns. Why would Dad do this to me? But making her father happy always seemed important, especially because of her mom's death. And of course, she still had to help Clem and Buster find the diamond they had lost, hidden somewhere on the set of the reality show.

How am I going to get through this stupid game? Dad said find the diamond, so I have to bail my brothers out. It's not like I lost it, but what's a girl to do when it's her family?

"C'mon, Shel. Let's go in." Clem grabbed her hand to help her out of the car, pulling hard and yanking her out of the backseat.

She stood in the warm breeze, her red hair blowing over her lips and mouth. She spat the hair out of her mouth.

The dust and the pungency of creosote trees filled her nostrils. Her mouth seemed to be jam packed with cotton balls. She ran her tongue over her dry lips. "I need water."

"Hey, lady, that's some tongue." A husky male voice spoke from behind her.

She assumed a clown must have snuck up behind her. *They are known for quietness. This one is far too quiet.* She whirled around ready to take on the dreaded creature and stopped awestruck when she saw the who--or what--behind the manly voice.

Eyes, like a glassy azure ocean on a summer day, held her frozen. Gray skin--wrinkled, peeled and ancient looking--framed young and vital eyes. Bedroom eyes, a bedroom voice to go with them and wavy black hair...

And what a bod. Cute zombie, for sure, but he looks too human for the undead. She shrugged. *I'm so glad he's not one of those horrible clowns.*

The average size young man-thing wore faded blue jeans, a tight blue t-shirt and cowboy boots. *Zombie cowboys? What will they think of next?*

"Huh...uh..." She couldn't believe all she could do was stammer.

The weird looking man chuckled at her embarrassment.

A warm flush crept up her neck and into her cheeks. *Don't laugh at me, mister. I really don't like being laughed at--ever since high school. She cringed at the memory of the humiliations she'd endured.*

The man-thing leaned forward and held out a hand. His grey skin appeared to be peeling as if from a bad sunburn. Gingerly, she placed her hand in his then pulled it away a little too quickly. *I wonder what's wrong with him that makes his skin peel?*

I don't know him but I also don't want to insult a guy I just met, then again he is a tallie. Like her father often warned her. *Never trust a person taller than you. Dad has way too many rules but in my experience too often tallies discriminate against little people like me.* Her entire family had dwarfism.

No one had inherited the average size gene. And being in the circus seemed to have jaded them all against tallies.

Except something about mister hunky was different. *He seems nice, if a little flirty.*

"Hi, my name's Reggie. My friends and I are Team Zombie. Are you the bachelorette?"

Zombies! Bachelorette? Oh yeah, the game show. She smiled and shrugged.

Five

"I SAID, WHAT TEAM ARE YOU THREE?"

Shelby looked at him uncomprehending. *The zombie speaks. Zombies, clowns and little people? I just entered the Twilight Zone.*

She shook her head. "Sorry. You startled me. I thought you were someone else."

"Who would that be?" His mottled brow wrinkled slightly and his blue-eyed gaze seemed genuinely concerned.

She shrugged, "Oh. It's not important."

Looking away to divert her attention to something other than hunky guy, she gazed up, up, up at the pitted aluminum wall of the giant sound stage. The immense size of the walls made her dizzy. She closed her eyes.

"Big. Isn't it?"

"Yeah. Big."

She opened her eyes and looked away from him to her left. The last thing she wanted to do was stare into his eyes. There were no signs of the clown she'd seen earlier. *Thank goodness.*

Looking back at Hunky, she saw a sloppy grin had crossed the zombie's strong-jawed features. *Aren't zombies supposed to be undead flesh-bots? They walk around like Frankenstein and they're mute or maybe they grunt, or something. This guy looks more like a regular guy than many of the so-called regular guys I've been on dates with. The guys I date, are either too tall, too short, too circusy, or have bad breath.* Shelby gazed at the zombie.

If anything Reggie's too handsome, with a sexy dimple in his cheek, wavy hair, a twinkle in his eye and he smells good.

He'll probably be eating my brain before this is over.

Shelby smiled and shook her head. "You're not a *real* zombie, are you? *Real* zombies--"

"Are stiff and mute and eat brains. Right?" Reggie finished her sentence.

She nodded, her mouth hung open. Realizing her mouth must look like a cavernous tunnel, she snapped it shut. *My foot tastes surprisingly good.*

Reggie shrugged and stuffed his hands into the pockets of his blue jeans. "Most of the ones I've seen are, sure. But, somehow, we escaped before the *Mambo*--that's a sort of Voodoo witch--had completed her spell. I'm certain she's really pissed about the whole thing. If we hadn't gotten away in time I'm sure we'd still be on that island as her slaves. I really can't explain it, I just live it."

Shelby stood still, wide-eyed as if in a trance as she listened intently to Reggie's story. *Guy's a zombie. Good looking but still a zombie. Too bad.*

"You okay?" Reggie touched her shoulder gently.

Shelby blinked and cleared her throat. She brushed his hand away from her shoulder. "I'd prefer if you didn't touch me." *He scares the crap outta me.* "I like my brain where it is." She offered a weak, apologetic smile. "Sorry. Horror movies are *not* my thing."

Reggie frowned then chuckled. "Me neither." He shook his head. "You have no idea how people treat those of us who are *different*."

Shelby nodded in agreement. *I've never considered fear of zombie's as prejudice before. Who woulda thought zombies had the same problems as little people?* "Yeah, I know what you mean."

She decided to change subject. Her brothers and the rest of Team Zombie had already gone ahead and left her alone with the charming zombie. "My brothers, Clem and Buster, over there." With a nod of her head, she indicated her brothers acting out their usual array of stupid circus jokes for the two other zombies. "We're Team Midget. And I'm Shelby."

"Well then, after you, Bachelorette Shelby." Reggie made a sweeping gesture with his arm as he bowed. He seemed a more gallant prince welcoming the princess to the castle than a brain eating freak.

Shelby couldn't help but grin at this act of chivalry, even though it annoyed her. *Does he really think I'm a pushover for such old-fashioned crap? It's not like I'm Snow White. To begin with she's a tallie. I'll be hurt. It's happened before, I have to protect myself.*

Prince Charming, the zombie? She shook her head. *This is all too weird.* A strong breeze swirled the fine golden sand about her feet as she approached the door her brothers and the other zombies had entered.

Reggie held the door open for her and she stepped inside.

You old smoothie.

Once inside, she froze in her tracks. The door *clunked* closed behind them. *Whoa! This sound stage is huge!* She took in a deep breath of the cool air.

The air conditioned warehouse-like space was a welcome change after the desert heat outside. Rows of lights ran the length of overhead walkways that spidered across the shadowy ceiling high above their heads.

The building had to be the size of three football fields and at least a hundred feet high. The air smelled of fresh cut wood.

In the distance stood a full size black, two-story house painted ink-black. *Amazing!* The black siding ran in overlapping layers up to multiple domes that comprised the roof. Along the edge of the domes were gilded railings. Two windows, reminiscent of eyes, bracketed the front door. It was like the house was watching them approach.

She whistled softly.

The curtained windows on the first floor glowed from the inside with an eerie yellow. A massive knocker in the shape of a gargoyle hung off the door. As Shelby studied the structure's odd architecture, she noticed the house looked familiar but she couldn't place where she'd seen it before. "I know this house."

"I've seen this house somewhere, too," Reggie agreed.

Without another word, Reggie walked away from her toward the house, maneuvering around the knot of cameras in front of the old house. She had to break into a run to keep up with him.

The vast space echoed his footsteps and her frantic running.

Typical tallie. They always forget we have shorter legs. She frowned. *It's sure weird there's no one around but us. Where are my brothers?* "Yeah," Shelby called after him huffing and puffing. She caught up with Reggie, and they stood side by side in front of the wood porch steps. Some of the boards were warped and the nail heads showed.

Buster then Clem walked out the black mansion's front door. Her eyes narrowed at her brothers.

They're making me nervous disappearing like that. She looked up at the dark house. *Creepy house,* she glanced at Reggie, *creepy zombies, now my brothers act creepy.*

Thick spider webs hung off the posts that held up the front porch. Shelby wasn't afraid of spiders, but she didn't want to run into the spider that made those webs. *He must be a big-un.*

Of course, this wasn't the *real* TV house, it just looked like the *real* TV house. *I wonder how this house fits into the reality show?*

"You wanta go inside?" Reggie moved toward the three steps that led to the porch.

She crossed her arms over her chest.

"Is something wrong?" Reggie gazed at her with a concerned frown wrinkling his forehead.

"Oh, no of course not."

She shook her head in disgust. *A reality show in an old, broken down house?* Her fists balled at her sides. *The things I do for my family.*

Buster stomped down the creaky steps with a wide smile and a yelp of joy as eager as a kid eating Christmas pudding.

"Hey, Shel," Clem walked down the steps behind Buster. "Isn't the house great? It's the old Addams Family house!" Clem gave a backward wave toward the house behind him.

Recognition set in. She recalled seeing this house on the oldie-moldy cable comedy channel that Clem and Buster watched *all* the time. She'd always assumed that house was a model, not a real house. Well, a *Hollywood-real* house anyway.

"Cool, huh?" Clem stopped and stood on her right side and Buster on her left. They were like brotherly bookends.

Shelby glanced at Buster. "You're enjoying this too?" He nodded, his eyes sweeping the house. *At least they're having fun.*

Reggie walked around and stood behind her and her two brothers.

She resented them when they acted like they were responsible for her safety. *I may be a girl, but I can take care of myself--I'm not a child.*

"Who's your friend?" Buster's eyes still focused on studying the twisted old house.

"Some zombie guy." No need to give her brothers ammunition.

"He looks a little like a tallie to me," Buster grunted.

"Yeah." Shelby shrugged.

Even though he was dreamy, there was no way a relationship with a tallie was in the cards for her. The vertically challenged had to stay with their own kind. No tallie would ever accept a little person anyway. *He hadn't done anything but be nice to me so far and make me drool over his wonderful voice, but no way am I gonna date the undead. Dating the nearly dead was bad enough.* She shook off invisible cobwebs. *Yuk!* She stifled a giggle.

"Hi," Reggie introduced himself. "My name's Reggie Kincade."

Her brothers turned toward him. "Buster and Clem Bass, and our sister Shelby. We're the world famous circus act, The Family Bass, though apparently for the purposes of the Big Art Films contract our father signed, we've been re-titled Team Midget--"

"That is *soooo* offensive." Shelby couldn't believe their father would agree to this. *Midgets? What a load of crap.* "We're little people, not midgets." Shelby harrumphed. "Midgets makes us sound like toys. We're human beings who deserve respect."

Reggie nodded, his expression serious. "We face the same discrimination, kind of."

"Where're your buddies?" Shelby looked around the studio. No one but the four of them stood outside the house. It was as if the world had suddenly ended. They were alone--accompanied only by the whirr of air conditioners and the shush of ropes moving in the warm air as hum of the air conditioner started.

"I think they're over at the office with Mr. Wills." Reggie pointed toward a squat single room office to the left of the Adam's house. A piece of skin fell from his hand and she shivered. *Disgusting. Guy's peeling like a banana.*

Reggie's grey face paled, and he slapped his other hand over the spot where the skin had fallen off.

"And where's the other team?" Buster's brow pinched as he scanned the sound stage.

Clem climbed the stairs and stepped onto the porch.

Buster walked up the steps to join Clem on the porch.

Shelby glanced at her watch. *Three o'clock. Where's Wills? He said to meet him here at three.*

When are we going get this show on the road? Waiting here is like waiting for a bus that never comes.

"They're clowns aren't they?" Shelby said as if it were obvious.

Reggie plunged his hands into his pockets and rocked back and forth on the balls of his feet and whistled off key.

Shelby's gaze flitted from her watch to glare at the zombie and knew her look said do-you-have-to-do-that?

He smiled, and stopped whistling. "Sorry." He shrugged.

Reggie followed Shelby after several seconds when she climbed the stairs to stand on the porch. *I hope he doesn't follow me. I don't like being studied. It makes me feel like an amoeba under a microscope. I wonder if he thinks my butt is too big? Or worse, too small.*

Boy, are his eyes ever blue. Who woulda thought a zombie would have such nice eyes? She snorted.

"Do you have coulrophobia?" Reggie crossed his arms and leaned against the railing that surrounded the porch and smiled gently. "Clowns--the fear of clowns--coulrophobia."

How does he know? Her eyes narrowed. "Yeah, those escapees from a horror flick--"

"I understand." Reggie nodded. "I used to have venustraphobia myself."

Shelby frowned. *The nerve--he cut me off. If he's trying to be friends, he's failing so far.* "What's that?"

"The fear of beautiful women." His mouth curled in a lopsided grin.

Shelby squirmed under his gaze. *Surely, he doesn't think I'm beautiful?* Her cheeks grew warm.

"Yeah, me too," chimed in Buster. Clem covered his mouth in a failed attempt to stifle a giggle.

"But I got better." Reggie chuckled.

Shelby's face grew warm and her legs shook. *No way is he gonna get to me.* She laughed uneasily to cover her discomfort. Like previous men in her life Reggie was slick with the words. *A little too slick.* Shelby had been let down by too many operators who just wanted a quick slap and tickle with a little woman. She wanted more than words, she wanted unconditional love. Actions spoke louder than a few well chosen words.

"Well, don't you worry, Shelby. I'm sure between myself and your brothers we'll be able to protect you from the clowns." His frown darkened his already gray complexion.

Shelby's eyes narrowed. *He's mocking me.* But his eyes. So sincere and *sooo* sexy. *People who cut me off are automatically on my double secret probation plan.*

After her first instinct-- fainting--her second instinct was to run when she saw a clown. Somehow, she would have to bury her fear and deal with the clowns since the contract tied her hands. *I will grit my teeth and get the job done. No clowns are gonna stop me.*

I'm going to be a blond surfer babe in Hawaii if it kills me.

Six

SHELBY ASKED A PASSING WORKMAN carrying an aluminum ladder under his arm if he knew where Mr. Wills was. He didn't. *Great. Wait in line. Wait here. Wait. The sooner we get this over with the sooner we can get the diamond, get out of here, and maybe avoid those clowns.*

Her brothers and Reggie's zombie friends seem to have bonded as soon as they showed up. They began by comparing lists of favorite movies and then moved on to a spirited game of I-spy-with-my-little-eye.

A half an hour after she had entered the sound stage, Wills--another little person and the show's producer--arrived accompanied by a tallie woman. Now this guy looked all slick in his white suit, ice-blue tie, and white shoes in a pimpy kinda way.

The blond woman on his arm wore black framed glasses on the end of her skinny nose. Her face was pinched as if she'd sucked on a lemon, a manila folder gripped tightly in her pale skeletal hands.

Wills didn't bother to apologize for making them wait but immediately began explaining the rules for the show. Shelby interrupted him.

"When do we get paid?" Shelby had never seen the payment in the contract. She rolled her eyes. *If I'm paid enough dough-ray-me, it just might be worth doing the show and of course we have to find the diamond but no one has to know that little detail but me and my brothers.*

A tolerant smile played across his thin lips. "So. Any *other* questions?"

Shelby watched as Wills paced back and forth while he spoke, ignoring her question about payment.

Wills grinned. "None? Good. Chipper will take care of your luggage." Wills black eyes shifted to gaze over the contestants' heads.

Shelby swiveled in her seat in order to follow his line of sight. A massive bald man, the size and shape of three Hulk Hogan's, appeared from the shadow of the right side of the house. His muscular arms hung down his sides, his chest was as wide as her and her three brothers together.

He was the Hulkster's twin, complete with shoulder length straw-blond hair and a droopy mustache. He dropped his heavily muscled arms to his sides, nodded to Wills, then turned and headed for the front door.

"Chipper will have your luggage in your rooms within the hour." He handed out numbered keys with paper tags with their names on them. Wills gave her one of his patented slippery grins as he handed her the key.

"As promised in your contracts," he pulled out three plain white envelopes from an inner pocket of his white seventies era leisure suit. He passed them to his dour tallie assistant. "Stephanie will pass these out. I think you'll find the amounts are as agreed in your contracts."

Stephanie handed an envelope to Reggie, her, and to the clown wearing green and white stripped baggy suit and purple wig. Clem eyed her, his brow wrinkled. "Sorry, bro I'm the oldest."

Shelby folded the envelope in half then stuffed it into a front pocket of her blue jeans.

Reggie did the same.

Buster smiled at her.

Clem held up his hands and shrugged.

But the one trait she shared with the clowns--they didn't trust anyone, and neither did she.

Wills rocked backed on his heels and smiled. "Now, I'd like to introduce my game master who will be guiding you through the game, Madame Toulest."

The door to the dark mansion opened, accompanied by the squeal of metal on metal.

Shelby winced.

Clem, Buster and Reggie stuck their fingers in their ears.

A woman who bore more than a striking resemblance to Morticia Addams slithered--yes, *slithered*--through the open door with the large gargoyle-shaped knocker.

Like her television sitcom look-a-like, her black, too-tight dress around her narrow hips, and her long legs forced her to shuffle rather than walk. Trailing curls of shiny, oil-black hair ran down her back to cover her bottom. Pancake flour colored skin, blood-red lips, and dark brooding eyes completed the look of the mystery she obviously hoped to convey--and succeeded.

Her somber, unflinching brown-eyed gaze paused on each contestant's face in turn.

The tallest tallie woman she had ever seen--*She must be at least a six footer*--the woman slithered to stand next to her boss. The odd woman towered over the three foot tall Wills like she was the whacked out wife of Jack's beanstalk giant.

The assistant, Stephanie disappeared into the shadows around the side the house.

The faux Morticia folded her thin arms across the swell of her bosom. Her long scarlet fingernails were at least eight inches long and curled inward at the tips. *Whoa! I wonder how she eats with those things?*

The scent of mint and fresh dirt filled the air wafting from Morticia. Wrinkling her nose, she decided this tallie woman must have come directly from the grave. *Or that's one weird perfume this broad is wearing.*

"Duhlings, Madame Toulest is pleased to be the master of ceremonies for the show."

The woman sounded like Natasha, of the Boris and Natasha in the Rocky and Bullwinkle cartoons. Shelby wondered if *moose* and *squirrel* could be far behind. *Girl, you watch more of that retro TV than you're willing to admit.*

Madame Toulest's brow arched as her dark eyes studied them. *She doesn't look pleased to be the hostess of a reality game show for a Z grade cable network.*

What a freakin' surprise.

But, as Shelby knew, sometimes in show business a paying gig's a gig you take when you have bills and need to eat. *I may not know how she eats with those fingernails but she must eat.*

Shelby glanced at Reggie. *I wonder what zombie's eat, if it's not brains?*

When she found the diamond, the money it would bring would change everything for the family Bass. *No more circus and Hawaii here I come.*

"Mr. Wills wishes me to explain the rules." Madame Toulest floated on her tentacle dress to stand across the porch from the assembled teams.

Buster and Clem looked at each other, sniffed under their arm pits, shrugged and sat crossed legged on the porch. Shelby stifled a laugh.

"Hey. Do I know you?" Reggie walked closer to their hostess, rubbing his chin with his finger like he had an itch, which he probably did.

The sooner they got going, the sooner they would be finished with this stupid game. *And, the sooner I'll be free of my obligation to my father. The surf's up somewhere in the world, big guy, and times a wastin'.*

Reggie winked at her, his indigo eyes twinkling. *Hmmm. Reggie's up to something.*

"Didn't you used to be the hostess of Friday Night Horrors, Channel 28 in Pokipsie?" Reggie pushed his hand through his hair, but stopped quickly. "You were called Mistress of the Night back then."

Madame Toulest's pasty face went slack and her hourglass shape trembled.

Out of the corner of her eye, Shelby saw Wills' coal black eyes narrow, and his tiny ears turned red. "Madame Toulest is the *best* host available for our program. I'll expect everyone…" Wills looked directly at Reggie, "to show her the proper respect. Is this understood?"

Everyone nodded, including Reggie, though his lips curled up in a mischievous grin.

Shelby rolled her eyes. *Doesn't he know anything about show business? Sure she may have been a late night horror movie hostess but work is work, dude.*

Madame Toulest smoothed the front of her black dress. Her fire engine red nails scrapped along the fabric. She cleared her throat, "Duhlings, the rules are simple, you must stay in this house for a full week. The team who has the most members left at the end of five days, and whoever has secured the prize within that time, will be declared the winner."

Toulest ignored Reggie's question.

Shelby shifted her gaze to the zombie. *I'm gonna find out what he knows about her. It might be a clue to finding the diamond.*

"Why is this show called Bachelorette: After the Prize?" Happy the horrible clown with black lips, that matched its black curly wig, asked in a clipped tone.

A twinkle appeared in Madame Toulest's brown eyes. "Ah, apparently, Mr. Wills hasn't told you," she paused for effect, "there is a prize at stake that many people would kill for. Consider the check each team has received as a down payment toward the much larger prize that will be awarded to the winner."

All gazes shifted to Shelby.

"And the bachelorette is *not* the prize," added Toulest.

"What? But then why is this show called Bachelorette: After the Prize?" blurted Shelby.

"Marketing," replied Toulest smugly.

"What? I don't get it." Reggie frowned.

"I do," interrupted Herbie, "I took marketing in college. If you want to capture the eighteen to thirty-five demographic, you have to cater to them." Herbie shrugged. "Sex sells."

Shelby glared at her brother. "I am *not* a sex object."

"And what might the prize be if it's not Shelby? Exactly?" Reggie crossed his arms over his chest, frowned as his brows pinched together.

Reggie cast a questioning look at Matt.

Matt shrugged, he obviously knew nothing. *Hmmm. That's interesting. I'll ask him about that too.*

"Eternal life is the prize." Wills rocked back and forth on his heels.

Seven

STUNNED SILENCE. Shelby looked to her right then to her left. The faces of the zombies, clowns and her brothers gaped at her. No one spoke. It was as if everyone were suddenly frozen in ice. *Attack of the ice cube men? Hmmm...interesting concept in the middle of a desert.*

Shelby snorted to break the spell. First, they all blinked, then they began animated conversations milling about the porch into a confusion of weirdness. Zombies with zombies, clowns with clowns, zombies with clowns, Herbie slapping a clown on its knee, and Clem looking to her for a group hug. *As if?*

Two of the clowns broke away to move to one end of the porch and began whispering to each other. *A clown plot is in the works.*

Matt and Herbie high fived each other. *When you're the undead, the eternal life bit sounds pretty good.* She could hear Reggie's shallow breathing and her brothers had the what-the...look on their faces.

Shelby jumped in her seat when a fan somewhere high above the studio floor clicked on and whirred with a rattle and a bang.

This is too good to be true. Eternal life? *Who does he think he's kidding?*

A husky laugh from behind her made her turn her head to see Reggie's hand on his stomach, his face split into a wide grin.

"What? Eternal life. Are you *joking*?" He laughed and doubled over.

Wills frowned. "No. Let me assure you this is no joke. The show's benefactor is offering the winning team eternal life."

"Benefactor? Who might that be?" Shelby glanced at Reggie.

He opened his mouth to speak, but she held an index finger to her lips to silence him. She smiled warmly. "Let me handle the details, big guy."

Reggie nodded at her with a wink. *Hmmm...team Shelby and Reggie. That has definite possibilities.* She glanced at her brothers who were shadow boxing with two clowns. *I love 'em, but teaming with a zombie's gotta be better than being on a team with my bros.*

Reggie seems cool. For sure, us as a team gig is a better idea than this lameo reality show's idea. Team Midget? Get real. And eternal life? Fairy tale junk. Besides he's tall. I may need a tall guy to reach the top shelves in the cupboards if the diamond is hidden there.

"My benefactor," Wills continued ignoring her question, "expects you all to try your best to stay for the full week--"

I hate being ignored. Just once, I'd like a straight answer from this guy.

"Hey, I don't get it," the clown with the black wig pointed at Wills. "You and the old bag keep telling us we have to stay in the house for a week. This won't be so tough. Sure the house could use a little paint, but it doesn't look so bad."

Wills' features softened into his all too familiar slime-creature persona. "I'm so glad you asked. You see the house is filled with surprises."

"Oh, com'on!" Shelby chuckled and snorted. "You're not going to tell us this place is filled with ghosts or dead people. Who believes in such stuff?"

The grin on Wills' face stayed frozen on his pudgy cheeks giving him a mannequin-like appearance. His black eyes scanned the group.

He's creeping me out.

"How do you explain Team Zombie? If there's no such things as ghosts, then how could there be zombies?" Wills mouth twisted into a thin line and his expression smug.

When he's right, he's right. Or I'm wrong.

"All right, Mr. Wills if there are such things as ghosts--and I'm not saying that I or anyone else here believes you--if there are ghosts then how do you know they're in that house? This house is only a Hollywood façade not a *real* house. And, what does any of this have to do with the show?"

Reggie crossed his arms over his chest and a raised his brow.

Wills shook his head and now his thin lips curled at the corners into a smirk. "No, Reggie that's where you're wrong. It's very real." He looked over his shoulder at Toulest who watched impassively from across the porch. "You see my benefactor spared no expense to bring in the Addams house for this show."

Shelby's mouth lost all of its moisture. *The house is real? What have we gotten into? I'm feeling a little creeped out by this. Zombies, clowns and midgets in the Addams Family house?*

"Don't forget you all must live in the house with the other two teams. The team who finds the prize must deliver it to me before midnight Friday the 13th --which is next Friday--one week from today. Other than that, there are no rules." Madame Toulest folded her arms.

Reggie walked to the opposite end of the porch then spun round to face Wills and Toulest. "Don't these reality shows involve voting? You know, the audience, or the judges, or the contestants vote team members off on each episode. At least that's what I've seen."

Wills shook his head. "Nope. This is it. No one will be voted off. You all just have to play along, and the winning team must bring me the prize."

Shelby walked to stand in front of Wills. "Where will you be? So we can bring you the prize when we find it."

Wills grinned. "Around."

"So when do we begin?" Happy looked, well positively happy.

She shuddered from having to look at the clown. *A week with three of them, how will I survive an encounter of the clown kind? Her stomach tightened as fear formed a knot deep inside her.*

"In ten minutes, we will commence a live broadcast. This will be the introductory episode." Madame Toulest's gaunt features formed a twisted smile.

Shelby cringed and wanted to find the nearest exit. *Yuk. She's sooo weird. She smiles like the undead.* Shelby glanced uneasily at Reggie's handsome features. *Then again, maybe that's not the best description.*

"You will all join me inside the house in the living room where I will introduce each member of the three teams to the audience. The show will be broadcasted twenty-four hours a day for the full week. There are multiple hidden cameras in every room."

Toulest walked toward the front door. "Mr. Wills will padlock the door behind us once he leaves. He will not unlock the door until next Friday at midnight."

Reggie took a step to follow Toulest inside the house. "What if we find the prize before Friday?"

The Morticia clone stopped and looked over her shoulder. A small smile played across her black lips. "You won't, so don't worry about it."

A knot of worry tightened in Shelby's stomach. *I'm gonna find the diamond and get out of here before Friday. Surely, they can't lock all the windows and doors, there has to a way to escape? I have to find it if I'm gonna get away with the diamond.*

If one of the others find the diamond before we do, then I'll have to go back to the circus and I'll never be a surfer babe.

Shelby followed behind her brothers as they followed the clowns then the zombies into the front door of the mysterious house..

She glanced at Reggie who had moved to stand next to Clem. *None of this seems to have fazed him. He's as cool as a glass of ice tea.*

Reggie walked to stand beside her then whispered, "You okay?"

She nodded.

The twin doors thumped closed behind them. Shelby sighed. *Locked doors are sooo not my thing. The stuff I have to do to get to Hawaii.*

~ * ~

Shelby stood beside a navy blue chair, ran a finger across the arm and it came away coated with thick dust. She stifled a sneeze.

Everything from the leather covered wing chairs, to the antique oak sideboard, and piano had a thick layer of gray dust. The color reminded her of zombie skin. *Ugh.*

Low lighting and a sickly yellow glow from the lamps set on dark stained end tables in the four corners of the room added to the gloom.

When the dust-covered piano played unexpectedly, Shelby jumped. Reggie took her hand in his.

No one sat at the piano playing. The music was a pretty decent rendition of *The Girl With The Strawberry Curls.*

Weird. Cool, but weird.

Madame Toulest appeared unfazed by the haunted piano playing itself as she slithered across the room in her tentacle dress.

Toulest was perched on the edge of a very scarred high-backed, and badly scratched rosewood chair, covered with paisley cushions. The chair creaked under its host's weight. She rested her bony elbows on the narrow arms of the chair. The woman looked like royalty examining her miserable subjects.

Reggie smiled with an amused glint in his eye. *He must be thinking how her brain matter is gonna taste after it's grilled on the barbecue.* She stared at her hand still in his. *Or maybe I'm dinner.* With a tight grin at the zombie, she pulled her hand out of his.

The three disgusting clowns were in a huddle, their arms around each other's shoulders.

Shelby sidestepped away from Reggie's side closer to Buster and shuddered. Clowns could be so clown-like.

Shelby's brothers were playing rock, paper, scissors. And they were both losing. She considered asking them what they were playing for but dismissed the idea. She smiled to herself. *I must have been adopted.* She snorted. They'd make better use of their time coming up with a plan to find the diamond they'd lost.

Three overstuffed navy blue couches formed a U-shape, with Madame Toulest's chair resting at the open end. The couches had ample room for each team. The Morticia-like woman waved her arm motioning for them to sit.

The clowns high fived each other then sat together on one of the couches.

Shelby tapped Clem on his shoulder and nodded to one of the still vacant couches facing Toulest. No way did she want to face the clowns the whole time.

One of the taller clowns--wearing a green and white stripped baggy suit, and a purple wig, it's face chalk white and it's lips bright red--smiled at her. Shelby swallowed hard and her legs trembled.

A tallie man wearing a black tuxedo and white shirt with a black bow tie entered the living room from the door to Toulest's right. His hair, the color of carrots, framed freckled skin so pale it almost glowed in the dark.

Her eyes narrowed. *Who is this guy? And where's Wills?* He didn't follow everyone into the house.

Something's fishy in Bermuda, Shel. She peered into the shadows above them. *Shouldn't there be a lot of studio lights?*

"Welcome to the first episode of *Bachelorette: After the Prize*, an original series from the Reality Network." *What is she doing? Is the show starting?* Toulest sat regally on the chair, her hands now folded in her lap. Her dark eyes focused on a wall with nothing on it. No pictures, no mirror and certainly no camera. *I've heard of an air guitar, sure, but never an air-camera.*

"To kick things off we thought our audience would enjoy meeting our cast: to my left we have Team Clown--Happy, Sparkles and Moist. These three will have you in stitches for the next week. Stay tuned to see their antics."

"Next to them, on their right is Team Zombie--Reggie, Herbie, and Matt. These three are will scare the pants off everyone for the next week. So stay tuned to see how many brains they eat!"

Shelby looked at Reggie.

Clem leaned closer, "Shel, do they really eat brains?" His whisper barely loud enough for her to hear.

"No. Of course not. We're on TV." *At least I hope not. Brain-eating zombies don't make good friends.*

"Yeah, right. I forgot."

She looked at Clem. *Is he joking?*

He faced straight ahead, his features not registering any hint of a grin. He glanced at her and nodded then turned his attention back to Toulest.

Shelby shook her head. *Nope. He's serious. Oh, brother.*

Toulest continued. "And finally we have Team Midget--Clem, Buster, and Shelby. They may be small, but there will be fireworks with this group."

Clem and Buster smiled and waved enthusiastically.

Shelby scowled and crossed her arms.

If she calls me a midget one more time...

Shelby stuck her tongue out at Madame Toulest. The smile on their hostess' face sagged briefly before she replaced it with a cold, thin lipped line.

Ha. Shelby smiled to herself. *Got ya. Take that, creepy old woman.*

Toulest finished explaining the rules of the show to the audience, same as she explained them to the contestants, then stood. Shelby and the others stood, too. *Let's do the wave.*

"If you would follow me, I'll guide you through the house where mayhem is about to take place." The Morticia clone stood and walked out of the living room and into the foyer. She slithered past Shelby, Clem and Buster forcing them to scatter or trip over her tentacles. *Hey! Watch it. We're standing here.*

Clem's face flushed a dark red, and his brow twisted in what she assumed to be anger. He smoothed his oil-black hair with one hand and patted his slight paunch.

"What the heck is the matter with you, Shel?" Buster, who had hair as red as Shelby's, and skin the color of alabaster, wore a scowl as deep as his brother. *The scowl twins strike again.*

"You're gonna get us fired. We're not gonna get paid and we need to get the--"

Clem elbowed Buster in the gut.

He grunted and bent over at the waist.

"Dad's gonna kill us." Buster's loud voice echoed in the quiet room.

Shelby knew what her brothers were going to say. They needed to find that stupid diamond.

"Stop!" Shelby shouted. Besides, they lost the stupid thing--she didn't.

"Do you really think this so-called 'gift of eternal life' is for real?"

"Clem, are you serious? This is Hollywood, for God's sake. *Nothing* is real." Shelby spoke between gritted teeth. *Don't they get it? The show's all fake. All we need is the diamond and we're done.* She looked around to see the others staring at them. *We just can't tell the whole world, yeah, we're thieves.* "You two watch *wa-a-ay* too much TV."

"Excuse me, Miss?"

Shelby turned away from Clem and Buster toward the sound of a feminine voice from behind her.

The clown Toulest had identified earlier as Moist--an odd name for sure--had moved off the couch and now stood looking down at her.

Shelby swallowed hard. Like a boxer who heard the bell sound, she tensed and her legs trembled. *Fight or flight?* Mentally she flipped a coin. It landed on fight.

"Listen, Clown. If you ever say anything to me ever again..." Shelby let the unspoken threat hang, but in reality her words were choked by the fear welled from the pit of her stomach.

"Take a chill pill," whispered Moist under her breath, her hands held up in mock surrender.

Shelby glared at the clown hoping she would just walk away.

The clown shook her head, her eyes turned down at the corners, then walked away.

"Hey, clown!" Buster eyed Moist, one eyebrow arched. "Why are you called Moist anyway? Isn't that kinda a funny name even for a clown?"

Moist studied Buster, shook *her* head.

Shelby hoped there were enough bedrooms that she would have major space between her and the clowns. *There better be a lot of air space between us.*

"Shelby! Are you listening to me?" Buster rapped her hard on the arm with his knuckles.

Shelby turned and frowned at Clem. She rubbed the spot where Buster had tagged her. "Sorry, guys."

Clem shook his head and placed his hand gently on her shoulder. "Well, sis you better get your act together. We've got to stick it out. We have to find the dia--" Clem's eyes went wide then flitted side to side.

Shelby shook her head. *Way ta go, bro. Now the TV guys are gonna know all about the diamond.*

~ * ~

The long, dimly lit hallway upstairs had six doors, three on either side. Shelby picked the one closet to the stairs and shoved open the door, which banged hard against the wall. She sighed and the tension knot in her back eased when there were no clowns inside the room. She rolled her neck.

Whew. Good. No clowns.

She let out a soft snort she hoped her brothers didn't hear. Her gaze shifted from inside the room to her brothers standing at the end of the corridor. The clowns disappeared into a room at the end of the hall, the zombies were in the bedroom across from the clowns. Her brothers watched her but didn't move from where they were standing. *They're such fraidy cats.*

She entered the room alone.

The room had only a steel framed bed with a green, yellow and pink comforter, a small pine nightstand next to it upon which sat a plastic lamp with a stained glass shade. One wall had a single wood framed window.

Clem startled her as he suddenly crowded in behind her. *I'd recognize that smell of bubble gum anywhere. Just call me the human shield.*

"Safe enough for you, bro?" Shelby glanced over her shoulder at her youngest brother.

Clem's face reddened.

Buster called out from across the hall. "Hey, this one's empty." Clem shrugged and left her room closing the door behind him.

Shelby ran for the bed and leapt off the carpet like a pole-vaulter to land on the mattress with a *whump* and a giggle.

I'm in the Addams family house with zombies and clowns to find a missing diamond, or win eternal life, or, hopefully, both. If someone one told me I'd be here right now, I'd have told them they had a one way ticket to the looney bin.

Shelby sighed. Now all she and her brothers had to do was find the Gnotborst diamond then blow this Popsicle stand. *Once it's night, when everyone's asleep, we'll retrieve the diamond. That is, if Clem remembers where he stashed it.*

Her brothers told her they'd stashed the diamond in an old house when the cops arrived early on the scene of the robbery. How were they supposed to know the Hole-in-One donut shop was next door to the jewelry store where the Gnotborst royal family had all their stuff appraised? Why didn't her brothers check out the donut shop? It's where the cops hang out.

But why did they have to stash it in this house? Surely they could have found one house that wasn't about to be moved to an old movie lot in the Nevada desert.

The bonus will be the prize. Whatever it really was, she was sure her brothers would steal it, too.

Life as circus little people had always been the perfect cover for the Family Bass' real occupation. They were professional thieves. A family tradition, Bass' always had been thieves, going back to her great-grandfather, Oscar Bass.

Shelby sighed. Thief, little person, circus performer, now reality show contestant. *Why me? All I really want is a taste of happiness in Hawaii catching waves. Is that so much to ask for?* Her eyes brimmed with tears but she managed to hold them at bay.

Imagine these contestants thinking they're going to win a major prize. *Ha! As if.* The Family Bass will be there way ahead of them all. They just haven't realized it yet.

Shelby folded her hands behind her head and sighed as she focused on a brown stain on the textured ceiling.

I wonder what that zombie guy, Reggie is doing?

~ * ~

Reggie sat in a wing chair near the window watching the artificial daylight fade into twilight through the library window. He glanced back into the room at the floor-to-ceiling bookshelves that lined three walls of the massive library. The myriad of titles caught his interest. *I used to enjoy reading.*

He buried his hands in the pockets of his blue jeans as he walked to the bookshelf to scan the titles. His noise wrinkled at the scent of mold. There were mysteries, science fiction, romances, cookbooks, and reference books on a variety of eclectic topics from apple farming to zoology.

He sighed. *If I read a hundred books or just one, what's the difference? We'll disintegrate before I have time to finish even one of them. Besides the prize is probably a year's supply of bubble gum. Eternal life? Does Wills think we were born yesterday?*

He moved back to the chair and sat down heavily causing an eruption of dust. He smiled grimly at the irony, knowing it wouldn't be long before he'd be part of the dust in the furniture. *At least I haven't lost my gallows humor.*

His mind drifted to the image of Shelby Bass. *I'd sure like to explore that little body.* He caught himself and his face grew warm. *Check that, 'ol buddy. Better watch what you say around the vertically challenged. I like her, and if I'm going to know here better, I don't want to offend her by calling her a midget or something. Like us zombies, little people are people, too.*

Mom would have appreciated the irony of my situation but Dad never understood me.

"Be a man. You are our only hope for the future of the Kingdom."

His father's angry words still echoed in his dreams. *I don't understand--why would Dad disown me? It's not my fault I'm a zombie. I'm still a prince of Gnotborst and heir to the throne.*

Maybe this is "the" test? As heir he had to go through a test devised by the current sitting monarch to prove his or her worthiness. *But regardless if I passed the test or not, the people of Gnotborst would never want a zombie king.*

Unless we can buy some radiation treatments soon, I won't be around even if they were willing to take me back.

Reggie shook his head as his eyes welled with tears. *It's hopeless. I'll never become the King of Gnotborst.*

A rap on the library door interrupted his thoughts. A frown creased his brow.

Reggie stood, walked to the door and gripped the brass knob firmly in his right hand opening it to reveal a smiling Shelby Bass standing alone in the hallway.

What's she doing here?

~ * ~

"Smells good, doesn't it?" Shelby nodded toward the hallway. The smell of roasted chicken wafted over them coming from the direction of the dining room.

Before he could respond, Shelby's stomach rumbled in the quiet of the hallway. "Sorry." Her face flushed red.

She looks so cute when she's embarrassed.

He realized he hadn't eaten since breakfast this morning at a roadside coffee stand. *Stale donuts aren't the breakfast of champions.*

"Wonder what's on the menu?"

Closing the library door behind him, he walked beside her along the long hallway lined with small tables with busts of ghouls, portraits of vampires, werewolves and ghosts from the late, late show. "Nice artwork, don't you think?"

Shelby nodded but held his elbow loosely in her delicate fingers as if afraid to touch him.

He felt her fingers tighten on his elbow. Glancing at her he saw her large blue eyes widen. *What's wrong?*

Under an archway, at the other end of the hallway, three clowns appeared. *Oh.* Clowns and Shelby didn't mix.

The one called Moist stopped and locked eyes with Reggie. "Ya'll coming' for grub?" Moist's feminine voice surprised him. He'd spoken to the other two earlier and they were definitely male.

Shelby's trembling fingers pinched his elbow tighter.

Ouch. I had no idea her fear was this bad.

Reggie called to the clown, "Yeah, we were just on our way."

"Wanta sit with us?" Moist offered.

Reggie sensed Shelby didn't want to rub elbows with a bunch of clowns. *Her coulrophobia is too ingrained.*

"Thanks but I think we'll sit with my friends."

Moist shrugged. "Shore, no sweat. Just wanta git ta know the competition a little 'foren we beat ya'll at the game." Moist walked away and disappeared into the dining room.

Shelby inhaled and exhaled quickly and her forehead beaded with perspiration.

Reggie whispered, "You okay?"

"No," Shelby breathed.

"I'm listening, Shelby."

"The clowns were supposed to catch Mom." Licking her lips her voice dropped to barely a whisper. "They didn't...and she..."

"I think we should eat," she let go of his elbow and sped ahead of him.

Reggie stood for several seconds watching her walk away. *I don't get her at all. Then again, how does any guy know what women really want?* He shook his head and hurried after her.

I'm such a lunk head. Shelby's team and his were competitors. *She isn't interested in me as a guy, they want to beat us to the prize.* But if Wills was telling the truth, then the prize had to be won by team zombie. *If we lose, we're dead.* He caught up to Shelby. When she turned around, he caught a slight smile twinkling in her eyes.

Girl, you, your brothers and the clowns have to lose. There's too much at stake.

Eight

SHELBY ENTERED THROUGH the doors into the middle of the large dining room. In the center of the room sat a thirty-foot long oak table and, along one wall, rows of stained glass windows. Heavy burgundy drapes framed them, held back by thick, twisted gold-colored ropes.

Ya gotta be kidding me. All this room needs to finish it off is a faux Dracula telling them he didn't drink "vine."

Will you get a load of that table? It's long enough for a family of fifty-two, including the jokers. The long table seemed to go on forever. She scanned the room. *But not a lot of chairs. I hope we don't start playing musical chairs or I'm gonna be fighting for a spot.*

Grouped at one end of the long table, already seated on elegantly carved dark rosewood chairs, were the three clowns. On the other side of the table sat Herbie and Matt.

Reggie's fellow zombies were engaged in an animated conversation, using their hands, with the clowns. Reggie sat farther down the table by himself. His eyes were studying one of the pictures hanging on the wall.

Shelby frowned. *Don't Reggie's buddies know those other guys are clowns?* She paused. *Shel, do you know how nuts you sound?*

The table's scarred wood, badly in need of refurbishing, absorbed the light coming from the chandelier hanging in the middle of the ceiling.

Clem and Buster's eyes were glazed over like they'd been into the beer on a Friday night. *But no way did they get any beer here.*

Earth to bros. She frowned. *What's wrong with them?*

48

Her brothers sat at the table and were at the same height as the tallies. *Huh, how is that possible?* She moved her head slightly to look underneath the table to get a better angle at the chairs.

The specially designed chairs had longer legs, with stepladder rungs affixed to the side, so they would be at eye level with the others. She looked around. *I wonder where the hidden cameras are?*

Warily, Shelby moved to take a seat in one of the specially designed chairs across from the clowns, beside her brothers.

Reggie stood then walked around to the other side of the table and sat next to the other two zombies seated beside the clowns. He smiled at his fellow zombies as if to say, "I'm with her, boys." With his chest puffed out like a peacock, Reggie suddenly snorted.

He snorts, too? Cool. Zombie boy and I have something in common.

Reggie picked up an empty chair carried it to the end of table and set it down next to her. Suddenly, he locked eyes with her.

Wow, cool. He's not a tallie anymore. We're at the same height..

Matt and Herbie had stopped talking to the clowns, instead they watched Shelby with disapproving frowns and both eyebrows arched.

She smiled at them. *There they go with that twin bit again. It's like they're joined at the hip.*

Matt and Herbie glanced at each other then shrugged and went back to telling the clowns about their three hour cruise to the island where they were made into zombies.

Shelby nudged Reggie's side so he would look at her, then she nodded her head toward Moist.

The clown didn't pay attention to the zombie's story and stared at her and Reggie.

"What?" Reggie leaned closer and whispered.

"Doesn't a clown looking at you make you uneasy?"

Reggie shrugged. "I don't know. Maybe she's just being friendly."

Shelby stared at him. *Is he crazy? Clowns are dangerous.* "Yeah, maybe."

Stephen King seems to think clowns are scary, and who would argue with him?

A painfully thin white haired man entered through a swinging door.

The man's features were wrinkled and gray with an undetermined age. The man looked like he could be at least a hundred.

Shelby shook her head.

Wills must enslave senior citizens on the side.

"Get the ancient butler," Reggie whispered.

The man, dressed in a formal yet old-fashioned tuxedo with black and white striped cravat and long tails that hung down his back. He wore white gloves on his hands, and he carried a silver serving tray with a silver cover over it.

"Dinner is served," the tuxedo-clad man announced in a scratchy voice.

Wills burst through the same swinging door with an unlit foot long cigar jammed between his lips, and Shelby jumped from the unexpected movement.

Wills chuckled and walked to spot at the center of the table closet to the door entrance the butler had used to enter the dining room. "Jeeves. Get me a chair, will ya."

Shelby frowned at Clem. *"Jeeves?"* He nodded.

Couldn't the production company at least have named the guy Lurch? He certainly looks like the guy from the old TV show.

Jeeves laid down the tray on the table then walked behind the clowns. He picked up a fourth special chair from against the wall under a portrait of a bearded lady.

Wills offered Shelby a mirthless smile. "All butlers are named Jeeves."

Reggie snorted. "That's not true. I know several named Franklin and Charles--"

Every set of eyes in the room turned to stare at Reggie. "Huh…I mean…at least…that's what I've heard."

"Well, son, in Hollywood every butler is named Jeeves."

Reggie looked at Shelby and shrugged.

Wills shifted his gaze to encompass the group. He removed the cigar from his mouth, then placed it next to the plate on the table in front of him. "Shall we enjoy this fine meal?"

Jeeves lifted the silver cover off the tray in the center of the table to reveal a whole roast pig with a green apple stuck in its mouth. An odor of spicy barbecue sauce filled the air.

Shelby eyed the ancient butler. *Impressive. He's stronger than he looks.*

"Looks yummy," Sparkles spoke in a falsetto. "I love my pork fat. Hmmm, hmmm good." A large wooden bowl brimming with Caesar salad sat beside the platter of pig.

The other clowns laughed uproariously as Sparkles licked his lips and rolled his eyes comically.

Shelby's looked around the room. *There have to be cameras around here somewhere. But where? Note to self: ask Wills. When I find the diamond, I don't want it to be on national television.*

Wills instructed Jeeves to serve the roast. The butler began to carve juicy slices from the pig's hindquarters.

She snatched the forest green napkin from the plate and stuffed it into the collar of her t-shirt.

Silly show with good food, who woulda thought?

Her mouth watered. And the food sure looked yummy.

She looked around at the Matt, Herbie, Reggie, the three clowns and her brothers digging into the succulent pork and Caesar salad.

Eat up boys and girl, it's gonna be a long week.

Nine

After dinner, Reggie accompanied Shelby upstairs to her bedroom. *A real gentleman zombie. For the undead, he's kinda sweet. If I didn't have work to do, I could begin to like him.*

She thanked him then closed the door and leaned her back against the cool wood, with her eyes closed.

Reggie was kinda cool but she couldn't let her attraction for him interfere with her *real* job.

Opening her eyes, she turned around and pressed one ear against the door. Once she heard the echo of his door closing, she'd get her brothers so they could start the search for the diamond.

The eternal life that Wills had talked about didn't exist. But there had to be a safe with money and jewels. A safe would be very real.

True, she hadn't believed in zombies until she had met Reggie. He was kinda nice in a different sort of way and so were his friends. *Since zombies are real maybe eternal life is real?* She snorted. *No way. Stupid idea. I must be losing my mind with all this talk of eternal life. No one lives forever, all we do is try to stake our little piece of happiness real estate. I deserve to be happy.*

With my luck, the prize is probably a new super bomb. The Whammo Peace Missile anyone? As if. Her heart pounded in her chest when she heard Reggie's door close.

Then again, if it is a weapon maybe we can pawn it or something and make a few extra bucks.

Her nose wrinkled. *This must be a smoking room. I don't remember smelling the smoke earlier.*

A noise from in front of her made her jump. Slowly she turned and pressed her back against the door. She closed her eyes tightly, her breathing rapid. Her heart beat harder in her ears. *I've never been so scared in my life.* "Is someone there?" she croaked.

Hands clapping sounded from the shadows of her room. She froze, her hands behind her flat against the door. Her heart leapt to her throat.

Listening for movement of where the sound came from. *Where are they?*

Feeling along the wall with her hand until she found the light switch, she slapped it on. She squeezed her eyes tighter due to the sudden burst of bright tight. Squinting, she blinked until her sight adjusted, then walked toward the closet where she had deduced the clapping sound came from.

With trembling fingers, she threw the closet door open. It creaked loudly on rusty hinges and slapped hard against the wall next to the bed as it opened. Inside was nothing but her suitcase. *Oh, is that all. Good.* The Hulk guy, Chipper, must have been here already.

Shelby laughed uneasily. *And I thought it was a ghost. Silly little 'ol me.* She released a deep breath.

To her right, out of the corner of one eye she saw a figure shrouded in shadow. She slowly turned her head toward the clown sitting in the wing back chair. Shelby froze at the sight of a clown's cold blue eyes staring back at her. *Oh, crap. A clown's in my room, baggy green and white pants and all.*

The white makeup didn't disguise its sardonic expression. The clown's blue eyes studied her with what seemed like a look of the judge at a hog calling contest at the county fair. *I spend way too much time at county fairs.*

The smell of smoke came from the burning tobacco of a thin cigarillo between its blood red lips. A trail of white smoke drifted upward from the glowing tip, filling the air. With a shudder, Shelby recognized the smoker.

Moist the clown had waited for her.

Ten

THE MOISTURE IN SHELBY'S MOUTH DISAPPEARED. Her heart beat hard in her ears and beads of sweat tickled her brow.

She closed her eyes and straightened her shoulders. *Com'on, girl you can face one of these loathsome clowns. No one beats Shelby Bass.*

"What are you doing in my room?" Her stomach muscles tightened, and she balled her fists at her sides. She hoped to look menacing. *I certainly don't feel menacing.*

Moist crossed her legs, which caused her over-sized clown shoes to flap. One gloved hand rested in her lap, the other held a thin cigar to her cherry red lips.

Shelby shifted from one foot to the other. *I gotta pee.*

Moist took a drag from her cigarillo. Her azure eyes and facial expression remained calm. The clown tilted her head back and blew a smoke ring into the air.

Shelby's eyes followed the smoke ring until it dissipated into nothingness at the ceiling. Her nose wrinkled. "And no one smokes in my room."

Moist sighed and with her free hand reached into the billowy folds of the white and green clown costume and pulled out a royal purple-colored glass ashtray. After stubbing out the small cigar, Moist set the ashtray on a side table next to the chair.

Moist shifted her lean body in the chair. "Yes. You're right. A filthy habit."

"Why. Are. You. In. My. Room." *I feel weak. I gotta sit down before I fall down.*

Shelby took two shaky steps toward the clown. *I sound like Mr. Spock.* She rolled her eyes. *What an idiot. Someone invades your space and you're afraid of her?* Shelby gave her head a shake. *I've got to clear my head because I'm not going to let a clown get to me. Never.*

She steadied herself with one hand on the bed and hoped her trembling legs weren't too obvious. *I don't want the clown to see my fear.* The butterflies in her stomach certainly weren't flying in formation.

"Coulrophobia? Right?"

Shelby frowned. "You're too smart for your own good." Anger dripped from her voice. Not at the clown, but at herself for letting her fear be read so easily.

"Yeah, but that's my job after all."

"You're a clown. Your only job is to amuse the kiddies."

Maybe I should join a fear of clowns anonymous support group. Hi, I'm a clownophobic, and my name is Shelby and I'm afraid of clowns.

The clown stood abruptly.

Shelby took a step back. Her knees trembled. *Must. Not. Make. Contact. With. The clown*

"If you're trying to get a rise out of me it won't work. I'm a product of the streets. I've met far tougher customers than *you*." Moist ripped off the glove on her right hand, stuck her fingers the collar of her suit, then pulled. The suit fell away down her body as a single piece. The one-piece suit landed in a pile of green and white stripes around Moist's booted feet.

Underneath her costume, Moist wore hip hugging blue jeans, a white cotton shirt, knotted at the waist exposing her belly button, and shiny, knee high leather black boots.

Oh, she has an inny.

The boots had six inch spiked heels so she towered over Shelby. *Whoa! This is wild! She must be the tallest tallie clown ever.*

Moist reached behind her head then pulled the white clown face off, to reveal pale, freckled skin and fiery hair, more orange than hers, tied in a bun. The mask hung in front under her chin. *Somebody call 911, a clown has disappeared!*

"The name is Armstrong, Aloha Armstrong! I'm an agent with The L.I.P.S. I'm here to help."

The tallie-woman-who-used-to-be-named-Moist kicked away the discarded disguise with the toe of her boot.

The tension in Shelby's shoulders eased. The clown was gone and now a beautiful, tall L.I.P.S. agent stood before her.

Hold on. The L.I.P.S.?

"What's The L.I.P.S.? And why are you doing some undercover work on a cheesy reality show? And why are you telling me any of this?"

Agent Armstrong smiled revealing perfect white teeth. "Good questions, Miss Bass." Armstrong pulled the black cord and released a tie holding her hair in place then shook her brassy red hair loose in a swirling display reminiscent of a model in a shampoo commercial.

Her hair cascaded about her shoulders like a fiery bird's nest. "To answer your first question, The Legal Integrated Protection Service, or The L.I.P.S., is a worldwide organization devoted to tracking down international bad people. We're the good guys."

Shelby rolled her eyes. "Yeah. Guys. Right." *Geez, hope Reggie doesn't lock his baby blues on her. She's gorgeous.* Shelby paused. *What's wrong with me? I'm not here to meet a guy. I'm after the diamond. Focus, girl. Focus.*

Agent Armstrong shifted her weight to her left side and crossed her arms over the swell of her ample breasts.

"Miss Bass--"

"Call me, Shelby." *She's a cop. I have to keep her off guard so she doesn't find out about the diamond.* "Oh, and that southern accent is terrible."

A whisper of a smile crossed Agent Armstrong's features. "Of course. Mis--excuse me--Shelby, we've been following your family's activities for the past several years, ever since your mother's unfortunate accident."

"It was no accident!" *Uh, oh. They've been following my family!* "Hey! Why have you been watching us?"

"We know *everything* about the Family Bass."

Shelby scowled at Aloha. *This has to be the biggest load bull poop, ever.* "Leave my room, Agent. I'm trying to sleep."

Aloha shrugged and slipped out of the room the lock clicking softly behind her.

Alone, Shelby climbed onto the bed and lay down onto her back staring at the ceiling. *Oh, crap. We are sooo done.*

~ * ~

Opening her eyes, Shelby squinted in the darkness as the only light came from the window where the artificial moonlight cast by the artificial moonlight that threw a soft, eerie glow over the bed. The drapes covering the window rustled from an artificial breeze. Shelby bolted upright in bed.

"Who's there?"

Silence. She sighed. *Must be the wind.* The sound of crickets chirping, probably sound effects, came from the direction of the window.

Wills obviously spared no expense to achieve Hollywood's version of realism. Her body involuntarily shook, not from cold. *I am so alone. Dad and my brothers have never understood me. They tell me my dreams are silly, that I'm a dreamer. All true, but it's me darn it, and I like who I am.*

Her eyes steadily adjusted to the low light. She ran her hands over the smooth down quilt covering her. The scent of cinnamon filled her senses.

"You okay?" *That voice is definitely male and definitely worried.*

"Reggie?"

The figure shrouded in the shadows of the room stood and moved closer. Finally, the shape hovered over her and the passionate blue eyes pierced her heart. *Reggie.* "Oh, thank goodness." *No clowns.* A feeling of relief washed over her. "Good."

Her head sank to the soft pillow. "Hmmmm…that's good," she murmured.

But what about Moist?

Is she really an agent for the L.I.P.S.? Shelby shook her head. *It's just a crazy enough name to be true. I better keep an eye on her. She could blow my opportunity to get the diamond back.*

She peered up at Reggie's wrinkled brow and caring eyes. Without thinking, her arms went round his neck and pulled his upper body on top of her. His arms enveloped her.

His hands are sure strong and yet still gentle. He feels surprisingly good for the undead. Nice.

Funny, when we're beside each other on the bed we're at eye level. Interesting, in bed everyone is equal. My first tallie is a zombie. Who woulda thought?

I think he wants to kiss but it isn't like I kiss zombies every other day. Oh, why not? It would certainly be different. She wanted to giggle at the thought this was another first, her first tallie kiss.

His lips touched hers with a gentleness that sent shock waves of passion through her. His lips were surprisingly soft against hers as she rubbed her hands over his lower back. His tongue slipped between her lips.

Hmmmm…zombies taste the same as alive little guys. Her hands wrapped around his back and she pulled him closer. *And he's not cold. I hope I don't break him. I wonder if zombies fall apart if you squeeze them too hard?*

His tongue dueled with hers, and she enjoyed the sensation of his taking control. His touch made her skin burn, sending shocks of pleasure through her. And she relished the way his mouth molded to hers. Hungry and passionate.

No. Shelby pulled her mouth away from his, stopped kissing, and pushed him away breaking their embrace. She looked at Reggie, her eyes wide. His brow wrinkled quizzically.

Hold on, this can't work. Not ever!

She made a promise a long time ago, that men weren't on the menu. Too many bad dates were a cure for loneliness. *Besides, I'm a thief. I steal things. I have a mission. I can't let men distract me from my goals.* She sat up, inhaled deeply to steady herself. *Oh, no, what am I doing? I have to stop.*

His grip loosened from around her waist, and Reggie's brow pinched, his eyes narrowed. "What is it?"

"Reggie, it's not that I--"

"I know," his gentle voice was like a summer breeze. "It could never work--"

She bowed her head. "Yeah, Reggie you're right, people would never understand a zombie and a little person being together. We'd be outcasts."

The ceiling light over the bed came on just as he opened his mouth to say more.

"Hey!" she covered her eyes with one hand.

Reggie blinked.

Shelby rolled away from him and off the bed to land on her feet with a soft *thump. Circus skills come in handy sometimes.*

Eleven

"CAN'T A PERSON GET A LITTLE PRIVACY round here?" Blinded by the overhead light Shelby shielded her eyes with one hand and squinted into the brightness trying to make out who had interrupted them.

"No. As a matter fact." The familiar voice barked out. The door slammed shut. *Too familiar.*

"Darn you, Armstrong how do you appear and disappear--"

Reggie, one hand over his eyes, blinking, stood next to the bed. "Who's Armstrong?"

Shelby uncovered one eye and instead of a beautiful woman, the white face of Moist the Clown now looked at both of them. *What's going on? Why is she back in her disguise?* Shelby's legs trembled. *Why does she have to dress as a clown?* She knew her fear wasn't rational but she hated clowns.

But it's a wonder I didn't see through her clown disguise. From what I've seen, she's a terrible clown. I hope she's a better L.I.P.S. agent. I'm sure not going to tell my brothers she's an agent until we have the diamond. I don't want them to lose focus, which they do all the time.

Things were definitely rotten in the state of weirdo land, never mind Denmark.

Moist, with a nod of her head, indicated a painting that hung on the wall to Shelby's right across the room from the bed. The canvas had the image of a large oak tree with a little blond haired girl dressed as Bo Peep sitting on a wooden bench beneath the branches. *Huh?*

Immediately Shelby understood. *We're on TV! I almost made a complete fool of myself. If we'd continued, we would have been the opening act on Friday night at the porn movies.* And if that happened, either her father or the embarrassment would have killed her. Her cheeks grew warm. *Agent Armstrong saved my butt. Crap. Now I owe her.*

Shelby cringed and her guts twisted in fear. She grabbed Reggie's forearm to steady herself. "Reggie. This is Moist. The clown."

Reggie nodded then moved to study the picture hanging over the three-drawer dresser across from the bed.

Shelby grabbed Moist's arm. "Hold on there, clowny. I'll go first." She motioned for Aloha to bend down so she could whisper in the clown's ear. "Did you know we were on camera when you took off your costume?" Shelby indicated the picture on the wall. "The cameras?"

Moist whispered, "I disabled them just long enough to reveal my secret." She pulled a device the size of a cell phone from the folds of her costume. She flashed it at Shelby then it disappeared back into her costume. "They would've thought it's a simple malfunction."

She must keep the kitchen sink hidden in there.

"Never leave home without your L.I.P.S. signal jammer." Moist grinned. "And in case you're wondering, yes, your performance with Reggie…very interesting. I saw it on the TV in my room."

Reggie turned to gaze at Moist with one eyebrow raised. "Yeah. I know. We met earlier. But who's Armstrong?"

Reggie looked to where Shelby was gazing and glanced back at the painting. Reggie's eyes grew wide and his gray skin paled. "You mean?" He pointed at the painting. "There are cameras in the bedrooms?"

She mouthed, "*Later.*"

He shrugged.

A sharp rap on the door interrupted them.

A small revolver appeared in Moist's right hand. *Oh, crap. She has a gun? Maybe it shoots a flag that says bang?*

Odd that Aloha seemed to be helping her but why? Shelby wished she knew the answer to that question. She wasn't afraid the agent would shoot her. *Being shot by a clown sounds too stupid for words, never mind embarrassing.*

Then again if Aloha did shoot her it would confirm her worst fears. *That'd be something wouldn't it?*

Moving to the left side of the door, Moist pressed her index finger to her lips. Then with her free hand, she turned the doorknob and swung the door open violently to reveal a frantic, wild-eyed Matt.

"Matt!" Reggie walked up to his friend and slapped him on the shoulder.

What is it with my room? It's like Grand Central Station.

Moist stepped back, the tension easing in her shoulders. The revolver disappeared back into the folds of her costume. *Maybe Reggie didn't notice?*

Reggie released Matt and moved to stand next to Shelby. He whispered, "Clown holster?" *He'd noticed. Great. Now he'll ask questions and she'll tell him she's a L.I.P.S. agent then the producers will stop the show before I can find the diamond and I'll never get to Hawaii. In other words, disaster.*

"I'll explain later," she whispered.

He grunted.

Matt's shoes shuffled back and forth like a child who needed to pee as he stood in the doorway. "Herbie's missing."

Herbie? Missing? How?

Reggie frowned. "Missing? What are you talking about? We're locked down inside this museum for the next week. No one can go *missing*. Are you sure he's not in the kitchen or something?"

"Yeah, I'm sure, Reg. Herbie's bed's next to mine. Last time I saw him he was asleep."

"At what time?"

"Five a.m. An hour ago."

Reggie placed a reassuring hand on Matt's shoulder and glanced at Shelby. "Matt and Herbie are very close. If anyone would know Herbie's missing it'd be Matt."

Shelby forehead wrinkled. *Great! Now we've got bigger problems than me gettin' the diamond.* "Maybe this is the first challenge?" she suggested.

"Yeah. Could be. Anything's possible." Reggie's brow furrowed and he moved to look out the window.

"If he left or someone took him away I would have woken up." The anger rose in Matt's voice. His watery gaze fell on Reggie. "Wouldn't I?"

Reggie turned to face Matt one eyebrow arched then shifted his gaze to Moist then lastly Shelby.

"Let's organize a search," suggested Moist.

Reggie snorted. "There's more than meets the red nose to you, Clowny."

Ignoring the sarcasm in Reggie's tone, Moist spoke first. "Yes, there is. Herbie's got to be around here somewhere." Moist smiled at Reggie.

Shelby's eyes narrowed. *Who died and made her the clown-slash-agent in charge?*

Reggie crossed his arms, his brow pinched and his blue eyes darkened as he focused his gaze again on Matt. "Don't worry, Matt, we'll find him."

A weak smile crossed Matt's pale-gray, peeling face.

Reggie walked past everyone into the hallway.

Matt followed him out.

Moist turned to follow the two zombies with a good-bye glance at Shelby.

~ * ~

The wooden floorboards creaked, and shuddered as the trap door in the floor opened and the thick, black, steel chain rattled as it moved. A cloud of musty air surrounded Happy as he climbed up from the dark, dank basement. He concentrated as he climbed the stairs in his size twenty-three shoes.

He stared at his feet as he climbed the last couple of steps. *One foot in front of the other.*

His once dusky red and powder blue clown suit was now covered in dust bunnies and cobwebs. His stomached still ached from the putrid smells of mold and brackish water in the basement. The stench lingered around him like a cheap hooker's perfume.

Yuk! That basement smells like the garbage dump behind Clown Town.

He slapped away the cobwebs on his arms and legs as he gazed down the hallway looking both ways. *What an awful place--stinky, damp, cobwebs and spiders the size of cats.* He frowned. *Anywhere's better than this crap hole.* He turned to look through the trap door still open at his feet. *What's keepin' Clem and Buster?* His eyes narrowed as he peered into the inky darkness. He called out, "Hey! Is anybody there?" His voice echoed. Silence.

Uh, oh. I think I lost them.

~ * ~

The "Where's Herbie" hunt was on.

Moist organized the search teams using a map of the house she just pulled from a hidden compartment in her clown costume. *That costume of hers is like Batman's utility belt--an accessory for every occasion.*

Shelby studied the clown-slash-agent's pasty face, garish red lips and green eye shadow. *Hard to believe there's a beautiful redhead in there.*

She shook her head then turned her attention to the map of the house spread over the oak end table. *I wonder what she's really after? At least she doesn't seem all that interested in me or my brothers. Not that I'm complaining.*

Reggie pointed to the basement on the map. "How about we start the search in the basement and work our way toward the top floor attic?"

Moist stood straight and a frown creased her forehead. "It's like he's disappeared off the face of the Earth, or at least the house."

"Wills wouldn't like that." Shelby pointed to the parlor but Moist spoke before she could add anything more.

"Reggie, why don't you and Matt start in the parlor? And I'll check the garage with Sparkles." Moist and Sparkles left for the garage accessible off the entryway.

Shelby was surprised when Clem, Buster, and Happy volunteered to search the basement. *I thought they'd had enough of the below ground places after they were in the basement already.*

I hope they're going to look for the diamond while they're down there. I wish we'd had a second to talk to devise a plan. All Shelby could do was hope that they kept the goal in mind while they searched.

She watched them go, but something about Clem and Buster was different. *They're not joking or fooling around like usual. I wish I knew what they're up to.*

"I'll look in the library." Shelby walked toward the library by herself. *I might find a clue to the location of a safe, maybe the diamond, and maybe the prize, if it exists that is.* Her eyes narrowed. *This game could be over for us sooner than later.*

They'd agreed each search team would meet in the foyer by the front door in twenty minutes.

Shelby walked into the library. Three of the four walls were lined with floor to ceiling bookshelves.

The library appeared to contain every hardcover volume since Guttenberg invented the printing press.

Reggie and Matt entered the library from the living room. Reggie's eyes were fixed on the floor as if in deep thought.

Shelby met Reggie in the middle of the room. He looked up when she cleared her throat. "What's wrong?"

"I dunno. But something's not right..." His voice trailed off just as Sparkles rushed into the room.

The closer he got the more he reeked of gasoline and perspiration. Shelby's nose wrinkled.

The clown's eyes were so wide she could see the whites around them. *Maybe he's like that kid in the movie and he sees dead people.* Which, considering where they were, didn't seem unreasonable.

"I can't find him," Sparkles squeaked out. His blue wig, chalk white makeup, purple bow tie, carrot orange shirt, and long toed clown shoes repulsed Shelby completely.

I guess Sparky means Herbie. "Yeah. Me neither." *I'm getting better at talking to clowns. Imagine.*

Aloha, still in her Moist disguise, entered behind Sparkles and her eyes scanned the group like a radar.

Shelby cringed. She was surrounded by these clowns from another nightmare. *I guess I've still a ways to go.* She regarded Agent Armstrong's disguise. *Let's not try to look like a spy shall we, Aloha?*

Maybe Reggie's right. Maybe I'm going to beat this clown-phobia after all. I'm talking to Aloha in her clown get up, and I just agreed with Sparkles.

Reggie offered her a reassuring smile. *Stranger things have happened.*

Sparkles shook his head frantically. "Not Herbie. Happy. I lost him." The distraught clown's hands shook, and his lean frame trembled. *He's gonna shake apart if he doesn't get control of himself.*

Sparkles stared at them. "This isn't like Happy. He's never left me alone."

Gosh, I actually feel sorry for the poor guy. She shook her head. "I thought you went to the garage with Moist?" Shelby indicated Aloha still in her clown disguise with a nod of her head.

Sparkles nodded. "I know something's happened...I know it."

Shelby frowned. "But how do you know he's missing?"

"I just know is all. He went to the basement. I saw it in my mind." The rest of his words were choked off by a sob.

Matt stepped forward and placed one hand on the distraught clown's shoulder. "I've heard of this. My psych 101 prof told us some people are more sensitive to cosmic forces than others. He believes extra sensory perception is a very real phenomenon. Sparkles must be psychic. He might know where Herbie is--"

Reggie snorted. "Oh com'on, Matt, don't be so stupid. As I recall, Professor Giggler lost his tenure and left the university in a straight jacket. Besides, even if Sparky has ESP it's not like he's a TV remote. It's not as if you press a button and *poof* you're on the right channel. No one can do things like that." Reggie nodded toward Shelby.

Sparkles' cheeks grew red through his thin white face paint and he squirmed.

Oh, you've got to be kidding, Shelby shrugged. *Then again, why not?* "Hold on, Reggie. Matt may be onto something." Shelby turned to face Sparkles. "You're physic aren't you?"

He nodded sheepishly. His gaze dropped to the floor.

We outed him. Shelby grimaced. *It seems everyone's got something in their bag of secrets, including me.* Shelby walked to the door. *I wonder where my brothers are?*

Shelby glanced at Reggie, who nodded.

66

Moist frowned and crossed her arms over her chest.

Shelby turned back to Sparkles, "So how does it work?"

"I can divine certain things from objects and certain close friends," he paused. His feet shuffled like a kid with his hand caught in the cookie jar and buried his hands in the folds of his purple clown pants.

"Well, you see, Happy and I are brothers. He raised me when Mom and Dad were killed by a circus train. They were walking on the tracks, and Mom's foot got caught in the one of the boards. Before Dad could free her, they…"

"I'm so sorry." Shelby used as gentle a tone in her voice as she could. Her heart still ached over the loss of her own mother. "What a horrible accident," she whispered.

"Too bad that wasn't an accident and his gift is called clairvoyance." Moist said from behind Shelby.

Shelby turned from Sparkles and faced the clown-slash-agent-slash-woman to confront her. *There she goes again--is every accident rigged? How does she know so much? My mom died in an accident. If someone killed her, I'm gonna get the name out of her.*

From the corner of her eye, she saw Reggie and Matt also turn to face Moist.

Moist held a black doctor's bag in her right hand. *Where did that come from? What else does she have hidden in her costume?* "What is it with you?"

"What do you mean?"

"Does every accident have to be fixed?" Shelby dropped her arms to her sides and balled her fists. "I mean, first you tell me my Mom's death isn't an accident, and now you're telling us this clown's family's tragedy isn't an accident? You better explain yourself."

Moist shook her head then nodded toward a large mirror affixed to the wall opposite the front door.

Oops! Great. The hidden cameras and microphones. *Girl, you've gotta learn better control. We're on this stupid reality show until we find the diamond.*

Wills and the viewers are really having a good laugh at our expense. *Wrong! I'm not about to give him the satisfaction.* A frown furrowed Shelby's brow.

She nodded to Moist showing that she understood and indicated with a wink that she had an idea. *It's time, Aloha--or should I say Moist?--and I teamed up.* "Why don't we take this outside?" *I prefer to think of this as a temporary truce. If she's going to assume the leader role on this show, I had better stick to her like glue.*

A trace of smile played across Moist's lips. *Good, she agrees.*

It's time to put that little L.I.P.S. jammer of hers to the test.

Once outside the house, she could use the jammer to give them enough privacy and then she could use the map and plan to defeat Wills and win this stupid game. *And I'll be able to search for the diamond without being watched. Perfect.*

Shelby walked toward the front door. She raised her hand to touch the doorknob and heard running footsteps behind her. Before she could react, something struck her from behind and pushed her to the floor. Extending her hands to check her fall she hit the carpeted floor hard. "Owww!" Pain seared her lower body and her hands stung.

Carpet burn really hurts!

She looked up to see who had hit her. *Reggie?* "Hey! What's the big idea?"

Reggie's forward momentum had brought his left forearm into contact with the doorknob. His body arched back, stiffened and his eyes opened wider than Shelby had ever seen on anyone. His blond hair stood straight up from his scalp as his entire body trembled.

Aloha rushed forward to hip check Reggie, like a pro hockey player would slam an opposing player into the boards, to knock him away from the electrified doorknob.

He collapsed to the carpet on his side, his teeth were clenched tight, his mouth formed a grimace, and a streak of drool ran down his chin.

After freeing him, Aloha, breathing in gasps, her head down, bent forward at the waist, rested her hands on her knees.

Reggie saved me! She stared at him lying trembling from the effects the electricity that coursed through him. *Oh, no. Is he dead?*

Wincing from the pain in her knees, Shelby got to her feet and raced to his side. She winced as she dropped to her haunches next to him. She grasped his right wrist in her fingers to search for a pulse. *It's there, but it's faint.* She placed one hand flat on his chest.

He's barely breathing.

Her father had the foresight to teach all of his children basic first aid. As he so often told them, "You never know when you'll need to help someone."

"How is he?" asked Aloha between gasps.

"He's alive. So far. Are you okay?" Shelby checked his wrist again. *There. His pulse is getting stronger.*

She watched his chest rise and fall more strongly than before. Scanning the rest of him revealed a reddish burn mark on his fingers where they had made contact with the doorknob. Other than the burn marks, there were no other obvious injuries. *I wish I knew more than basic first aid. Reggie, please don't die.*

Reggie's entire body shuddered, and he coughed several times.

She held her breath and waited.

His beautiful blue eyes blinked hard several times. "Sh...el...by?" He coughed.

Shelby exhaled, looked up and glared at the mirror over the fireplace. "Is anyone gonna call 911?"

Sparkles looked at Matt. "Who she talking to?"

Matt grunted. "The cameras."

"Oh." Sparkles nodded

"And I don't think so." Shelby whispered.

"What?" Matt looked at her, his brow wrinkled.

"No one's going to call 911. We're on our own." Shelby rose to her feet and dusted off her thighs with her hands.

"Double oh." Sparkles moved to stand over Reggie. "He doesn't look so good."

Shelby glared at Sparkles. *Great. But I think he's right. We're on our own in this crazy house, even if someone gets hurt. Some of us might actually die. Double great.*

She looked back at Reggie as he opened his eyes to slits and groaned.

He's alive.

He coughed and rose to his elbows. Shelby pressed her hand flat on his chest forcing him to lie back on the carpet. Reggie's eyes closed again then he moaned softly.

What do I do? I'm a circus performer, not a doctor.

"Lie still." Reggie almost sacrificed himself to save me from being electrocuted. *How can I ever repay him?*

"Some shock, eh?" He smiled weakly, and a sly grin turned up at the corners of his mouth. His voice was barely above a whisper.

"The door's booby trapped," Reggie paused to cough.

Matt walked to stand next to Reggie and shook his head. "Reggie is the one who keeps us together. He's the only one knows how to sew." He glanced at Shelby. "We're going to fall apart if anything happens to him."

Shelby looked at Aloha. L.I.P.S. agents must have medical training. *Maybe she has a medical lab hidden in her costume.* "Aloha, huh, I mean Moist do you know first aid?"

Moist shrugged. "Nope, sorry. It isn't in the required LIPS training. We're expendable."

Shelby rolled her eyes. *Maybe L.I.P.S. agents carry a little black suicide capsule too.*

Matt looked at Sparkles and mouthed, "L.I.P.S.?"

Sparkles shrugged.

Now she's done it. How're we gonna be a team if everyone knows she's not a clown?

Aloha shrugged. *Some secret agent she is.*

Reggie's eyes fluttered.

She turned her attention to the wounded zombie. "You saved me. How did you know?" She ran a hand over his smoking blond hair. *Yuk.* She withdrew her hand and ran it down her pant leg. "Huh, thanks."

"I didn't," his voice sounded strained. "Something looked wrong."

"You could have died." Shelby stood.

She wanted to tell Reggie she cared about him, but she didn't want to fall into the hands of Wills and his boss who wanted artificial drama for the show.

The eye in the sky, or the walls, or the pictures watched their every move. Every reality show she'd ever watched tried to create tension where none existed to increase ratings.

I hope no one watches so I can get away with the diamond undetected. Her gaze dropped to Reggie. *And, of course, I don't want to be hurt if I fall for the big stupid lug.* She sighed to herself.

Goofball probably saved my life. There's nothing artificial about that.

She moved to stand by the curtained windows beside the front door and crossed her arms. *But I can't let my heart rule my common sense. This isn't some goofy soap opera, and he's not an actor. This job is headed south like a runaway tractor.* She looked down at Reggie again. *This was supposed to be a simple--steal back the diamond my brothers lost and scram. Easy. But I'm falling for this zombie guy. This accident and missing clowns and zombies complicates everything.* Her eyes narrowed. *And something is definitely dirty at Big Ass films. Why do jobs always get so messy?*

"Hmmm. No. I don't think anyone is supposed to get killed." Moist knelt on one knee with her face an inch from the door handle studying it closely.

The L.I.P.S. agent examined the evidence. The name of her organization might be silly, but at least she seemed to act like a professional. *Or at least like the government agents I've seen on TV, if they dressed in funny costumes that is.*

With two fingers, Moist yanked a wire attached to the handle causing a shower of sparks to shoot out, then she lifted a black wire away with her index finger, and followed the line to the door frame where it ran down the side into a small freshly drilled hole in the floor. There were minute wood shavings around the hole.

"What do you mean?" Shelby waved her hand to indicate Reggie. "He's hurt!"

Moist nodded toward the floor. "He'll be fine." Then her brows pinched together wrinkling her brow. "I suspect if we followed the wire to its source, we'd find a generator hidden somewhere in the house."

She placed the wire back on the doorknob then stood. "I don't think the voltage is enough to kill."

Moist placed her hands on her hips. "But I suspect there are similar booby traps around all the exits." Moist used her foot to toe the hole in the floor where the wire disappeared. "Whoever's behind this is devious." Moist's emerald eyes narrowed. "I hope we don't run into too many of these traps." She shifted her gaze to Reggie. "They may not kill, but they do seem to hurt."

Shelby rolled her eyes. *Duh.*

Matt chuckled and Reggie groaned.

Moist scanned the group. "We're all in this together."

Shelby considered Moist's words. *She's right* . This accident--if that's what it was, is a sign that somehow they had to form a team. But could two clowns--one who's really a secret agent named Aloha Armstrong--two zombies and a little woman with the ambition to get to Hawaii no matter what the cost really work and play well together without killing each other?

Only time would tell. *I just hope Moist-slash-Aloha doesn't expect we'll be BFF's.*

Twelve

SHELBY WATCHED THE TRAP DOOR in the floor slowly open.

I can't help but worry when Clem and Buster are out of my sight in this house . She eyed the trap door. *Especially since Happy disappeared down there.* She smiled to herself. *I'd never tell them this, but I love them.*

The trap door creaked loudly and heavy chains attached to the heavy wooden door rattled as it thudded into place.

Shelby felt relief when Clem's head appeared through the opening, then his upper torso and finally his legs.

Buster followed close behind.

They were both breathing hard from the climb, their clothes filthy and their faces streaked with soot.

Shelby had to hide a smile behind her hand. She pretended to yawn to disguise a laugh. *They look like Pig Pen clones.* "Any luck, guys?"

Clem shook his head. *Nuts!*

Shelby glanced toward the open door to the library at the end of the wide hallway. Moist had left them saying she'd be back after she fixed the door.

Whatever she did must've worked. That L.I.P.S. gizmo shut down the electrical booby trap that nearly took out Reggie. She glanced at Reggie lying on the carpet.

Reggie had partially recovered from the shock and managed to raise himself up on his elbows.

As promised, Moist returned in time to help Reggie stand, placing one arm around his waist and helping him to his feet.

"Thanks," he grunted.

"We didn't find any sign of Herbie." Clem shook his head filling the air with a cloud of black dust.

Shelby stole a glance at Reggie. How quickly she'd grown to love the mischievous glint in his blue eyes. *Those eyes. Wow! Sexy.* A shiver of remembered lust from the kiss earlier shivered down Shelby's spine

"We're going upstairs. I need to take a shower." Buster snorted in disgust.

Clem nodded and followed his brother up the stairs to their bedroom.

Moist, with her arm wrapped around Reggie's waist to support him, looked at Shelby.

Reggie offered a weak smile.

"Hey!" Sparkles stamped his foot. "What about Happy? He's still missing ya know!"

Matt nodded and added, "We still need to find Herbie--"

"--and Happy," Sparkles adamantly thumped a fist into a wall.

Shelby turned to watch her two brothers scramble up the staircase until the sooty twins disappeared from view. *I hope they don't go missing, too. Man, I just don't know what to think anymore. I have a crush on a zombie, a wannabe BFF who's in reality a secret agent disguised as a clown, and we have no leads on the diamond.* "It just aint fair," she muttered, shaking her head.

Moist nodded. "You're quite right."

Shelby looked at Moist. *Oops. Did just say that out loud?*

Moist continued as if she didn't realize Shelby's error. "There is only one place no one has searched yet. The kitchen." Moist turned to Shelby. "Why don't you take Reggie and go back to the library?"

"Why?" Shelby crossed her arms, "Are you trying to get rid of us?"

Moist arched one eyebrow. "Miss Bass, did you look for hidden panels or passageways behind the bookcases?"

Shelby shook her head. *Uh, oh. I hope she doesn't realize I'm looking for hidden passages. I'm just a little ole circus little person, what do I know about hidden passages and safes?* "How would I know if there are hidden passages behind the shelves?"

"Elementary, my dear Miss Bass."

Shelby scowled at the clown woman. *What's with the "Miss" crap? Great. Aloha thinks she's the L.I.P.S. answer to Sherlock Holmes.*

"Did you detect the odor of cinnamon in your room when you woke up?"

Shelby nodded slowly.

"Well, Miss Bass, I don't wear perfume that contains extracts of cinnamon. Frankly, I prefer a good Chanel product."

"You mean someone else was in my room?" Shelby shivered. *Creepy or what?*

Moist nodded. "I'm certain of it. I detected the odor of cinnamon when I came into the room the first time. I couldn't be certain until now…secret passages are common in these old houses. And, knowing the producers of this show, I'm sure some were added." The tilt of her head suggested that everyone should know this fact.

Yeah. Obvious. Ri-i-ight.

Shelby had heard of such a thing. In the movies, sure. But in real life? *Naw. Impossible. On the other hand, what if unknown weirdoes were sneaking around inside the walls of the old house like rats?* Chills ran down her spine.

Reggie's brow pinched together in a scowl. "Hey, how is it you know so much? You're a clown, but you talk like a cop."

Shelby took Reggie's hand in hers. His hair still stood straight up like a fright wig. She squeezed her lips together so she wouldn't laugh.

He looks so cute.

At the touch of her hand, he gazed down at her. His scowl faded into a tender smile.

"Do you trust me?" she asked, with a chuckle

"Of course not." He eyed her and wiggled his eyebrows comically. "We are competitors after all."

She giggled. *Reggie is not only incredibly sexy for a zombie but he's the funniest undead guy I ever met. Maybe I've finally met a nice guy.*

All those dating websites and late night chat lines only produced rat bags. *When I got up this morning, the last thing I thought I'd meet is a really cool undead zombie that I like. Too bad, I have to dump him when we find the diamond.* Her gaze shifted to him. *This is gonna be harder than I thought. Why is my timing always bad when it comes to men?*

Reggie's gaze shifted back to Moist, "It's just you're drawing some pretty crazy conclusions based on very little evidence. I mean you're a clown, not a cop--" He paused to gaze at Shelby.

She squeezed his hand and then loosened her grip and patted his hand. "It's the shock. Don't worry. For now, you and I have to go to the library. Okay?" *I need her. The longer they think she's a clown, the more time for me to use her to find the diamond.*

He shrugged. "None of this is making any sense but, all right, why not?"

Shelby turned to face Moist and gave the woman from L.I.P.S. a sardonic smile. "And where are you three going to be? Miss Clown?" Shelby arched an eyebrow.

Moist grimaced. "Matt, Sparkles, and I are going to the kitchen. I'm hoping we'll find a clue there about our two missing friends. From what I've heard, food seems to be high on their priority list." Moist shook her head and started for the kitchen. "This must be one of the goofiest challenges--finding missing team members--in the history of reality shows," Moist muttered as she walked away.

Matt and Sparkles looked at each other with stupid grins on their faces and nodded. *A zombie, a clown, and a secret agent--mix 'em together and what ya got? A confused mess that smells like dead fish, tells bad jokes, and has secret weapons in its tighty-whities.*

The expressions on the zombie and the clown's faces were eager like kids on the playground. Moist's frown and eye rolling as she walked away must have meant she hated being saddled with these two.

Shelby smiled. *Now she knows how I feel most of the time around my brothers.*

"Okay. We'll meet back in the foyer in twenty minutes." Reggie blurted.

Shelby shook her head. *I hope his shock wears off soon.*

Moist turned and lead the way into the dining room. Matt and Sparkles trailed behind.

As Shelby recalled from the map Moist had shown them, the door to the kitchen was through the dining room. With hidden doors and passageways in the walls, who knew what was up, down, or sideways in this crazy house? *We need the map she has to find the diamond.*

Reggie followed Shelby into the library. The twin oak doors were covered with elaborate carvings of deer and bears etched into the dark wood. Reggie opened the doors using the brass snakehead-shaped handles then, once she was inside, he closed the doors behind them with a dull *thud.*

The room itself smelled of ancient dust and stale cigar smoke that had permeated the long maroon-colored drapes covering the murky windows. The drapes were badly in need of cleaning, discolored by grease spots and dirt.

A thick Persian rug in a deep red wine color with ornate patterns of gold thread through the fabric to create images of lions, elephants, and giraffes covered the floor. Whoever built this room certainly liked their wild animal imagery. Shelby stole a furtive glance at Reggie. *Grrrr.*

Shelby moved toward the right wall and stared at a shelf of books. "Nora Roberts? Tom Clancy?"

She plucked a hardbound volume off the shelf and held out the book. "And look, Ludlum."

Reggie walked toward her and accepted the offered volume. The jacket was in pristine condition as if it has never been handled.

Briefly, their fingers grazed each other's. Her hand froze in mid-air for a moment in time, as if the air had suddenly been sucked from the room. Her eyes caught on his, and she drew in a breath. *Oh, my…*

Pulling her hand away, she broke the connection. *Air. I need air.*

Shelby inhaled deeply. *Oh, boy. He got me good. Man, he's making this hard for me. I can't let him get to me.*

Reggie offered her a crooked smile, then flipped open the book. His eyes darted back and forth across the pages. He stopped reading and his brow furrowed.

"What's wrong?" Shelby moved closer until she stood on his right side.

"The pages. They're blank."

He lowered the book to show her.

She gazed at the plain white paper. He fanned the pages. *Empty all right.* There weren't even any lines.

"I don't get it." He flipped the pages.

The library and books must be a Hollywood illusion.

Fake. "Everything's fake," she murmured. "But if that's true then what happened to Happy and Herbie? Why are they missing? That part of this show, if it is a show, is very real." *Too real for me. I'm still not convinced this is a show at all. I haven't seen any TV equipment or cameramen.*

"But if that's true then what happened to Herbie and Happy?" Reggie was following her line of reasoning.

The heavy library doors creaked open and Shelby jumped.

Sparkles stood in the entryway.

Shelby breathed a sigh of relief.

"Hey! Shelby! Reggie! Guys! You won't believe it!" He breathed in and out heavily as if he just ran to the room. *This is one excitable clown.*

"What is *it*?" Reggie's head bobbed in time to Sparkle's bouncing up and down like a Mexican jumping bean.

"They found Happy?" offered Shelby

Sparkles stopping jumping and stared at Shelby.

"How did you know?" Sparkles frowned and cocked his head like a confused puppy.

Shelby shrugged. "Elementary, my dear fellow contestants." *More like obvious I'd say.* "Good news travels fast?"

"Did you find Herbie, too?" The clown shook his head. Reggie frowned and crossed his arms.

The corners of Reggie's mouth curled and he crossed his arms over his chest, still holding the book. "If that's so obvious then are you psychic, too?"

Shelby chuckled and moved to another shelf of books. "No. Sorry. It's just that Sparky here seemed so attached to his friend. I assumed his good news had to be Happy had been found." Shelby turned her head and placed her index finger against her temple. "Logic, my friends."

A book thudded to the floor barely missing her arm. She looked up to see books above her tumble off the shelf as if they'd been pushed from the inside. They fell straight down to land with *thuds* all around her like a hail of angry prose. She covered her head with her arms and ran away from the storm of novels. A heavy volume struck her forearm just as she cleared the raining titles, leaving an angry red welt on her skin. "Owww! That hurt!"

The others stood far enough away they weren't being hit, but they still ran around like chickens being chased by the fox and yelling like it was a fire drill. Matt and Sparkles ran out the door in a panic screaming, "Tim-m-mber-r-r!"

Reggie rushed to her and wrapped an arm round her waist, lifted her off the floor, then carried her to a wing chair.

Reggie placed her gently in the chair. *I feel a little woozy.*

Aloha who had also come in earlier, now swiped at books using another book in her hands to deflect them away from Reggie and Shelby. *Cool.*

Shelby raised her head to gaze upon the small mountain of hardbacks where she once stood. "Whew. That was close." Her breath came in ragged gasps. *I used to think of reading was a safe hobby, now I'm not so sure.*

Thirteen

Sparkles sat on a stool at one corner of the table in the kitchen. The group had retreated there after the near miss by an avalanche of literature.

Shelby hoped the kitchen would be safer than standing beneath a mountain of books that might bury you any second.

Sparkles' red-rimmed eyes were unfocused. He sat on a stool next to her. *He looks okay, for a clown.* Shelby shook her head.

When I find the crazy librarian responsible for the bruise on my arm, I'm gonna kick his butt to Timbuktu.

After checking to make sure everyone was okay, Moist left them alone saying she had to find the bathroom.

On the counter next to the stainless steel fridge sat a plant that looked a lot like a Venus flytrap on steroids. Reggie waved at her nodding at the plant's massive bulb shaped mouth. "Think this thing eats zombies?"

Shelby chuckled. "Naw, it probably likes vampires better." She watched the plant's mouth open then snap shut just shy of Reggie's fingertips.

Shelby raised one eyebrow and indicated the obviously hungry plant with a tilt of her head. Reggie looked at the plant with its open jaw and yanked his hand away. "Hey! I'm *not* a snack."

Shelby shrugged. "Oh, well, I guess zombies are tasty too." She winked at him. *I really gotta stop encouraging him and look for the diamond. But I can't help it he's fun.*

Directly in front of her, on another wall was a large stainless steel fridge and a walk-in freezer. A large granite center island with a hardwood cutting board and twin tan-colored porcelain sink with old fashioned brass fixtures sat in the middle of the kitchen.

The kitchen smelled of fresh thyme, basil, and garlic. And no wonder. At one end of the rack of pots, hanging from hooks, were dried herbs and a bunch of garlic bulbs enclosed in a small net bag.

"I wonder if Herbie's okay?" Reggie walked to a shelf between the fridge and the walk in freezer against the wall that contained five wooden shelves of clear glass jars of various sizes.

She felt for him. If her brothers were missing, she'd be frantic by now.

"Hey, some of these jars are labeled bats' wing and eye of newt." He turned another jar around in order to read the label, "and there's even three marked toads toes." He picked one up, "Large toads toes." He shrugged. "I guess they come in more than one size. Who knew?"

Sparkles looked up and snorted, "Wow! Really? Neat." *The clown lives.*

Matt had his head in the open fridge.

Shelby chuckled. "Must be a witch's cauldron around here somewhere. The garlic must be to scare off vampires." She walked over toward Reggie and waved her hand over the zombie eating plant. It snapped at the air missing her fingers by inches. "No food this time. Too bad for you, little fella."

But what are toad toes for? She glanced at Matt who took a bite out of a red apple in his hand. She rolled her eyes.

Shelby shook her head in wonderment. *Since this is supposed to be the Addams family house, it isn't exactly a stretch if these other herbs had monster attraction properties. Zombies are re-defining what I used to think as weird. Do we ever really know normal? People have been treating me as strange since birth. And I'm certainly not weird.*

She walked over to look inside the fridge and saw shelves lined with glass jars filled with unidentifiable green, pink, red, and blueberry-blue liquids. Shelby wrinkled her nose at the smells of sour meat and mold and slammed the fridge door closed. She wiped her hands on a gray towel that hung off the oven handle of the gas stove across the room. *Ewww!*

Shelby backed away from the fridge and spun around to find her face buried in Reggie's muscular butt cheeks. *Oops!*

"Hey! What's the idea?"

She stepped back to extricate herself. "Huh. Sorry. I didn't mean..." A rush of heat spread up her neck, and she knew her cheeks were the color of a fire engine.

Moist appeared through the door and tripped. She stopped from falling by grabbing the counter edge with both hands. Her eyebrows were arched, her emerald eyes wide.

"Happy! I found him--" Moist's eyes focused on her feet as she held onto the other side of the stainless steel counter across from Shelby

What is she talking about? Moving closer to the counter Shelby rose on the tips of her toes so she could peer over the counter.

Sure enough, Happy lay flat on his back on the floor. His eyes were closed, but Shelby could see his chest rise and fall. His black wig had slipped toward one side a little, but other than that, his makeup and his fake nose looked perfect. There wasn't any blood and his clown costume, while dirty with soot, was relatively unscathed.

"Now if we can only find Colonel Mustard with the lead pipe in the library," she murmured.

"Who?" Obviously, Reggie wasn't a fan of the board game *Clue*. *Guy needs an education about classic board games.* "Never mind, big guy."

"Al--uh--Moist?" Shelby moved around the counter and knelt next to Moist, who moved her hands over Happy's head and chest looking for injuries. "How is he?"

Moist had removed the clown's black wig to reveal Happy's smooth, bald head. On his forehead under the wig was a huge bump the size of a goose egg, which meant he either fell and struck his head or someone hit him.

Moist's eyes narrowed. "I don't know. Do you?"

Shelby grunted then reached for Happy's wrist. His pulse was faster than normal. Happy's mouth hung open. She placed two fingers over the clown's mouth. His hot breath blew against her skin. *He's breathing too fast.*

Without his wig and by the lines on his face, she saw he was a very old man.

He looks older than Dad, and my father's the oldest man in the world.

"He's the oldest clown in the business." Sparkles eyes drooped at the corners. "An amazing guy who most people think is much younger." He hung his head. "It's the high pitched voice."

Shelby nodded. "Well, if we only had a first aid kit we can help him to retain that title for several years yet."

As if on cue, Reggie rushed to kneel beside the wounded clown with a first aid kit--in a red pack with a white cross on the plastic lid--tucked under his left arm. He squatted next to Shelby. *Very good, big guy.*

Sparkles rushed around the counter and knelt next to the injured clown across from Reggie.

Shelby sat back on her haunches at Happy's feet. *What is this a football huddle?* "Guys, the air is getting a little thin in here. Sparky, why don't you boil some water?" She looked at Aloha in her Moist disguise. "And Moist, why don't you find...something...anything."

Moist nodded and disappeared out the door she'd come back through. *Yeah. I knew it. She didn't have to go to the bathroom. I wonder where she really went? I've gotta keep my eye on her.*

She heard Sparkles grunt as he turned on the tap at the sink followed by the sound of water beginning to fill a steel pot.

Satisfied she'd given the clown something to keep him out of the way, she turned her attention back to the injured clown. "Let's see what we have in here." She took the first aid kit that Reggie had laid out on the floor and bent forward to study the clown's features more closely. *This doesn't look so bad. Mild concussion by the look of it. I've worse bumps when I was a barista at Planet Coffee.*

"Where did you get the first aid kit?"

"I found it on the floor in the corner by the fridge."

Shelby lifted her eyes and smiled wryly at him. "I suppose a ghost left it there?" The level of weirdness had just gone up a notch. *Maybe a ghost knocked Happy out, too.*

Peering inside, she saw a collection of cloth bandages, band-aids, tubes of ointment, and antiseptics.

Reggie reached into the bag and pulled out packs that looked like the ketchup that accompanied a meal from a fast food restaurant.

"Smelling salts," he handed her a packet. "This'll wake him up. Tear off one corner and hold it under his nose."

She tore off the perforated corner. The sharp chemical scent of the smelling salts filled the air. Shelby placed the open end of the packet under Happy's nose.

Happy's eyes popped open, and a groan erupted from between his black lips. With one hand, he grasped his throat as if he were choking.

"Hey! What the...?" he sputtered.

Shelby threw the packet to the tiled floor and placed one hand on his shoulder to keep him from rising too quickly.

Reggie held five fingers in front of the clown's face. "How many fingers do I have?"

"The same as me?" Happy placed the palm of his right hand on his forehead. "Owww! My head hurts." He shoved Reggie's hand away. "Ya got an aspirin?"

"Does the kit have a compress?"

Sparkles walked toward them and stood holding a large pot of water that sloshed over the sides. The tip of his tongue curled out the right side of his mouth. *Cold water? Unbelievable.* Shelby smiled at him, "*Boil* the water." *Gotta keep these guys busy so they don't get in my way.*

"Oh? Sorry." He turned around and disappeared toward the stove across the kitchen.

Shelby stood and walked over to the sink to pluck a dishcloth off the edge and soaked it with cold water from the tap. She held the damp cloth out to Reggie.

Reggie folded it lengthwise then placed it carefully across Happy's forehead.

"Can you understand me?" Shelby studied the dazed clown.

Happy looked at her uncomprehending. "Huh. Yeah. I think so?" Happy placed one hand on the dishcloth and winced as he closed his eyes.

Reggie leaned forward. "Did you see who hit you?"

The clown opened his eyes and looked at Reggie, "Someone hit me?"

Reggie sighed. "I don't think we're going to get much from him. Too bad, I hoped he'd help us find Herbie. Help me get him up, then we can carry him upstairs."

"Do I look like I can carry a tallie?" *How soon they forget.*

Reggie avoided her look and his shoulders slumped. "Huh, sorry. Sparkles and I'll carry him upstairs. Okay?"

"Yeah. Good thinking." *Once a tallie, always a tallie. It's so hard to trust tallie's.* She looked at his handsome features and gentle eyes begging for her forgiveness. *He's sorry. I gotta lighten up, but after years of being discriminated against, it's so hard.*

She glanced over her shoulder at Sparkles who pushed and pulled buttons trying to figure out how the stove worked so he could boil the water. "Forget it, Sparkles. Help Reggie carry Happy upstairs."

Reggie and Sparkles disappeared through the door leading to the dining room with the injured clown's arms thrown over their shoulders.

Moist stood on the other side of the door, her hands buried in the folds of her clown costume. She walked into the kitchen after Reggie and Sparkles were gone. "No ghosts out there." She shrugged.

Shelby smiled. *Funny lady.* "Why don't we check the library? Since Happy turned up in here, we might find Herbie in there. Makes sense right?" She paused and Moist nodded. "On the condition that you promise me if we find a secret passage we'll investigate. Agreed?"

Finally, after a longer pause Moist nodded. "Okay. Agreed. Two sets of eyes are better than one. You better tell me if you find Herbie--or anything else."

"Like what?" Shelby asked innocently.

"Like the prize." Moist raised an eyebrow. "Or *anything* else."

"Yeah, the prize, right." *I wonder if she knows about the diamond?* "But what about the cameras?"

Moist cast her a wry smile and patted the left side of her costume with the palm of one hand. The smile faded until she patted the other side and smiled with satisfaction.

Thought ya lost that L.I.P.S. damper thingy, didn't ya?

"Not to worry about that, Shelby." She winked.

They shook hands tentatively. *We're in for a bumpy ride.*

Fourteen

SHELBY ENTERED THE LIBRARY in Moist's shadow. *It must be way hot in that clown suit.* She eyed the folds of the green and white striped clown disguise. *Wonder if she keeps an air conditioner in there? She seems to have everything else.*

Shelby walked up to the mountain of books that had fallen off the shelves to examine them more closely. "There has to be a secret passage around here somewhere." *And, I haven't been alone to talk with Clem or Buster to see what they've discovered since they went for showers.*

They better find the diamond quickly or they'd have to be locked in this house for the whole week. *And I really don't want to stay.*

Moist scanned the titles on irregular stack of books. "Yeah. Must be."

Shelby pulled out *War and Peace* out of the pile. She had misjudged the weight and almost dropped it. *Man, this thing is heavy. Oh, yeah Reggie showed me the pages are blank. Seems like a waste of paper to me.* She shrugged.

Shelby grunted as she carried the heavy red leather-bound book to one of the side tables placed next to a chocolate brown chair. She sat and the seat cushion expelled a *whiff* of dust that tickled her nostrils.

She wiggled her nose then laid the book on the edge of side table and opened it to the middle. As she'd suspected this, too, was a faux book. Just like the one earlier, the pages were blank.

After letting the book fall to the floor, Shelby stood and walked to the door leading to the hallway.

This isn't getting me any closer to the diamond. I gotta find my brothers. Maybe they're having better luck than I am.

"Hey! Where're you going?" Moist called after her. "We have a lot more--"

Shelby didn't hear the rest of the L.I.P.S. agent's words as the doors slammed shut separating them.

Once alone in her room she felt the tension that had grown into a knot in her back released first in her shoulders then travel down her back. She sighed as she at last began to relax. *I'll talk to Clem and Buster tomorrow. I'm too tired and that damn diamond isn't going anywhere. And Herbie is probably fine. I hope.*

~ * ~

Shelby entered the dining room the next morning. *One day down and only six to go.* Her stomach grumbled.

Jeeves, still dressed in his formal tuxedo, served scrambled eggs from a silver serving platter.

Reggie picked listlessly at the food on his plate, while Aloha, still in her Moist the clown getup, and Sparkles were having an animated conversation comparing makeup tips. Happy shoveled as much eggs and bacon into his mouth as he could. *He certainly hasn't lost his appetite. Is it starve a cold and feed a head wound?* She shrugged.

She watched with disgust as her brothers also stuffed their faces with thick pancakes floating in syrup and greasy bacon.

Ewww. My bros are such pigs.

Toulest sat at the head of the table not eating, just watching. Her dark eyes were free of emotion. *She's not very friendly, is she?*

Everyone was here except, of course, the missing zombie, poor Herbie. *I hope he's okay.* She glanced at Reggie and wondered how he was holding it together with one of his best friends still missing.

She shifted her gaze to Toulest. *I wonder what our hostess has dreamed up for us today?*

Reggie sat at the end of the long dining table, an empty chair next to him, which was just the right height for her. She smiled to herself.

At least some good is coming out of this stupid show. He's learning about little peoples' needs and I am leaning to accept the undead, a L.I.P.S. agent, and even clowns. Shelby shook her head. *Who woulda thought?*

As she walked toward him, he glanced up from the syrup soggy pancake on his plate.

His eyes went wide when he saw her coming toward him. A generous and sexy smile appeared on his face with each step she took. *I'm like Cinderella making her grand entrance at the palace ball. You go, girl.*

He stood as she came up beside him. "Is this seat taken?"

"Why, no." Bowing as if she were a queen, he pulled the chair back from the table with one smooth motion. She climbed up the side of the chair and took her seat.

He sat down again.

"Oh, really! Cut the crap will ya," Matt snorted in disgust. "Why don't you two get a room?"

"That will be enough, Mr. Butcher," Madame Toulest spoke from her seat in the exact midpoint of the table. "There'll be no rough language here."

Shelby rolled her eyes and gazed over at Reggie who grinned and shrugged. *Rough language?*

A white china teapot with a matching teacup and saucer rested on the table in front of Toulest. A small plate with a piece of dry rye toast sat untouched to her right. Try as she might Shelby couldn't read Toulest's expression. The eyes were free of emotion. *It's like looking at dead eyes.*

An involuntary shiver ran down Shelby's spine. *She's so strange, I wonder if she's even real?*

The palms of Toulest's long-fingered skeletal hands rested on the gray, green, and white tablecloth.

She gazed intently at each contestant before finally coming to rest on a sheepish looking Matt.

"Is Happy okay?" Sparkles asked, his tone feisty.

Toulest turned her dark gaze on the clown. "Mr. Happy is fine--"

"Yeah, for now," Reggie put down his fork his voice angry. "But Herbie's still missing. What about him?"

Her left eyebrow arched and her lips pursed into a thin, cruel smile. She regarded Reggie with obvious distain. "I'm certain Mr. Holmes is also fine."

"How can you be so sure?" Shelby glowered at their hostess. "And you nearly killed Reggie. Why are the doors rigged? Are these the challenges?"

Toulest picked up a fork in her left hand. It *tinked* as she placed it on her plate. She took her cloth napkin from her lap and dabbed the corners of her lips. She dropped the crumpled napkin on the table next to the plate. Her dead black gaze focused on Shelby.

Uh-oh. She looks a little crazed.

Toulest shifted her gaze to the large mirror on the wall behind Shelby and nodded her head.

Shelby glanced at the mirror and frowned. *My eyes look tired.*

The camera must be behind the mirror, like in my bedroom. The cameras must be activated by motion detectors. Actually, that makes sense, why would anyone want to watch someone sleeping? She smiled to herself. *That'd be pretty dull.*

"No one will be hurt. This is a television show, Miss Bass. As with real life, there are many challenges, some of which you've already experienced." She glanced at Reggie. "But I assure you no one will permanently injured."

"People are missing and some of us have been hurt." Shelby's fingers touched the purple bruise where the book struck her arm. She winced. "Give us a good reason why should we believe you? You're a cheap late-late show horror movie hostess." Shelby frowned. *How am I going to beat a motioned detector and retrieve the diamond without anyone seeing me?*

"Madame Toulest, if you're so certain Herbie is fine then where is he? Exactly?" Reggie leaned forward in his chair and eyed their hostess.

Toulest rose from her seat and walked toward the door that led to the kitchen on the other side of the dining room from the door to the hallway. Her floor length black dress *shushed* as it moved across the carpet. "I'll have a word with Jeeves. He knows every inch of this house. If anyone knows it's him." She paused and her dark eyes scanned the group. "I'll be back in a moment."

She disappeared through the door to the kitchen.

After several seconds of silence, Shelby looked down the table to see her brothers were attacking their breakfasts again.

Herbie's missing in action, they're eating, and what about the diamond?

"I'll give her five minutes to come back with answers. While we wait, do you want some coffee?" Reggie stood and walked to the sideboard where a silver coffee pot sat, steam rising from the spout. "You'd better eat something," Reggie returned with the coffee pot and filled her cup with coffee.

Shelby shook her head.

"Are you joking? Herbie's missing! He might be hurt or even dead. Why are you all just sitting around stuffing your faces?" She stopped when she realized all eyes were on her. "What?"

A brief smile crossed Reggie's lips. "I care more then you know but we have to keep our strength up if we're going to find him. I'm happy you care about someone you don't even know." He frowned and checked his watch. "I'm worried."

Reggie's lips pursed into a thin line, and he pushed his fingers through his hair so roughly a piece of his gray skin stuck in his hair.

Ewww. But he is a zombie after all. "Believe me when I say I care about Herbie. We've been through a lot together. Matt, Herbie, and I are like a band of zombie brothers."

Reggie shook his head. "Going AWOL just isn't him," he paused and his eyes misted over. "Shelby, I'm really worried."

Like a block of ice in the summer sun, Shelby's heart softened toward Reggie. "When you put it that way, yeah, I guess I better eat." She leaned forward to rest her chin in her hand and looked deeply into the cool, blue pools of his eyes.

"I'm sorry I jumped all over you. It's just that with clowns, and you being nearly electrocuted, and--" She spoke in a hushed tone.

Reggie held up his hand to stop her. "It's okay, there's no need to apologize. I understand."

"Finally," Sparkles snorted. "Can we eat, or is this soap opera gonna to go on all morning?"

Shelby erupted with a laugh and patted Reggie's forearm. "Don't worry Reggie. We'll find Herbie."

"I don't think Toulest's coming back." Sparkles spoke through a mouthful of toast.

Shelby looked at the clown. "Why not?"

"It's been too long and she took her purse." The clown shrugged.

"Anyone else see her purse?" Shelby scanned around the table. Happy Reggie, and Moist shook their heads.

Great. We've been had. She's gone and who knows when she'll be back. I guess we're on our own again.

~ * ~

Shelby followed Reggie, Moist, Matt and Sparkles into the hall. Sure enough, no Toulest. *Where did she go?*

"Let's go back to library," suggested Moist.

"Why?" Reggie locked gazes with the agent disguised as a clown.

"Because I have a map,"

Reggie nodded. "Oh. Does it show any secret passageways?"

"Maybe."

Sparkles mouth formed an O shape. "A secret passage? Cool."

~ * ~

Once they were back in the library, Shelby scanned the wall of fake books her eyes drifted to the top shelf fifteen feet above her head. She looked down and checked her watch. *It's nearly noon. We've been at this for too long. We should have found a clue to finding Herbie by now.* She stretched her arms over her head and yawned.

Shortly after breakfast, Happy went to lie down complaining about a headache. Moist volunteered to stay back and play nurse for Happy while they searched.

Matt stood scanning a shelf of cookbooks. So far, all he'd mentioned was Martha Stewart's book on great vending machine dinners.

Piles of books remained right where they'd landed last night, stark evidence of yesterday's avalanche of literature. *Good thing we got out of here when we did or I'd have been buried under a complete set of encyclopedias and that's a heavy word count.*

That was wa-a-ay too close for comfort.

So far, the books remaining on the shelves hadn't fallen off.

Clem and Buster had found a brass chess set on a table near the windows facing the outside. The gold and silver characters were shaped like dragons and elves. They were playing checkers with the chess set.

Shelby shook her head and a small smile played over her lips. Simple guys, but good brothers.

A book fell off the shelf to land at Shelby's feet with a *thump*. Out of the corner of her eye, she saw Sparkles and Matt jump. *Nervous boys? Me, too, but I'm not gonna show it.*

She placed her balled fists against her hips. "I'm sure something made those books fall off the shelves. There has to a secret passage behind these books." Her eyes narrowed. "Someone didn't want us to find it so they created the book storm to chase us outta here. I'm sure of it."

Shelby turned attention back to examining the shelf of books in front of her. One title caught her attention. *Stranger in a Strange Land* by Robert A. Heinlein. *Hmmm...message?* She looked again at Sparkles. *We're all in this together, little people, zombies and even clowns. We should be working together.*

She walked over to Sparkles and placed a comforting hand on his forearm. *Who'd a thought I'd ever feel empathy for a clown?* "We're not looking for ghosts, Sparky. We're looking for the reason the books fell off the shelves. I think there are hidden passages behind the books and someone doesn't want us to find them." She dropped her hand to her side. "And I think this will lead us to Herbie."

And, I hope, to the treasure if there is one and the diamond. She didn't think that her brothers had managed to hide the diamond so well. But running from the police could mess with your mind. So the damn thing could be anywhere.

"Okay then, let's keep looking. What do you say?" She glanced at Reggie.

He nodded and grinned deepening the dimple on his left cheek. *Good, he agrees. Besides he's the cutest undead guy I ever met.*

"Before anyone else decides to jump ship," she added.

Not that once we have the diamond we aren't going to find a tunnel that leads my brothers and me outta here. She looked at Reggie. *And leave everyone high and dry.* She winced. *I feel bad to have to dump Reggie and the others. My sense of right and wrong is playing tennis right now, and right seems to be winning forty-love.*

Sparkles grunted and walked back to a shelf of children's books.

"I'm bored." Clem stood and stretched.

Buster pocketed a silver dragon and stood as well. "We should go upstairs and search the bedrooms for hidden doors and secret passageways."

"Okay boys, but I think we need to find my purse, too. I left the bag somewhere, and I'm hoping you are helping to look, right?" *They better not be going to read their comic books. What they need to do is find that diamond.* Shelby frowned. *They have to get serious about why we're here and she hoped her hint helped.*

Clem looked at her before he walked out the door and winked.

Whew. I think they understand. At least I hope so.

Shelby looked around. "Hmmm…we should find Toulest. She's been gone for a long time. She never did come back from the kitchen."

"I'll look for her," Reggie offered.

"Good idea," Shelby agreed.

Shelby suppressed the butterflies in her stomach that surfaced as she watched him leave the room.

Reggie disappeared out the library door closing it with a *thump* behind him.

If anything happens to him, I don't know what I'd do.

Fifteen

REGGIE RETURNED TO THE LIBRARY carrying four burnished steel flashlights. Everyone looked up from the pages of the books when he entered from the hall.

"She wasn't there?" Sparkles voice squeaked.

Reggie shook his head.

"Jeeves?" Sparkles added.

"Herbie?" asked Matt.

Reggie shook his head again and offered a flashlight to Shelby.

"What do we need these for?" Shelby accepted the heavy flashlight, hefting the weight in both hands.

He then handed one each to Matt and Sparkles.

Sparkles kept switching his light on and off.

The last one Reggie slipped into his belt and shrugged. "When we find the hidden passage ways they might be dark."

"Good thinking, big guy." Shelby grinned.

Sparkles and Matt began flipping volumes off the shelves. A rainstorm of books landed on the carpet filling the air with dust.

Shelby shrugged then, with a nod at Reggie, she set the flashlight on an oak end table, walked to another shelf, and began pulling books off the lower shelf, two at a time. "There has to be hidden entrance here somewhere."

Reggie moved to stand over her and reached for a thick volume of the Complete Works of William Shakespeare above her head. He grunted as he used both hands to pick up the heavy book off the shelf. Walking over to a table, he sat the book down, flipping the first few pages open.

"Little heavy there, Tex?" Shelby grinned at him then walked over to the next bookshelf and pulled off a few titles. *Figures. Westerns. A whole shelf of Zane Grey.*

Shelby glanced at Matt, who set the flashlight on the carpeted floor next to him, as he pulled more books off another shelf with his gray fingers.

Looking over at Sparkles, she saw the clown had a stack of Dr. Seuss books piled in front of him. He studied the covers then flipped them open and snorted in disgust when the pages were blank. He then threw them one after the other in a growing pile behind him.

We're putting a lot of work into this and still no sign of a safe, or secret passage. I'm beginning to think we'll never find the diamond, the prize or our missing friend.

Expecting to find blank pages like all the books, she opened the cover of another Zane Grey western. Bold-faced black typed words were printed on the page. *What the...? It isn't blank.*

"Ah, Reggie. I think you better take a look at this."

"Ummm...what?" He didn't look up from the thick volume of Shakespeare.

"This book--" All the books she'd looked at so far were blank. *Why is this one different?*

"What book?" His voice had a trace of impatience.

"A Zane Grey. It's not blank." Fanning the pages, the book had writing on each page.

She heard Reggie grunt as he stood and then he moved beside her. His eyes darted back and forth as he scanned the pages. His hip brushed against hers as he bent over the book to look more closely at the words.

A shiver ran through her.

He poked the page with his index finger. "I don't get it. Why is this book real when the others aren't?" He frowned and scratched at his cheek absentmindedly. "It has to mean something." He shrugged. "I wish I knew what."

His eyes studied the empty slot in the bookshelf as he fanned the pages with his fingers. "It'd be cool if this is a clue to finding the prize."

Or better yet the diamond.

Matt stood and walked over to join them. He left a trail of gray dust behind him.

Reggie grimaced but didn't say anything.

What's the use in telling Matt he's shedding? She looked around Reggie's tennis shoes and, sure enough, there were traces of grey dust around them as well. She winced. *Hard to imagine Matt, Reggie and Herbie turning into dust bunnies. Man, it's not fair. I have to find a way to save them.* She looked at Reggie. *I like the guy.*

Sparkles stepped in front of Matt and stood on the toes of his clown trying to reach a book off a higher shelf but tripped over Matt's Nikes and stumbled backward away from the shelf. Arms wind milling, and unable to stay on his feet, he fell and landed hard with a dull *thud* on the carpet.

"Watch it!" cried Matt, looking at the clown seated on the floor. "This is my space, pal!"

Shelby threw up her arms in disgust. "Com'on, guys, work with me. Let's stop playing games and help find Herbie. A book with words *might* be a clue."

Rubbing her temples, she tried to concentrate.

Maybe. Her eyes narrowed.

Matt moved closer to her. "But what does it mean? Will we find Herbie behind the bookcase?"

"That's one possibility, but I don't know exactly. I think this house must have secrets. It's obviously not a normal house." Shelby pointed to the stuffed moose head hanging off the wall over the door. The animal had only one antler and its eyes were crossed-eyed. "I mean does that look *normal* to you?"

Reggie chuckled and nodded. "I see what you mean."

The twin doors to library burst open. Jeeves entered carrying a tray with a silver teapot and four red rose patterned teacups with matching saucers sitting on it. The fragrant odor of Earl Grey filled the musty air.

"You scared us, Jeeves," Shelby's voice dripped with faux anger. *Never hurts to let them think you're mad. Actually, I'm glad he's back. He might know where Herbie is.*

Jeeves set the tray on an empty end table between two leather wing chairs then straightened to his full height of over six feet, cleared his throat, "Sorry, Miss. I thought your party looked parched. A cup of tea might brighten your mood and refresh the spirit."

Shelby nodded slowly, she knew her face had pinched into a scowl. "How did you know we were in here? Have you seen Herbie? And where are Wills and Toulest?"

"I'm afraid I wouldn't know where Mr. Herbie is, Miss. As for Madame Toulest, I'm afraid I am not privileged with such information."

"Oh, c'mon now." Reggie scowled at the unfazed butler. "You have to know what's going on around here."

Jeeves gazed at Reggie his features unmoved by his sudden outburst of emotion. "I beg to differ, sir. I am merely the hired help. My duties are to serve the meals and ensure your comfort."

Sparkles frowned. "If that's true, then where are the video games?" The clown nodded at Matt with a grin on his face. "I *love* video games."

"I'm afraid, Mr. Sparkles, I do not know of any video games here."

He doesn't seem to know much of anything. I better put a stop to this.

"Yes, of course, Jeeves. Thank you."

With barely a detectable nod of his head, Jeeves bowed slightly at the waist then left the room by walking backward--which is a weird thing to see--until he disappeared through the oak doors closing them behind him.

"Where were we?" Reggie asked.

Matt followed Sparkles as he walked over to the table and each poured themselves a cup of steaming copper-colored tea from the pot. They slurped loudly as they drank.

Reggie frowned clearly annoyed. "Hey you two, leave that stuff. We have work to do. I wouldn't be surprised if it's poisoned."

Shelby looked at Reggie. *Where'd that come from? But then, I'm worried too.* Falling books and a booby-trapped door were hard to forget.

Reggie's mouth formed a grim line. He shrugged. "Given what we've seen, you never know."

"Yeah, good thinking, Reggie."

Matt and Sparkles must have thought so, too. They looked wide-eyed at each other then put the teacups back on the table as if they were on fire.

Shelby grinned at the zombie and the clown then moved to one of the empty wing chairs and sat.

The producers want us to panic. Panic makes a better show. Shelby's hands formed tight fists.

She glanced at Reggie, Aloha, Sparkles and Matt then shrugged. *They're okay. I like them.* She rolled her eyes. *And I thought this would be a simple job where my brothers and I would get back and diamond and then leave this show and these people behind. Now I have to see this through. I just can't desert them--it'd be wrong.*

"You don't think Herbie's *dead,* do you?" Reggie ran his fingers through his thick blond curls. *Nice hair for a zombie-boy.*

Matt and Sparkles edged toward the door.

Shelby stood and placed her hands on her hips and glared at them. Both of them stopped and stood perfectly still as if they were the wax versions of a clown and a zombie. "Where are you two going?"

"We're leaving." Matt's eyes drooped at the corners, and Sparkles' hands were trembling.

"We're scared," added the clown.

"We all are guys," Reggie interrupted, "but there's nowhere to run anyway. We're locked in the house and we can't leave until the week is over. And I don't think Herbie's dead."

Shelby nodded and began to pace the carpet. "Herbie's got to be hidden behind a wall. And somewhere in the library, there has to be a secret door. It's the only thing that makes any sense."

Her brow furrowed. *Diversion tactic number one hundred one, create doubt.* Shelby walked over to the bookshelf and again scanned the titles. "I *could* be wrong ya know. The pages with printing could mean something completely different." She paused. "There's only one way to know for sure."

Reggie waved his hand toward the walls of books remaining on the floor-to-ceiling shelves lining the three long walls. "They're thousands of books to look through. They might as well be grains of sand on a beach.

It's going to take a lot of searching, and a lot of luck, to find a particular book that is the key to unlocking a secret door, if there is one. And besides we still need to find Herbie."

This is Sunday. One day gone. Six to go. Her stomach knotted. *I've got to find the Gnotborst diamond. To heck with the prize. After my brothers and I get what we really came for, I'll worry about getting us out of here.* She glanced at Reggie out of the corner of one eye. *Then maybe I'll let him in on the Bass family secret.* She winced. *I hope he understands.*

Sixteen

SHELBY GLANCED AT HER WATCH. *Six o'clock. Monday's pass way too slowly.* They'd been pulling books off shelves for hours. *Nothing.* The pile of discarded books had grown to a mountain challenging the size of the avalanche from earlier. *They're the biggest molehills I've ever seen.*

Shelby's eyelids were leaden, and her legs were jelly. *I'm sooo tired. I never want to see another book as long as I live. And still no secret passage. This isn't making sense. There has to be a passageway around here somewhere.*

The twin oak doors to the foyer from the dining room burst open once again. "Dinner is served," Jeeves announced in his butlerish monotone.

In her position, Shelby could see behind the butler, through the library doors, Buster and Clem stood together. They were speaking in muffled tones so she couldn't hear what they were talking about.

Have they found a clue to the whereabouts of the diamond? Clem and Buster haven't missed a meal since they were in diapers

Jeeves left the room leaving the doors open.

Shelby looked back at the wall of books and sighed. She looked over at Matt on the top step of the stepladder. It slid along the floor to ceiling bookcases on a track built into the shelves.

What's the use? I'm fed up with looking. And I'm sick of books. We're not going to find another one with printed pages, or a secret passage behind them. Besides, I'm starving.

Sparkles yelped from across the room, "Book ahoy!"

He shook a thick volume above his head with both hands and smiled from ear to ear. *He's found the book with the clue we need!*

Sparkles hefted the book from the shelf with both hands and with a grunt carried the thick volume to a table. Matt scrambled down the ladder and Reggie stood up from where he knelt checking the lowest shelves. He came over to stand beside Shelby who'd moved closer to the table where Sparkles had set the book.

It certainly isn't the abridged version.

The Child's Collection of Grimm's Fairytales sat closed on the table.

She excitedly slapped the clown on the back of his thigh to congratulate him. *I thought we'd never find us another one, but thank goodness for Sparky.*

Sparkles' green eyes narrowed in the center of a circle of pasty white makeup, and his white forehead wrinkled. He rubbed the spot where she'd hit him then fanned the books pages with his fingers.

The clown raised his eyes to gaze at Shelby. He threw open the pages and they all leaned in to get a closer look. The pages were blank.

Sparkles looked at her. His eyes were so sad she wanted to cry. "It's hopeless." He sighed. "We're never gonna find the secret passageway or Herbie." He paused his shoulders slumped. "Let's go grab some dinner and recharge our batteries. We can bring our food back and keep going."

Boy, do I ever feel the same way but we can't give up. "We're all frustrated and tired." Shelby patted the clown's arm.

Reggie's eyes narrowed and his hands balled into fists at his sides. "I'm not giving up. Ever. We don't need food, we need to find Herbie." *Wow. He said zombie's need food for fuel to stay alive. I guess Herbie's more important to him than hamburger.*

She shifted her gaze to the open doors. Her brothers were gone. *That's funny, they've never missed a meal in their lives.* "Has anyone seen my brothers?" Reggie and Sparkles shook their heads in unison.

Where could they be? She nibbled her lip. *Maybe they went to eat without us.*

"What are we going to do with Happy?" said Sparkles.

Shelby gently patted Sparkles arm. "Don't worry he'll be fine. He's upstairs in bed all ready."

So far no one had found any hidden passageways in the kitchen, or her brothers would have been screaming in here like fire trucks. If anything was hidden, her brothers would have found the prize or diamond. After all, she had to admit they were pretty good thieves. *They just can't hang on to what they steal. Imagine losing the Gnotborst diamond, the largest, most valuable single gem in the world.*

Shelby rolled her shoulders to loosen her tired muscles. *But hey, no one's perfect. Maybe the bros found a safe and they're trying to figure the combination?* She shook her head. *Wishful thinking, girl. Today hasn't been one my better days.*

She looked around at the others who shuffled like they were all zombies. A frown creased her brow. *And why hasn't Moist come back after taking Happy upstairs?* Her heart sank. *Is everyone missing? Girl, you are gettin' wa-a-ay too paranoid.*

The heavy fairytale book slid off the table to land with a *thud* on the carpet.

What the...? Did it just move by itself? Instinctively she covered her eyes expecting another literary deluge. Nothing happened. She opened one eye to see Reggie bend down to retrieve the fallen book. Her legs trembled.

As he knelt, he glanced over his shoulder at Shelby. His indigo eyes danced with excitement. *A near miss must be a sign.*

He slowly opened the book his face squished in a wince.

Blank. Another dud? So much for signs.

"This sucks," he murmured.

Shelby looked at the zombie. At least we haven't heard from a ghost. *Maybe it's missing, too.*

Seventeen

SHELBY PACED BACK AND FORTH. *It's late. Too late. And I've got itchy feet.* "I gotta do *something*, anything," she murmured.

Reggie's footsteps *thumped* as he, too, paced the carpet beside the long dining room table. His hands were locked behind his back, and his brow was wrinkled in concentration. None of them had eaten a thing. Her stomach rumbled. *But we're getting close to something. I just wish I knew which something it is, the diamond, the prize, or Herbie.*

Matt sat on a dining room chair and stared out the dark windows.

Sparkles picked at the pork chop and cabbage on his plate.

Her plate sat empty on the dining table while she paced. *Funny how your hunger disappears when life throws the unexpected at you.*

She glanced at her watch. *Seven-thirty.* "Where can they be?"

When her brothers failed to appear for dinner by six thirty she'd become even more worried. Aloha had eaten half her pork chop and one forkful of cabbage.

Shelby smiled weakly at the disguised L.I.P.S. agent. *She isn't in the mood to eat either, obviously.*

Her gaze drifted over to Happy, who sat across from her devouring a whole apple pie, shoveling crust and cooked apple into his mouth. "Hey, Happy." The clown stopped in mid-chew to stare at her. Hard to believe anything could be worse than a clown chewing, but a clown with his mouth full was actually worse.

"Yeah?" Happy mumbled around his mouthful of pie.

Shelby glanced at the empty chairs specially designed for little people. "Have you seen my brothers?"

"Nope," he shook his head.

First Herbie, now Clem and Buster are MIA. I hope there looking for the diamond. Her brow wrinkled. She paced more quickly. *And I hope they're okay.*

Jeeves appeared carrying a plate filled with freshly cooked pork chops. He approached her, but she shook her head. *Jeeves might know where they are.* She looked into his perpetually sad blue eyes. "Jeeves, have you seen my brothers?"

"No, Mademoiselle Bass. I have not. Mr. Matt was already here when I rang the dinner bell. Only Mademoiselle Moist, Mr. Happy, Mr. Sparkles, then you, and Mr. Reggie showed up." He shook his head. "No one else I'm afraid."

Shelby looked at Moist. *Do the clowns have to wear those clown outfits all the time? There gonna get a little stinky if they don't change their clothes soon. The only thing worse than a clown is a smelly clown.*

Moist looked up from her plate. "I passed them in the hallway on my way back from the bathroom. They didn't come back?"

"No," Shelby eyed Moist, "they didn't." So if Jeeves rang the bell and they were seen coming back from the bathroom where were they? *Now I'm really worried.*

"It's no use," Matt sounded defeated and pushed his hand through his hair. "We have to get out of here. We have to go to the cops."

Reggie frowned. "Sure. And what do we tell them? A zombie and two midgets--" he glanced at Shelby--"Uh, I mean two *little people* are missing, and a clown has been hit on the head. And all this took place in the course of a reality show in which the prize is eternal life."

"Somehow, I don't see the cops taking us seriously," said Reggie, "Besides we have no evidence that anyone is in danger."

"Except me," he shifted his gaze to Happy who still wore the bandage around his head. *This is a TV show, isn't it?*

Shelby didn't want the police involved. She and her brothers had enough heat on them. The cops had never found the missing Gnotborst diamond. Before they'd left home, the detectives had asked a lot of question around the circus. Also, her brothers told her they noticed a few times they were being tailed. *Only the cops have no idea they lost the diamond--they think we still have it.*

"He's right." She nodded. "It's more likely the tabloids would be interested in the drama of this mess than the cops."

Oops! I hope I didn't over play my hand. After all, Aloha is a type of cop. If she knew what they were after, she might call in the local cops. Not a bad idea if they had a phone that worked. And if they knew how to open the doors without being shocked or objects falling on their heads or disappearing or whatever else Wills had planned for them.

Shelby stole an uncertain glance at Moist. Despite the L.I.P.S. agent's earlier verbal slippage, the others didn't yet seem to suspect the clown was an undercover federal agent.

I hope she hasn't formed a secret alliance with anyone here. But if she has with who would be the most likely candidate? Shelby scanned the faces of her dinner companions.

Moist looked down at her plate and speared a piece of chicken with her fork. "We can't even prove that three of our party have been kidnapped. We're only suspecting Herbie, Clem and Buster are missing. We have no ransom note. Nor do we have any physical evidence of foul play. For all we know they could be hiding, part of the game...of course there are other possibilities."

Reggie stood so quickly his chair flew backward and fell to the carpeted floor with a heavy *thud*. "I'm going to look for Shelby's brothers and my pal, Herbie. I'm willing to bet there is a secret door upstairs in one of the bedrooms and I'm going to find it. None of them would disappear on purpose."

I like a man of action. Hey, could thing I formed an alliance with Reggie. I'll need a tallie to reach the diamond if it's out of my reach. "I'm coming with you." *He seems to like me so maybe I can talk him into to helping me.*

She imagined Reggie with a mischievous smile dressed in swim trunks, his washboard stomach glistening with salt water. He held a surfboard on a white sandy beach, the surf crashing in the background.

Ahhh. Hawaii.

"Reggie, do you want me to come along?"

He stopped to look at her, his eyebrows were raised. "Yeah, sure. But I'm going alone. It's too dangerous." Reggie shattered her perfect image of him as her tanned surfer boy on a Hawaiian beach.

Crap. He saw right through me.

"Listen, pal, I worked at Starbucks. If you don't think it's dangerous being three foot two around all that hot coffee, try getting on your knees and live in my world some time. I'm going with you."

Reggie's blue eyes studied her, his square jaw set in determination. "No. You're not."

I don't believe this guy. He still thinks he's going alone. He's assuming there's danger. Sure, someone has been hit on the head, but they'd have to reach me first and I duck really well.

She shook her head and rose from her chair. *Courage, girl. Stand tall.* "No way. It's my brothers who're missing and I'm going. And no testosterone fueled zombie is gonna stop me."

A loud tapping on a plate made her look away from Reggie. Turning to face the sound, she saw Aloha with her hands folded over each other on the tabletop. The disguised agent cleared her throat. "What did you say?"

"That I'm going with Reggie--"

"No, after that," Moist waved her fork impatiently like a conductor's baton.

"Testosterone fueled zombie?"

"Yes." Moist frowned and placed her fork on her plate with the *click* of metal against china.

"So?"

"Zombies." Moist's green eyes travelled over the rest of the group.

Reggie looked at Shelby then together they looked at Moist like she'd suddenly grown two heads.

Moist grinned sheepishly. "I'm a bit of a fan. Well, actually I have every one of the Zombies albums, CD's, and singles--"

"Never mind that," snapped Shelby, "what has the Zombies got to do with the Herbie being missing?"

Matt and Sparkles stood up from the table and started to dance around while Matt played air drums and Sparkles simulated playing an air guitar that would make Clapton proud. *The all-star-dead-with-a-clown band?* Shelby stifled a laugh. *Too funny.*

Moist grinned. "I should explain. As you know, like many rocker bands of the sixties, the Zombies went through a period of addiction problems. When they recovered they gave an interview to *Rolling Stone* titled 'Me and Mr. McGoo'."

"I get it." Reggie crossed his arms over his chest a grin crossing his features.

Shelby frowned at him. "What is there to get? Moist doesn't know what she's talking about. Old rock and roll singers, zombies, clowns, and little people have nothing in common. When I get outta here my friends back home are never gonna believe I appeared on this silly-ass show. Even I don't believe it and I'm living it."

Moist ignored Shelby's outburst, "I expect somewhere in the well stocked library is a collection of Rolling Stone articles. If we can find the one with the interview with my pals the Zombies, we'll find our next breadcrumb."

Moist folded her hands over her chest and stared at the table. *Is she kidding? Like she knows the Zombies personally?*

"Sorry to burst your balloons, clowny, but isn't this *all* a bit of a stretch? I'm going upstairs to search, you can do whatever you want. How about as an alternative plan, Sparkles and Matt can go back to library while Reggie and I go upstairs and look for a hidden door."

At the mention of their names, Matt and Sparkles ceased playing their imaginary instruments and looked at Shelby with enthusiastic grins on their faces. "Yeah, we'd love to read old *Rolling Stone* mags. Wouldn't we Sparky?" Sparkles nodded eager to help.

That ought to keep everyone busy. Now all I have to do is convince Reggie to help me and the diamond will soon be back in Bass hands. She paused to gaze at the zombie. *Maybe I should take him to Hawaii with me. A zombie is not exactly what I had in mind for my blond surfer boy but we seem to be getting along and he's certainly handsome. Hmmmm...I wonder if gray skin tans?*

Moist shrugged and rose from the chair. "Sure thing, Shel. How you waste your time is no business of mine. I'll stick with the boys and go to the library."

You can lead a clown to water but you can't make the secret agent underneath drink it. Shelby shrugged and walked toward the door. "Okay, then let's go." Reggie walked up beside her. *A girl and her loyal zombie companion.* She chuckled to herself. *I'm so cool.*

Jeeves entered through the swinging door from the kitchen carrying a silver tray just as Shelby opened the dining room door.

"No dessert?" Jeeves' tone reflected his offense that they were departing before he served dessert.

"That's okay, Jeeves. You eat it." *I don't care much for desserts, anyway.*

Reggie grinned at her and he took her hand in his. *His hand is sure warm. Oh, man, I don't want to let go of him, ever.* She reveled in the way he looked at her as if she were the only woman who existed, and the gentle tone of his voice sent shivers down her spine. *I love the way his eyes sparkle when he looks at me. It's like we've known each other all our lives.*

Reluctantly, she let go of his hand. *When he touches me, whoa!* Her face felt warm. "Shall we?" She turned and went out to the foyer.

"I told you they were gonna get a room." Matt groaned.

Eighteen

REGGIE WALKED AHEAD OF HER in the hallway going toward his room. There were weathered floorboards visible through holes in the thick wine red rug. Reggie's long strides were fast separating them.

Oops. He's getting away. Shelby hurried to keep up. "Hey, zombie-boy, hold up." He glanced over his shoulder and winced then slowed his pace and she quickly caught up.

Some of the teams had to share a room due to space limitations in the run down house. Matt, Herbie, and Reggie shared one. Reggie opened the door to his room and held it for her.

She eyed the sixth bedroom door as she entered. *We haven't looked in there yet.* There might be a major clue in the sixth bedroom--it might be where the secret door was.

She scanned Reggie's room as she entered. "You know, I'm wondering about that sixth bedroom." Shelby jumped when Reggie kicked the door shut behind her with his foot.

We're alone. Cool. "Something on your mind?" *I like really this man.*

Her breath caught when Reggie suddenly wrapped his strong arms around her waist, picked her up and spun her around. Now eye level, she gazed directly into the eyes that had been fascinating her since she met him. She pressed her lips against his. *Hmmmm. Yummy.*

Eagerly, she pressed her body into his. Her tongue slipped easily into his mouth, and she dueled hungrily with him for supremacy.

Hmmm. Pork chops, cabbage and zombie--what a wonderful combination.

For several fleeting seconds, Shelby wanted to urge him to take her to one of the three single beds against the wall. *I better not. He might tear and that would be bad. And a little icky, but we can't all be perfect can we?* Reluctantly, she broke off the kiss.

Darn those hidden television cameras. She gazed longingly into his eyes. *If only we'd met under different circumstances.*

She forced her eyes to drop away from his gaze. "I don't think this is the right time," she whispered. Shelby hoped he wasn't too disappointed. *I know I am.*

Looking back into his blue eyes made her ache with their shared passion.

He's shown me through his actions that he is gentle, caring and he really is into me. I'm falling in love with this man. I don' want to but I can't help myself. We come from different worlds. He's a zombie and a tallie. And I'm a little person and not undead. A relationship between us could never work. Her heart beat hard in her chest, and her breathing became rapid.

If I steal the diamond and the prize, I can get out of my life of crime and be in Hawaii the next day. He won't want to go to Hawaii with me. Bodies rot faster in the tropical heat. Do I want freedom, or to stay and take a chance at love with a man who I think I'm falling for, and who's likely to turn to dust sooner than later? She sighed, her hands held tightly in her lap. *This isn't fair.*

"You okay?" Reggie studied her, his brow wrinkled his eyes curious.

She shook her head and closed her eyes.

"All I know, Shelby, is I want you."

And, given the current state of his peeling flesh, who knew how long they would enjoy being together? What's the shelf life of half-made zombies? *It was a good thing that Mambo didn't finish her magic spell or Reggie would be really be undead.* Unfortunately, he wasn't going to last forever. *As usual, girl, your timing is wa-a-ay off. Story of my life--fall for the wrong guy at the wrong time.*

She gazed into his eyes and placed one hand on his right cheek. "I don't think it would work between us." Her heart seemed to skip a beat. *Did I just say that out loud?*

"Yes." His words seemed to catch. He swallowed hard and his eyes brimmed with tears. "You're right, of course," Reggie's voice was huskier now.

Shelby's body slumped like balloon that had the air let out. *If only we could find the prize. If it's real, we could have a shot. If Wills is lying, then for sure there'll be no us and I'll end up all alone in Hawaii in my little grass shack. Great.*

After unwinding her arms from his neck and her legs from his waist, she slid down his muscular frame to the floor. On the way down, she rubbed over the telltale bulge that demonstrated their passion was mutual.

Her face grew warm. She averted her eyes from his gaze.

This must be the cold shower episode of the show. "We should go. I wonder if the basement is very dark?"

"Let's check the closet before we go," suggested Reggie

Shelby nodded. *Sure why not?*

He walked to the closet door and listened very carefully by pressing an ear to the door. He shook his head stepped back and swung it open on its creaky hinges. Inside, on the floor were two small black soft-sided suitcases, which looked more like backpacks with handles.

He stepped inside, pulled the suitcases out one at a time, and handed them to Shelby.

She grunted from their weight and placed them side by side on the worn burnt orange carpet behind her. Though the suitcases were large enough, they were too light to be hiding her brothers.

He knelt and rubbed his hands along the floorboards of the closet looking for hidden switches or latches.

A soft moan from the direction of one of the beds behind them made Shelby freeze.

Reggie looked over his shoulder at her.

Shelby shrugged. Listening intently, there was another moan from the furthest bed shoved against the wall. "I'll check it out," she whispered to Reggie. When he moved to follow her, she shook head.

In for a penny, in for a buck. One of these days, I'm gonna regret being so brave. Shelby sucked in a breath then tiptoed toward the bed. She stood over the bed studying the human-shaped lump in the middle until she abruptly pulled back the pink rose-colored bedspread.

111

She let the cover slip from her fingers and drop to the floor.

With the cover gone, she saw a little person curled in a fetal position lying on his side facing away from her toward the wall. The dark brown curls on his head looked familiar as did his baggy blue jeans. *He sure snores.*

Hmmm...I recognize that snore. But why are his hands and feet tied?

Her pulse raced. The man was one of her missing brothers. *Clem?* A blue and white polka dot handkerchief covered his mouth. *Why? Who did this to him?* "Reggie. Help me," she whispered urgently her excitement rising.

Reggie hurried to her side. He pulled at the ropes holding her brother.

With trembling fingers, she managed to undo the ropes around his hands.

Shelby whipped the handkerchief off his mouth to find gray duct tape underneath. "Clem! Are you okay?" her eyes brimmed with tears. Shelby took his right hand in hers and stroked his wrist gently. *Please be okay, bro I couldn't bear it if anything happened to one of you.*

Gently, she pulled the duct tape off his mouth. His gray-blue eyes were open, but stared straight ahead.

She resisted the urge to wrap her arms around Clem, certain if she did she would only add to his discomfort. She had to force herself not to touch him for fear of hurting him any further. *Crap, crap, crap, crap. I gotta do something!*

Reggie still struggled to untie the knots around his ankles.

"Be careful there, zombie-boy! This is my brother."

She looked at Reggie and mouthed an apology. He nodded.

Reggie grunted, the tip of his tongue stuck out one side of his mouth. "I'm trying, but I just can't get the rope undone."

He shouted in triumph as the ropes finally pulled apart.

Clem moaned weakly.

Shelby supported Clem with one hand behind his back and gazed helplessly at Reggie. "Is he going to be okay?"

Reggie shrugged. "I don't know, but since none of us so far has been seriously hurt, I expect he will recover. By the look of him I'd say he's been drugged."

Suppressing her fear of hurting him with one finger Shelby gently poked her brother's arm. "Wake up, Clementine Bishop Oscar Bass! We need to know where Buster and Herbie are! You're the only one who knows. Wake up!"

Reggie chuckled. "Clementine?"

"Yeah. My Mom's a fan of the classics"

"Classics?" Reggie walked to a nearby chair and sat down. He used the sleeve of his shirt to wipe the perspiration off his forehead.

"Yeah, you know? *My Darling Clementine*--the song."

Reggie nodded then wrinkled his forehead. "Shelby?"

"As in, the best car Ford ever built is the Mustang." She shrugged. "Classics come in all forms." She shrugged. "Mom had a lot of hobbies."

Reggie shook his head. "It doesn't look like he's going be coherent for some time. I'll get him some water then maybe we better leave him on the bed and wait?"

"Yeah. Good idea." She glanced at her stricken brother. *I'm worried. I'd hate anything to happen to Clem or Buster.* Her stomach tightened and she blinked away tears. *Especially after losing Mom.*

Clem emitted a soft sigh as he rolled on his side back into a fetal position. He stuck his thumb in his mouth and snored loudly. *So much for water.*

"He's going to cut down a few trees with that saw." Reggie joked with a brief smile. His eyes narrowed. "Shouldn't we tell the others we found Clem, and that Buster isn't with him?" His gray brow wrinkled. "He might lying somewhere hurt, too."

Shelby shook her head as her eyes dropped back to her brother. Her fingers gently brushed his cheek. "I don't know, but I'd rather wait to see if Clem wakes up. He'll know where Buster is." She looked up at Reggie. "And he might know where Herbie is, too."

She gazed at the sleeping Clem. "He snores so darned loud back home the rest of us had to start wearing earplugs." *Home. I never thought I'd miss his snoring.* She sighed. "Good times."

"Think we should look under the bed for Buster?" suggested Reggie.

"Sure, if you want." She took one of Clem's hands in hers.

Reggie nodded. He knelt beside the bed next to her then his head disappeared under it.

His head came out from under the bed. "Empty."

Shelby rolled her eyes. "Yeah. Our luck holds. All bad. Problem is he's the only lead we have in finding Herbie and Buster, and I don't want to leave him alone."

"Do you want something to drink while we wait for him to wake up?" Reggie offered.

"Sure." Shelby shrugged. "That would be great."

"Iced tea? Lemonade?"

"Apple juice, I saw some in the fridge earlier." Shelby released Clem's hand and sat on one of the two wood chairs resting against the wall on either side of the closet door.

The bedroom door burst open, and Jeeves entered carrying a tray upon which rested two glasses of apple juice.

Shelby cast Reggie a bemused grin and rolled her eyes. "I'd *really* like to know how he does that."

Jeeves set the tray on a night table then left, closing the bedroom door behind him.

A red flush crept up Reggie's grey neck to his cheeks, and he averted his gaze to look at the floor.

"Is something wrong?"

"I have to tell you something. Something important."

Uh, oh. Here it comes, the big brush off. I'm just the fly on the shoulder of life. Shoo, fly, shoo. I guess I offended him.

"I used to be Sir Reginald Kincade of Gnotborst--*used to be* being the operative phrase."

"Gnotborst?" *Oh, crap. The Gnotborst diamond is from Gnotborst. Act casual, girl, he doesn't know the Bass' stole it.* "Is that in Europe? The place with the really tasty sausages?"

"Huh. Well, yes actually, my kingdom does have a tradition of fine smoked meat products."

Shelby chuckled. *Naw. He's pulling my leg. A prince? Oldest line in the book. What's he gonna tell me next, he's with the CIA?* "Oh, com'on, zombie-boy. You expect me to buy that line? A sir? A lord of some kingdom? Com'on *really*. What a load of--"

The bedroom door flew open. "It's true." An all too familiar feminine voice from a shrouded figure in the doorway interrupted them.

It was the voice of Aloha, L.I.P.S.-special-agent-of-the-weirdo-files, Armstrong disguised as a clown named Moist.

Shelby threw up her hands. *How does she do that?* Mulder and Scully would be shocked if they knew who'd replaced them. For sure, they'd be horrified upon seeing Aloha in her Moist get up. FBI agents didn't like to think of themselves as clowns. She stifled a giggle at the mental image of Mulder in a Bozo suit. *What's the use? This is too silly for words.*

Moist swung the door aside with her hand and stood with her hands on her hips. *That's some pose.*

Shelby put a hand to her mouth to mask the unwanted giggle. Removing her hand from her mouth, "Don't you *ever* knock?"

"Uuuh. I…" Moist stopped, she couldn't come up with a response.

Moist straightened her shoulders and her eyebrows pinched into a frown. "It's true. We have a file on Reginald Morton Philip James Kearney, fourteenth Earl of Gnotborst, also known as Reggie K., nuclear physics graduate student, and bad white boy rapper of the Phi Beta Kappa fraternity."

Shelby looked at Reggie. He grinned sheepishly and shrugged. *Rapper, huh? Yeah right.*

"His father, King Gustav the Third, is Gnotborst's Ambassador to the United States. Disavowed by his father when he became a zombie, Reggie harbors resentment. Since turning zom he and his frat boys have taken to finding radium they claim slows down their inevitable disintegration."

Reggie's ears turned bright reddish-grey, but he didn't say a word.

"The ambassador told everyone his son died in an unfortunate sausage machine accident. Of course, *we* know different. *We* always do."

Shelby shook her head. *I kissed a prince? Cool. Too bad, we stole his family jewel. Man, If he finds out we stole the diamond any chance of an us-- never mind that he's a zombie--is gonna go sour for sure*

"Way ta go, Ms. Genius G-woman. Mulder and Scully would be proud. Zombies, clowns, and federal agents on a reality show." Shelby drummed her fingers against the chair arm. 'This is about as X Files as it gets."

"You're FBI!" Reggie rose from kneeling by the bed, his eyes travelling from Shelby to Moist, then back again.

"Damn." Moist lowered her head and slapped her forehead with the palm of her hand. "No, I'm *not* FBI. I work for the Legal Integrated Protection Service."

Shelby pointed a thumb at the painting hung on the wall over the four-drawer dresser of a black pussycat with its back raised in attack mode, its lips pulled back and its teeth bared as if hissing in anger. "America, meet Moist the Clown, also known as Aloha Armstrong, the woman from L.I.P.S."

Aloha unzipped the front of her Moist the clown costume and let it drop to a heap at her feet. She stood with her hands on her hips, her red curly hair cascading about her shoulders, wearing spandex tights and a sleeveless tee shirt that emphasized the swell of her bosom.

Reggie smiled and crossed his arms. "I knew there was something different about you."

~ * ~

The soft bed felt good. Buried under the covers that were so warm, Shelby felt like she could stay hidden here all day. *Welcome to your artificial day.* She smiled, rolled onto her back, and stretched her arms over her head.

Rising off the bed, she waddled across the carpet to the washroom. *Knock, knock.*

She hesitated and wasn't about to open the door to just anyone without confirmation of who or what was on the other side. *My room is like Grand Central Station, and it's a little early for visitors.*

"Yeah. Who is it?" She called out one hand flat on the door.

"It's me. Agent Armstrong."

Shelby sighed and opened the door.

What's with her? She looks like she slept in her clothes. At least the clown disguise is gone.

Shelby yawned and scratched her scalp then kicked the door closed with her sock encased foot.

Aloha's fiery red hair dangled askew over her forehead and dark circles under her green eyes made her look like death warmed over. *Aloha obviously hasn't slept a wink.*

"Hey. What ya been up to?" Shelby stifled another yawn.

"I didn't want to say anything last night, but the note I found in the book of fairytales is very revealing." Aloha hesitated her eyes avoiding Shelby's her shoulders were tight.

"I thought the book was blank like the others?"

Aloha nodded. "It was but I managed to palm a note I found after the last page."

She didn't tell us about the note until now? "I'll bite, why did you palm it?"

"I had to conduct some inquiries."

Shelby's eyes narrowed. *Is she in touch with someone one the outside?*

"Okay, but revealing? How?" *C'mon how much worse can it get? I hope she has good news about Buster and Herbie.*

"The note said the contestants upstairs will be soon be missing *permanently.*"

Fear twisted like an oily snake in Shelby's belly. "Why didn't you tell us this last night?"

Her heart leapt into her throat. "Oh, my! Why didn't I think of this before? C'mon, Aloha." Shelby threw open the door, leaned into the hallway, cupped her mouth in her right hand and yelled, "Fire!"

Following Shelby's lead without question, Aloha slid past her and ran up and down the hallway shouting, "Fire!"

Shelby watched as a Clem, Sparkles, Happy, Reggie and Matt stumbled sleepily into the hallway. *It's a stampede of weirdoes but I had to get everyone out of bed somehow and yelling fire works every time.*

Herbie and Buster were still missing but everyone else stared at them, confused.

Aloha stood with her hands on her hips next to Shelby, a smile of satisfaction on her fine boned features. "We did it. Now what?"

Shelby slapped Aloha hard across her thigh, looked up, and grinned at the startled agent.

"Hey! What's that for?" Aloha rubbed her upper thigh.

My Zombie Prince

"That is for not telling us last night about the danger we were in before we went to bed. Did you expect us to wake up missing? You want the prize all to yourself don't you?"

"What? Shelby, have you lost your mind? I didn't finish telling you what's going on." She paused to rub her thigh then continued, "After I read the note again I discovered another message on the same paper, written underneath the first one in disappearing ink. The other message appeared when I held the paper under a black light I carry in my makeup kit."

"What made you think to look? Shelby turned toward the bathroom intending to brush her teeth. *Morning breath, yuk.*

Reggie approached them, while the others scurried for the protection of their rooms. But actually, it was smart of her to get them out of their rooms to verify they were all okay. *Gotta love those side benefits.*

She turned her attention back to Aloha. "And what did it say?"

"Beware the joker in a deck of fifty-two."

Reggie blinked and looked at Aloha. "And what does that mean, exactly *Agent Moist--*"

"It's Armstrong, actually. Aloha Armstrong."

"You're joking." Reggie scanned her up and down then laughed. He placed his balled fists on his hips and regarded her as eyebrow cocked skeptically. "I mean look at you. I thought Shelby was making that up."

Aloha's eyes narrowed. "*No,* I'm not this is the way I usually dress. And I don't know what the message means. What I do know is if there is a joker in a deck of fifty-two cards then one card is missing, and the joker is thus the only wild card in the deck."

Reggie nodded. "Based on what game?"

Shelby eyed him dryly. "Nothing about this situation makes sense."

"So who's the wildcard?" Reggie asked moving to sit in the chair by the window.

"Clem has been missing so we need to ask him where people go when they disappear. He'll know where Herbie and Buster are." Shelby went into the bathroom and started brushing her teeth.

"And who's the missing card in the deck?" he added. Reggie crossed his legs, and Aloha sat on the unmade bed.

Shelby called out from the bathroom with a mouthful of toothpaste. "Ya know, there are days I wish I had one of those bat computers."

Nineteen

Shelby and Reggie followed Aloha into the library. The agent's movements were spider-like, her hands pressed flat against the wall shifting side to side as her eyes flitted back and forth as if she expected an incoming threat at any second.

Shelby watched this with an amused grin. *Oh, brother. She thinks she's a commando or something.*

Reggie had taken Shelby's hand in his.

She looked up at him. He didn't seem to notice Aloha's strange movements. *His brow is pinched and his gaze seemed unfocused, so serious. I hope he's okay.*

Matt and Sparkles walked in and closed the twin doors of the library behind them with a *thump* then headed for a wall of bookshelves.

Shelby hoped it wouldn't take long to find the collection of Rolling Stone interviews.

She recalled seeing something that might have been the magazine's cover on the seventh shelf from the floor on the north wall. She only knew which direction because in the center of the Persian rug is a pattern of a compass with N, E, S, and W at each of the corners of the diamond shape.

Balancing on the top step of the ladder, Aloha shouted "Ah-ha!"

That's wa-a-ay too easy.

"I found it," Aloha patted the spine of the large book. "Sorry, fellas but I'm going to need your help." She clambered to the floor pointing at the book above her head.

After she stepped down, Matt scrambled to the top of the stepladder.

120

Sparkles climbed half way up to grab the edge of the oversized volume in order to help the zombie carry the heavy book down the ladder.

Why don't they just drop it? Shelby looked around at the piles of books. *They've been known to fall.*

Matt stood at the bottom of the stepladder with the book in his hands.

Whoa. That's some book. And no wonder, since it contained all of the interviews the magazine had ever published, it probably had a million pages.

Aloha cleared off a sturdy looking side table with the sweep of an arm. A crazy-eyed moose head clock flew off the table landing on its one antler, which snapped off upon impact.

It looks better without antlers.

Aloha helped the two men wrestle the book onto the table.

"Whew!" Matt wiped away the beads of sweat from his forehead with the back of his hand. "I've been neglecting my workouts." His eyes widened, a flap of skin fell away like a banana peel from the back of his hand.

"Say, Matt how did you become a zombie?" Sparkles sat down on a chair as he focused on the pages of the Rolling Stone book. The cover had a picture of a smiling Britney Spears. He lifted the cover and glided his finger down the table of contents. He hadn't seen the flap of skin come away. At least the pages of this book weren't blank.

Matt reached into his pants pocket and retrieved a safety pin. He winced as he deftly used it the secure the loose skin.

Ewww.

Aloha rolled her eyes. "Doesn't that hurt?"

Matt stiffened as he finished with the safety pin. "Only when I laugh," his voice was a terse whisper. He smirked at his joke, but the pained expression made it obvious jokes were the last thing he meant.

"Good," chimed in Sparkles muffled voice from between the pages of the massive book where he studied a picture of Sonny and Cher in their hippy days, oblivious to his companions.

Aloha smiled at Matt. "Tell me later."

Whoa ho, what's going on here?

Sparkles looked up from the book and chuckled. "What will you tell me later?" He shook his head. "Why don't you tell me now?"

Aloha patted Sparkles' shoulder. "Yes, of course."

Sparkles shook his head and muttered something unintelligible under his breath.

Matt followed as Aloha moved to the table as Sparkles turned back to the index page.

The index showed the contents, including a who's who of the past forty years of rock music--The Beatles, The Rolling Stones, Eric Clapton, and, yes, the Zombies.

Aloha ran her finger down the index page until, on page 1383, she found the Zombies interview. She held her breath then opened the book--she had to use both hands because the combined pages were so heavy. The book made a *thunk* as she dropped the pages onto the table.

It's about as far from a bedtime reader as you can get.

Aloha smiled in triumph then plucked a piece of yellow note paper from between the pages with the Zombies interview and opened it.

A note! Another real clue. Aloha's green eyes became gradually wider and wider as she read.

"What is it?" Shelby rose to the tips of her toes and tried to peer at the note, but still couldn't read it.

"Uh, oh," Aloha huffed.

"What, what?" Reggie crowded closer, and Shelby could smell his musky aftershave.

The L.I.P.S. agent suddenly sprinted for the door, Shelby stepped back to avoid being run over.

"We have to get upstairs right now!"

Aloha pulled the door handle, and her hand flew roughly back. She winced and waved her hand as if she'd hurt it. The doors were locked.

Matt watched, his jaw slack, his eyes wide.

Sparkles burst into tears. "It's not fair," he wailed.

Reggie went to stand behind the distraught clown and rubbed his back with the palm of one hand.

Shelby crossed her arms over her chest. *I've a feeling the door is not gonna open.*

Aloha rubbed her hands together as if warming them over a fire then used both hands to pull hard on both door handles. She grunted, but the door remained closed. Breathing hard, Aloha stepped back a few paces, lowered her shoulder, then ran at one of the doors. She slammed against it hard and stumbled backward.

"Ouch!" Aloha gripped her shoulder where it had struck the door. "Crap that hurts!" Matt joined her.

Sparkles hugged his legs to his body, his feet resting on the chairs edge as tears slid down his cheeks. "Trapped," he wailed. "I hate being trapped."

Matt and Aloha looked at each and nodded. Heads down they stood side by side and charged the door. A chorus of yells of pain followed, but the door didn't move.

"That hurt," gasped Matt. Breathing hard he looked at Aloha.

Aloha nodded at him then shifted her eyes to glare at the door.

"Please tell me I nearly killed myself for a reason." Matt rested his hands on his knees.

"The note says the contestants upstairs will be soon be missing *permanently,*" Aloha hissed between gritted teeth.

Shelby slapped her forehead with the flat of her hand. "Great. It's the same as the other note! They've wasted our time."

Aloha stumbled to a wing chair and dropped into it heavily. Her breath came in gasps. She straightened and moved her right arm up and down like a windmill. "Sorry, Matt. I had no idea we'd come up against an immovable object."

Matt sighed, his fingers gripped his shoulder as he straightened and made his way to another winged chair. A forest of beaded sweat coated his gray forehead, and he gasped from what Shelby could see was clearly pain.

He must be able to feel extreme pain and not those small skin tears that opened on the back of his hand.

Shelby snorted in disgust. "Matt's right, if we don't get up there right away the others will be missing."

"What do they mean by missing?"

"I don't know for sure but whatever *it* is, isn't good." Aloha grunted as she shifted her weight in the chair. "That much I do know."

She pointed at the note that now lay on the floor.

"The note says we're all going to go missing by midnight and it's almost that now."

Shelby followed Aloha's gaze to the moose head clock. Her heart froze when she saw the time. *She's right it's ten to twelve. We've got to get upstairs.* "Oh, crap. How're we gonna get out of here?"

Aloha sighed and rubbed her sore shoulder.

"We're not gonna give up are we?" chimed in Reggie.

Sparkles stopped mumbling and crying, then looked at Aloha. The frown on Sparkles' features had disappeared replaced by a look of grim determination. His gaze darted between the doors and the maroon curtains that framed the floor to ceiling windows.

Sparkles stood and spun on his heel then marched across to the far side of the room. He lowered his head as if he were a bull about to charge a matador's cape. Aloha raised her arms in protest, but the enraged clown took off at breakneck speed headed right at the door.

Shelby winced and closed her eyes afraid to watch. His clown shoes made a muffled *thud* as he ran across the carpet. The cool breeze swept against her skin as he passed her in the chair.

The floor trembled as Sparkles came into contact with the door, accompanied by a tremendous cracking noise that sounded like thunder echoing across the desert foothills as it filled the room.

Slowly she opened one eye, the shards of wood from the door frame lay scattered about the floor. But the doors still weren't open. *How is that possible?*

Opening both eyes, Shelby peered at Sparkles who lay face down, his arms at his sides in front of the messed up door.

He isn't moving. Oh, my God.

Reggie ran toward the clown and knelt beside him. "Is he dead?" Shelby jumped off her chair and ran to keel beside Reggie.

Without answering, Aloha ran to clown and knelt next to him. Reggie placed two fingers on the clown's neck to check for his pulse. Aloha ran her hands over the clown to check for injuries.

"I doubt it, but he should be," Matt still hovered over the Rolling Stones book. Slowly the door that refused to budge fell to the floor with a loud *thud*. It missed them all with inches to spare.

"Oh, crap," Shelby exclaimed softly her voice trembling. "That scared me into next week."

Twenty

ALOHA MANAGED TO REVIVE SPARKLES. Though he was dazed Sparkles didn't appear to be seriously hurt.

Shelby followed Aloha as they looked in one of the bedrooms to continue the search for Buster and Herbie, while Matt, Reggie, and Sparkles went to Happy's room to get him.

Clem stood in the doorway one hand braced against the doorframe. *I'd say he looks a little green around the gills, if he had gills.*

"I'd like to help," he offered his voice weak.

Shelby shrugged. *I've seen him cram himself into a car with twelve other little people after a party plenty of times so why not?*

"I thought you were missing." Matt chuckled.

Oh, brother.

"Missing? Me?" Clem shook his head. "Not me. I'm found."

Shelby rolled her eyes. *Oh, brother.* She grimaced. *He's not gonna be much help finding Buster and the diamond. As soon as he is coherent, I need to find out what they've found so far. Damn them, I'm in the dark. We've gotta find the diamond. I'm losing focus.*

Reggie frowned and stroked his chin with his fingertips. "Ya know," he began, "I really like to get out of here but we have to find everyone before we exit stage left."

Shelby nodded. "I agree but what about the prize?" She stopped in front of the bedroom door and shifted her gaze to Reggie. "I think you boys need it to survive."

He shrugged. "There are more important things at stake."

Shelby regarded him with a slight frown. *There are?* "Like what?"

"I don't know. You and your brothers?" His shoulders slumped. "We zombies aren't going to last much longer anyway."

Aren't we the little defeatist? "Yeah, I guess so but right now we have to solve the mystery of the missing Bass brother and Herbie."

This sounds like a fractured version of a Catherine Coulter suspense novel.

She shifted her attention to the bedroom door then used her fingers of her right hand to slowly push. The hinges squeaked in the quiet. The door opened to reveal a room very much like the others.

On the wall opposite the doorway hung the two ubiquitous paintings of cats, which no doubt disguised the cameras that were watching their every move. The brass bed sat with its rose-colored quilt positioned beneath the window. The sheer curtains moved in time with the artificial breeze from the studio outside--Shelby froze.

Outside? The window is open? She raced to the open window. *We still need a way out when we find the diamond and this might be it.*

"Don't!" yelled Aloha from the doorway.

Ignoring Aloha, Shelby placed her hands under the window frame and yanked upward on it with all her strength. "Don't worry, Aloha I'm getting you all out of here if it's the last thing I do." *Then I can search for the diamond and my brother without interference. If I find the prize, and it's what Wills claims it is then I'll come after Reggie and his friends and save them.*

She grunted as the window slid slowly upward rubbing on the sliders on either side. Shelby reached deep down, put her full strength into her arms, and with brute strength pushed the window open. Beads of sweat tickled her forehead.

But no matter how hard she pulled up, the window pushed down slowly and slowly. Her eyes were wide with fear as the window pressed back against her hands as if an unseen power resisted her.

"Help me!" *It's like the window has a mind of its own.* Her arms over her head pressed harder against the window frame, as she used the floor for extra leverage. Despite straining and pushing up as hard as she could the window continued to shut. Her feet slipped and she grunted, sweat slid down her forehead stinging her eyes. Shelby looked over her shoulder at Aloha for support.

The L.I.P.S. agent had her arms crossed and had a sardonic expression on her face. She shook her head. "It's useless, Shel. Let go."

Shelby decided retreat was the only option left so she relaxed her fingers and pulled away. *Uh, oh. I'm stuck like a fly to flypaper.*

Someone had laid another trap. *Stupid! I fell right into the spider's web.*

"Help me," she pleaded desperately.

Aloha moved beside her and knelt down. Her head moved around the frame as her green eyes studied the structure and Shelby's hands that were stuck to the top carefully.

"Hurry up will ya?" The window continued its downward movement, getting closer and closer to crushing her fingers.

Aloha offered a brief smile and a reassuring nod. She patted Shelby's shoulder then stood and scanned Matt, Reggie and Clem's faces. They nodded.

"You wanta flip a coin?" The L.I.P.S. agent raised an eyebrow. *What's she waiting for?*

"No, please after you." Reggie bowed slightly from the waist. *Now what is he waiting for?*

Shelby could only watch as the window slid steadily, slowly lower and lower with each passing second. It wouldn't be long before her fingers were history. She pulled and pulled her fingers from the frame, pain shot up her arms. The fingers and the palm of her hand were held tight against the wood.

I really don't wanta lose my fingers. Good thing I didn't take up the piano.

Behind her Shelby heard the sound of wood cracking. *Now what?*

Aloha reappeared at her right side with the leg of a chair in her hands gripped like a baseball bat. *What's she gonna do with that?*

The L.I.P.S. agent stuffed the thick oak chair leg into the remaining gap. It fit perfectly and stopped the window's downward progress.

Shelby exhaled loudly. "That's too clos--"

A thunderous crack reached her ears just before shards of wood hit her body. The wooden leg had splintered as the frame crushed the wood into kindling.

Whoa! Bad news! This thing must be a prop from a Terminator movie.

Aloha frowned then disappeared behind her again.

Reggie, Matt and Clem a came over and together they began to push on the window to stop if from closing but still it inched downward. They grunted and sweat trickled down their faces.

Shelby could hear Aloha running water in the bathroom.

"Hey," yelled Shelby, "nothing's working…" *I'm soooo doomed. It's just ridiculous to die by window. It's not fair.*

And it's a heck of a time to haveta pee. Uh, oh. Her bladder took the opportunity to throb to remind her of its nearly full condition to the point of exploding.

"Don't worry, my friend. You're not done yet." Aloha reappeared carrying a wet towel covered in soapy bubbles. The three men took a step back. Reggie grasped Aloha's arm and said, "Do whatever it takes."

Aloha nodded grimly then he let go of her. She rubbed the slippery, soaked towel over Shelby's hands coating them in billowing bubbles, "Okay. Try it now. Pull."

Pulling gently, then harder and harder still, Shelby just couldn't wrench her fingers away from the window frame.

Aloha ran the soaked towel over the window frame and Shelby's fingers and hands.

Yanking, jerking again and again until, finally, after the soap and water had soaked into the wood, Shelby could feel her fingers begin to loosen.

"More. Put on more soap," she breathed.

Aloha applied the soapy towel repeatedly again and again at a furious pace.

Almost there. The window continued its downward descent. Only a half inch left between her fingers and the sill.

With grunt and one last tug, Shelby freed her hands and fell backward landing on her backside. "Aggghhh!"

Reggie looked at Matt and Clem and grinned. "See? I told ya Aloha would save her. She's a professional government agent."

"Like James Bond," agreed Matt.

Rising on her elbows Shelby watched in horror as the window settled to the bottom of the window frame coming to rest with a soft *thud.*

Her heart still beat faster than normal, and her mouth felt like she'd been chewing on cotton balls. She licked her lips and her body trembled.

Man, that was wa-a-ay too close for comfort. She glared at Matt, Reggie and Clem. "Thanks a lot, you guys."

Reggie grimaced. Matt and Clem looked at each other and shrugged.

Staring uncomprehendingly at her hands as if she seeing them for the first time, she counted her fingers. They were a little red and a sore. She breathed a sigh of relief.

"But thanks to you, Aloha, I may play the piano one day. I owe you one. And I owe you an apology for doubting you." *Ten. Yup. All there.*

"No worries. You were upset. I understand frustration." Aloha frowned and crossed her arms, "believe me." Aloha unfolded her arms and held out one hand, which Shelby took in hers, and Aloha pulled her to her feet.

"You're okay for a tallie--"

"What's a *tallie*?"

Shelby's face grew warm. *My ignorant underwear is showing. Stupid, girl.*

"Sorry, I meant for a L.I.P.S. agent." Shelby hesitated. *Should I explain the slang?* "A tallie is anyone who isn't a little person," her voice trailed off. *Oops. I hope I didn't offend her.*

Aloha laughed. "An apt description I'd say."

Shelby smiled. *I'm beginning to really like this woman. Maybe Aloha isn't the threat she'd seemed at first. Sure, she could throw them all in jail, but no one's perfect are they?* The L.I.P.S. agent seemed intelligent, resourceful, and useful to have around when you were up to your neck in danger. *Funny how things work out sometimes.*

"Anyway, thanks."

The L.I.P.S. agent snorted. "I'm getting tired of this megalomaniac and his little mind games. I'm beginning to think the prize is so much hot air, and he gets his kicks out of torturing us regular folks. I think we better round up everyone and have a little talk with Madame Toulest and that butler. That's *if* Jeeves' a *real* butler."

Russ Crossley

Aloha punched a fist into one hand.
She winced then shook off the pain. "It's game over."
Yeah. Whatever. Man, I really gotta pee.

Twenty One

ALOHA AND SHELBY WERE ALONE in the library. Shelby went to a wingchair in the middle of the room next to a small round oak side table with a brass reading lamp on it. She climbed into the chair.

"We need to talk. The others can wait outside." The sound of fists being pounded on wood came from the direction of the library door. "I locked it," Shelby said matter of factly. Aloha nodded.

"So what's the deal?" Aloha shifted her weight to her left foot, her arms were crossed over her chest. She had the classic pose of the skeptic, especially with the scowl across her features.

Shelby sniffed air. *This must be what day two smells like. Except it's the same musty air as days one and two. Four musty days to go.*

Man, library air is stuffy. Books covered the rug stacked in haphazard piles. Chairs were pulled into a circle and most of the shelves were bare. The mini-avalanche still sat in front of one shelf.

The pounding on the door stopped.

"You and I have to work together." Shelby crossed her legs.

"Why?"

Shelby shrugged. "I have the brains, you have the investigative skills. It would be the perfect fit." She eyes the federal agent. "You're after someone. I don't know who and frankly I don't care. But if you and I find the prize then I expect we'll find whoever you're after." She paused to let a brief smile curl the corners of her mouth. "Am I right?"

The eyebrow over Aloha's left eye arched and she sat in the wingchair on the other the side of the end table from Shelby's. Aloha's eyes were deadly and earnest.

"What I know for sure is this so-called reality show isn't a game."

She's right. But I need her on my side if I'm going to find the prize, and the diamond.

"Yeah. You're right, Aloha." She gazed toward the window. "I really am scared for my brother and the others." *And myself.* "I know this is serious stuff."

"You bet your *butt* missing people are serious," Aloha scowled at Shelby.

As if on cue, Jeeves entered the library. Matt, Sparkles, Happy, Clem and Reggie stumbled in behind the butler in tangled mob of shouts, grunts, and tangled limbs.

Short of breath Reggie gasped, "The door," he gasped again dragging in a lungful of air, "locked."

Reggie leaned forward, placed his gray hands on his thighs, and took in deep breaths. *He looks a little worse for wear. I hope he's okay.*

"We thought you were in trouble," Matt bent over, his hands on his knees.

"We were talking is all." Shelby gazed at Aloha. "After all, Aloha did save me."

"We should have broken down the door." Happy moved to an empty chair set near the thick maroon drapes framing the floor of ceiling windows and sat down. He looked a little woozy on his feet.

"I'm not doing *that* again," Sparkles rolled his eyes obviously referring to his earlier misadventure of running headlong into a locked door.

Aloha stepped in front of the butler, forcing him to halt. "Mr. Jeeves. Tell us all you know about this game and what is going on with the missing players."

The butler's placid features changed as Aloha moved closer to him. His gray eyes narrowed. Jeeves cleared his throat. "I received a dispatch from a Mr. Wills claiming he represented Big Art Films offering me a position at twice my normal rate for a week long engagement."

"And you accepted?"

Jeeves gray-white eyebrows shot up on his forehead in surprise. "When I say twice my normal rate, I mean my *yearly* rate, not my weekly rate. I'm not a common streetwalker. I do *not* rent by the hour."

His nostrils flared. "Of course, I accepted. Now what is this all about? And what business is it of yours what jobs I accept, if may I ask, *Mademoiselle*?" Jeeves, his angular face turning a distinct shade of purple. Shelby saw his hands were trembling. *He's one angry dude.*

"Take it easy, old boy." Aloha winked at Shelby with a smile on her lips.

Shelby's lips formed a tight smile. *We're getting to him and he knows more than he's saying, but time is growing short.*

"I'll ask the questions because I'm with the Legal Investigative Protection Services. It's my job to ask questions."

He scanned her from head to toe and snorted.

"You knew me as Moist the clown."

Jeeves mouth formed a thin line and a frown creased his brow. "A clown is a federal agent? Really, Mademoiselle?" he eyed her skeptically.

"Sticks and stones," Aloha grinned at Shelby who nodded.

Shelby frowned.

"Who are you really working for?" Happy moved to stand in front of the butler.

"Yeah. And what's your shoe size?" added Sparkles.

Happy looked at Sparkles. "Shoe size?"

Sparkles shrugged. "Ya know, in case we find footprints under the windows. Like on CSI."

Happy nodded. "Yeah. That makes sense."

Reggie moved to stand by the window his hands in his pockets. "C'mon fellas. Be serious." He stepped forward, pulled his right hand from his pocket and slapped Jeeves on the back, which made a loud *smack.* The butler winced. "Now com'on, Jeevesie, my boy, tell us who hired you and why."

Jeeves rolled his shoulders, and his mouth curled slightly at one corner. "The employment request came to me via electronic means. I believe you young people refer to it as *e-mail.*"

"Yes, of course." Shelby shuffled forward in her chair then dropped to land on her feet.

Aloha locked her hands behind her back and glared at him. *Intimidation factor--six. Engage.* "This, e-mail--did it say anything else?"

Jeeves shrugged. "Just the usual. Time and date of arrival. And the anticipated date of departure." His brow creased and scratched his chin between his index finger and thumb. "That's odd."

Aloha eyed the butler suspiciously. "Tell me."

"Well, if I'm not mistaken the date of departure is scheduled for two days from now. I would have expected my end date to be Saturday when the game ends, not Wednesday."

Two days? Uh, oh.

"Greenwich mean time?" Matt piped up.

"Oh, don't be so stupid." Sparkles tapped the back of Matt's head with the palm of his hand. "Everybody knows that only applies to England, Scotland, Wales, Ireland and the island of Tongo."

Matt nodded as he gingerly tested the back of his head with his fingers.

Reggie mouthed *Tongo?*

Shelby chuckled.

Jeeves ignored everyone and walked toward the exit doors.

"Whoa. Where do you think you're goin', Mr. Butler?" Aloha stepped up from behind to place a hand on Jeeves shoulder to signal him to wait.

"I'm going to retrieve the copy of the message. I kept it." He regarded Shelby dryly. "I expect you'll wish to see it, Miss Bass. I'm sure you'll want to dust it for prints, run DNA tests, or whatever other CSI-type experiments your American bobbies are wont to conduct."

His eyes were expressionless and his nose slightly elevated to show them his obvious superiority.

Snooty guy.

"I've watched your American television shows, droll as they may be."

"And I have a lot more questions for you, Jeeves." Shelby wagged a finger at him. "Like, where are our missing friends, and how do get out of here, and where is the prize?" Her brow furrowed. "All serious stuff, ya know."

"Yes, Mademoiselle, of course."

Aloha let go of Jeeves shoulder and dropped her hand to her side. "You can go, but I'd like Matt, Clem and Sparkles to go with you."

"If you insist."

"I do."

Jeeves, nose firmly in the air, rushed out the door. Matt followed quickly and finally Sparkles and Clem hustled out the door after them.

Shelby smiled.

Clem and Sparkles ran like cartoon roadrunners racing to keep ahead of the hungry coyote.

After they were gone, Aloha chuckled, her mood bubbly like it was New Years Eve. *Does she look pleased with herself or what*? You'd think she'd solved the big case. *As if.*

"Now for Madame Toulest," Aloha's eyes narrowed. "Where is she?"

~ * ~

Shelby found Toulest seated at one end of the over-long table in the dining room. Aloha and Reggie accompanied her, and they each took a seat on either side of the table bracketing Toulest.

Their hostess sipped from a red rose decorated teacup and the silver tea set sat that sat on the table within easy reach. *Afternoon tea?* Shelby glanced at her watch. *How time flies.*

Her grim expression revealed that the former late night horror movie hostess wasn't too happy to see the clown, now L.I.P.S. agent, the zombie, or Shelby.

Aloha sat facing Toulest after turning the chair slightly to her left. She had her arms crossed and her brow was creased by a frown.

Aloha started the questioning. "Did Wills hire you?"

"No." Morticia sipped her tea. Her hands didn't tremble.

"Oh, really?"

"Yes." Toulest set her cup on the matching saucer in front of her. "I received a call from--" Her body straightened and Toulest's pasty features twisted as if she were in excruciating pain.

What the...?

"You have until midnight tonight...after that...it'll be too late..." She gasped, and her raspy voice strained for the words.

Toulest collapsed face down, her head narrowly missing the teacup and saucer. The force of the impact sent the cup and saucer skittering across the table over the side to fall to carpet.

Toulest's breath rattled, her body sagged as the air went out of her lungs like air escaping a balloon. She lay unmoving, her arms dangling beside her.

Shelby looked in turn at Reggie and Aloha, then back at the stricken woman. "What happened? Is she okay?"

Aloha reached over and grasped Toulest left wrist in her fingers. An eyebrow arched and she looked at Shelby. "There's no heart beat."

Shelby jumped off the chair and walked around Toulest's chair. There was a large knife sticking out from the middle of her back. The blade was buried to the finger guard. A ragged tear ran down the chair back behind her where the knife had torn through the fabric.

She had to sit in the one chair in here with a fabric back. Shelby shook her head. *Who woulda thought?*

Shelby licked her lips. "Guys, someone stuck a knife through the chair right into her back. I think the stakes of this show have just been kicked up a few notches."

Oh, man I don't like the looks of this. I'm here to steal back a diamond, not to get killed.

Reggie walked up beside her and dropped to one knee. He enveloped her in his arms and held her close.

She pressed hard against him. The steady beat of his heart came through her shirt.

Now, I'm scared.

"Hold on," Aloha raised both hands. "This stinks to high heaven. Don't you see, this is all a little too theatrical? We're trapped in this house with people mysteriously disappearing then suddenly re-appearing. Now we have a dead," she waved her hand at the dead woman as if searching for the right description, "A dead ghoul." She wiggled her eyebrows. "This could be a trick." Aloha stood, crossed her arms and began to pace. "Madame Toulest might not be *really* dead. This may be part of the show." She stopped and gazed at Reggie. "We have been fooled before."

"Yeah, of course," Reggie groaned. "But, com'on isn't it obvious she's dead." The zombie held one of Toulest's limp wrists up then let go. Her arm smacked the table.

He walked over to the drapes beside one of the floor to ceiling windows and pulled until on it until the rings snapped and it fell to the floor. Aloha helped him pick the heavy drapes off the floor then together they carried the heavy material to the table and threw the draperies over their late hostess.

Aloha could be right. "I agree with Aloha." Shelby nodded. "Toulest's sudden death bothers me too. It seems too predictable. Like it's in the script."

Aloha shook her head, her eyes drooped at the corners. "I should have known this would happen."

I knew it. She's been up to something all along. Never can trust a cop even if she's your BFF. "What have you done?" Shelby felt her face grow cold.

Aloha lowered her head to avoid Shelby's stare. "I lied to my boss." Her voice soft and recalcitrant. "If I was on official status, the cavalry would have shown up by now." Her eyes drifted to cover covered body of Toulest. "And maybe she wouldn't be dead."

"What do you mean?" asked Shelby in a squeaky voice.

"I didn't tell anyone I came here--I'm on leave...sort of...well..." She held her index and middle finger barely apart, "it's actually this close to leave."

Yikes! Ya got to be kiddin'. "No one knows you're here?"

Aloha shook her head looking like a scolded puppy. "So, the marines aren't coming?" asked Shelby. Again, Aloha shook her head.

Shelby hung her head and her heart beat faster. Her voice trembled. "That's just great."

Shelby rubbed her eyes with the heels of her hands. *Great. We're the fly caught in the web. The doors and windows are booby-trapped. No one can get in, and we can't get out and the army, the air force, and the marines won't be busting through the door anytime soon to save the day and Toulest is dead. Maybe.*

"Well, then tell us why you're here if it's not on official L.I.P.S. business."

"Hmmmm," Reggie nodded. He winked at her. "I get the distinct feeling all is not lost." He glanced at the picture hung over the sideboard where an empty silver serving tray sat. "Aloha may be on to something important.

Toulest's death looks like pure theatre played out for us to generate panic."

Shelby felt the tension in her shoulders ease slightly. "That makes sense to me."

Aloha's gaze fixed on her feet. "But I'm kinda embarrassed."

Shelby lowered her voice. "As embarrassed as us getting locked in a stupid house for a stupider reality TV show?"

"Yeah," echoed Reggie.

Shelby gave the zombie her best give-it-a-rest look.

He nodded he understood.

She offered him a thin-lipped smile. *I appreciate the help zombie-boy.*

Aloha nodded. "I'm on suspension at L.I.P.S., but I've been working on the Arnold Zero file for two years and I have to catch him. He's escaped our clutches many times. An informant revealed Arnold Zero's connected to this reality show." She shrugged. "At least that's what the informant told me, and I think he's the mysterious benefactor Wills talked about."

Shelby motioned to Aloha she wanted her to come closer. When she did Shelby whispered in her ear, "Do you think you should be talking about this stuff when the cameras are on us?"

Aloha looked her in the eye and smiled. "Damper field."

"Oh." *Both these LIPS agents come fully equipped. Cool.*

"Zero?" Reggie sat down again his brow furrowed and his arms lay on the table. "That's a strange name."

Shelby blurted, "I know him."

Aloha's gaze locked on hers as she stopped pacing.

Shelby grinned. "Arnold Zero owns the circus my brothers and I work for."

Matt, Clem and Sparkles stumbled through door to land in a tangled heap of arms and legs at their feet.

Great. Another interruption. Just when things were getting interesting. "What is it?" Shelby crossed her arms.

Matt grunted and managed to extract himself from the tangle and stand up. He brushed carpet lint off the arms of his navy blue sweater. There were several tears visible on the grey skin on his face, and his eyes were glazed over.

"We found something." Matt trembled.

Reggie rushed to his friend's side and circled his waist with one arm. He threw his other arm around Matt's shoulder and looked over his shoulder at Shelby. "I have to go to my room to retrieve my repair kit."

Matt, one arm thrown across his friend's broad shoulders, hobbled to an empty chair. Once there, Reggie eased him down gently. Matt smiled weakly at them.

Reggie placed a comforting hand on Matt's shoulder, "It'll be okay, buddy. I'll be right back. Please keep an eye on him, Shelby."

Grunting and groaning, Clem and Sparkles managed to untangle themselves and stand. "Is he okay, sis?" Clem brushed carpet lint off his clothes and his hair.

With a sly smile at her brother, she nodded then approached Matt to get a closer look at the tears in his gray skin.

Man, those look nasty. "Does that hurt?"

"Only when I laugh." Matt's pained expression said otherwise.

Reggie rushed out the door without another word. His hurried footfalls retreated down the hallway.

Shelby could smell garlic and dry skin coming from Matt. Her nose wrinkled.

Ewww, he doesn't smell so good.

"You okay?" Shelby's nose wrinkled.

"The library…" he coughed.

Gee, I hope he's all right. She wanted to touch him to comfort him, but her reluctance intensified when he coughed again. *Yuk! I wonder if he's contagious?*

"What about it?" Clem stepped forward.

"We found it."

"Found what?" Sparkles took a step closer to Matt.

I hate twenty questions. Why can't people just give us a straight answer on these reality shows? I swear everyone's a drama queen. She looked at Matt. *Or in his case a drama zombie.*

"The entrance to hell," the zombie finally managed gasp out between gritted teeth.

Twenty Two

"WHAT DO YOU THINK Madame Toulest meant when she said we had until midnight?" Shelby watched Reggie weave the light colored thread through the skin on Matt's cheek. He had returned with what he called a zombie repair kit.

Aloha and Clem went ahead to the library to see what hell looked like. Happy went with them.

Shelby decided to stay behind to see if she could help Reggie with his zombie repair work. Sparkles stayed with her to keep Matt company. She offered the clown a brief smile that was more grimace than smile. *Clowns. They still creep me out.* She shivered then looked away.

Reggie nodded grimly then refocused on Matt, his brow wrinkled with concentration. *He's gonna make somebody a good wife one day.*

Matt sat unmoving, sideways in the chair with his arm laying casually off the chair back.

He didn't flinch as the needle pierced his skin over and over again.

She studied Reggie working on his friend. "You're pretty good. I thought you told me you were into nuclear science? Maybe you shoulda been a doctor. Or a seamstress. You're pretty good at that."

Reggie chuckled as he used the needle to pull the thread through Matt's gray flesh again and again. "Yeah. You know, Shelby if we don't find a more permanent solution soon, the tears in our skin are going to get worse and more frequent until I can't fix Matt or Herbie anymore--"

Reggie fell silent.

While she didn't know for certain, Shelby suspected exactly what the ending of this tale would be. *Reality usually wins. What was I thinking? I'm such a fool.*

Reggie's a zombie and a prince or a duke or something, and I'm just a little person and a thief. Like he's gonna whisk me away on his white horse and I'll live happily ever after.

She cooed at Matt as she ran a hand gently over his blond hair. His red-rimmed eyes looked up at her sending a deep sense of loss through her. *More likely Reggie and the other zombie's are gonna fall to pieces and I'll be left holding the thread.*

She looked at Reggie still working his sewing magic on Matt's torn flesh. *Boy there sure are a lot of rips. A lot more than before--that can't be good.*

Her brow wrinkled. *It's time to find the prize--the real prize, not the silly Hollywood nonsense. Eternal life, or doomsday bombs, or golden magical statues, or the Holy Grail? What a lot of crapola. The diamond is my prize and my ticket to Hawaii and a new life.*

Finding the Gnotborst diamond is supposed to be the priority for me, and my brothers. It's our job. She watched Reggie sew a tear along Matt's forehead. *Everything--everyone is second to finding the diamond no matter how much you care about them.* Her heart felt heavy and she pushed away the memory of Reggie's strong arms enveloping her and the beating of his heart against her chest.

She blinked to clear her mind and the tears that blurred her vision. *What's wrong with me?*

She wiped her eyes with the back of one hand.

The diamond had to be somewhere in the house. *But where?* One thing was certain, it wasn't in the library. *But these old houses always have secret places where the owners hide stuff. I just have to find one. Easy right? Right.*

According to movie mythology, the cliché hiding place for safes was behind paintings, or you tugged the arm of a statue or something. *Naw. They don't have any statues unless you count that cross-eyed moose head. As if.*

Shelby tapped Reggie on his shoulder. He glanced at her and stopped in mid-sew. "I'm a little busy can't whatever it is wait?"

She shook her head. "There's a dead woman--killed with a knife, one of my brother's is missing, Herbie's missing, and now the gates to hell have been opened by a zombie, a clown and my brother Clem, and a clown named Moist--a name, by the way, that I have no idea what it means--who is in reality a government agent, are on their way to hell. I think we got problems."

Matt suddenly jumped to his feet, flapped his arms like a bird, and jumped around like he had a hot foot. *Zombies can dance. Very cool.*

"C'mon, you guys. We have to get downstairs--" Matt's voice bordered on panic. "Aloha's in danger."

Shelby frowned. "Matt, for goodness sake, you don't think we believe the gates to hell have really opened, do you?"

Matt stopped dancing about. "Well, yeah, actually."

Reggie placed one hand on his friend's shoulder. "Okay, Matt take it easy we'll go downstairs with you." He winked at Shelby.

She shrugged. *What ya gonna do?*

"You believe me, don't you, Reggie?"

"Sure I do, Matt, sure."

Matt walked out the dining room door leaving it to swing back and forth behind him. Reggie, Sparkles and Shelby quickly followed him into the hallway.

Some headline: Zombie Goes Off Half-Cocked.

Their hurried footsteps echoed around them as the trio rushed to catch up to the frantic zombie. When they arrived outside the library, the doors were closed and Matt stood in front of them pointing his index at them. His mouth hung open.

That's strange. The doors should be open.

A bright light could be seen coming from beneath the bottom of the door. A faint scent of smoke from wood burning wafted in the air.

Where there's smoke there's fire? Is hell really on the other side of the door? Shelby looked at Reggie and frowned.

He shrugged.

Matt grabbed one of the door handles and pulled on it. "Owww! It's hot!" He waved his hand madly in the air leaping about then buried it between his thighs his jaw clenched in a grimace.

Matt must have pulled hard enough, the door banged hard against the wall as it flew open.

A searing hot wind burst through the now open door blowing Shelby and the two zombies off their feet. She landed hard on her behind while Matt, who was in front of her, fell partially on her legs. Reggie rolled over and over to finally stop with his head against the hall wall. Sparkles held his hands in front of his face as a shield. His over-sized clown shoes had no tread on the soles so while he stood still he slid backward along the carpet blown by the wind. "Hey!" The clown yelled.

What's happening?

Reggie struggled to his feet to face the wind created by the blast of the fire shooting through the library door licking and crackling like a wild beast. *This is nuts!*

With both hands held up to block the heat, Reggie leaned into the wind and took one step forward then one more until he made it behind the open door using it as a shield. Sweat dripped off his face and his cheeks puffed in and out.

"You okay?" Shelby yelled into the wind.

The wind must have carried her words away because Reggie didn't acknowledge her as he ran his shoulder hard into the door and grunted. He stumbled backward after bouncing off the overheated wood until, with a satisfying *click,* the heat and the wind disappeared behind the closed door.

He did it! Sweat dripped from Reggie's chin and his legs wobbled as he stumbled away from the door. He stopped himself from falling by placing one hand flat on the wall. His breathing came in gasps. "You okay?" Shelby asked as she rose to her feet.

Reggie turned round his back against the wall and slid to land heavily on the carpet with a muffled thump and a groan. He placed his arms behind him against the wall. Sweat dripped down his temple, cheeks and off his chin. He inhaled and exhaled deeply as if he just ran a marathon.

"Whew! So that's what hell looks like? Amazing!" Matt shook his head.

Sparkles chuckled nervously as he approached from behind. His hair was blown back on his head giving him the illusion of speed even when standing motionless.

Matt looked at Sparkles grinned then looked at Shelby. "This is no joke," Matt's lips formed a grim line. "That fire's not natural. There are forces at work here we don't understand."

Matt's obviously referring to some supernatural force. But ghosts don't set fires. People do.

Reggie bent forward, his hands on his thighs. He raised his head and stared at his friend. "Matt, where are Aloha, Jeeves, Happy and Clem?"

"Uuuh." Matt pointed at the door then scrambled backward on his hands like a crab.

Oh, crap. Shelby sniffed the air. *Hmmm. Odd. The smoke's barely detectable now. These walls must be fireproof. For the megalomaniac who has everything.*

She stared at the closed door as her shoulders slumped. "I'm afraid if they're in there, they're toast," her voice cracked with emotion.

~ * ~

Aloha watched the flames lick at the walls surrounding the entrance to the secret passage until it shut behind them protecting them from the heat and flame that had engulfed the room.

Why am I always in the wrong place at the wrong time? She glanced at Happy, whose soot-stained white makeup made him look less than Happy. *He came with me so he must be really thinking he's in the wrong place.*

"You okay, Clem?" The little man had dove onto his belly into the passageway like a championship high diver. He rolled over, grinned and gave her a thumbs up sign.

When the flames burst out simultaneously in all the corners of the library, Jeeves had grabbed the wall sconce and pulled on it. The hinged sconce was attached to a mechanism that activated a lock. Immediately a wall of books opened to reveal a hidden tunnel.

It's as if he knew the sconce is the key to open the wall.

The fire happened too fast. Gas jets that must have been hidden in the floor had burst to life quickly engulfing the books, the carpet, the drapes, and everything else with furious speed. The engulfment of the room happened with unnatural speed.

Aloha crouched low in the semi-dark tunnel. *At least Clem can stand upright. The tunnel must have been designed with little people in mind.* Aloha grunted. *A perfect escape route for Zero.*

Aloha's fingers brushed the damp wall. "Yuk." She rubbed her hand on her pant leg.

"What's the matter with you?" Aloha looked up at the sound of the familiar voice and saw Reggie's pale gray features.

"I thought we left you outside?"

With a wry grin, Reggie shook his head. "You're not going to lose me that easily." He crouched low, turned, and hurried further into the tunnel following Jeeves who took the lead because he said he knew the way through these tunnels.

Aloha frowned. *Okay. Now this is strange. If he's here, where's Shelby? Those two have been joined at the hip lately. He sounds different as if he's not really Reggie.* She shook her head. *But he looks like Reggie. I best keep a close eye on him and see if I can spot if he's in disguise. I'm not the only one who's good at disguises.*

The tunnel walls were slick with what looked like moss and ripe with the smell of mold and decay. The old-fashioned brass candleholder she held in her right hand was now the only light.

The library fire had made it impossible to go back they way they came. Aloha knew she had to take the lead at some point if they were going to go deeper into the tunnel no matter where it led.

The snap of Aloha's boots echoed off the walls as she followed the others.

Too bad, I couldn't get to those flashlights. I should have kept on the clown costume then I'd have the extra pockets to carry them in. Best laid plans don't always work out the way you want them to.

Aloha counted heads. *A clown, a butler, a little person, a zombie and me.* She squinted at Reggie. *Wait a minute. I thought he stayed behind? Strange.* She shook her head. *I must be confused by the fire. Near death experiences tend to make me less clear.* She smirked. *Been in one too many of those situations on other L.I.P.S.' cases.*

That left Matt, and Shelby, Sparkles and, of course, the still missing Herbie and Buster. *They probably think we're dead.*

Reggie and Shelby seemed pretty sweet on each other. And why wouldn't he be with her? Of course, there's more going on than a mere reality show. There were real dangers here. *I have to protect these people, even the undead ones, and even if he's sweet on a little person.*

And it bugs the crap out of me I can't find Zero. She frowned. *I'm a L.I.P.S. agent for goodness sake. The L.I.P.S. always gets our man or woman.*

Her suspicions would have to wait. The more immediate problem was how do they get out of this damp tunnel. *Before we turn into mushrooms.* She touched the wall with the flat of her hand. She immediately withdrew her hand and ran it down her jeans. *Slimy. Yuck.*

"Cool, huh?" At least Happy looked happy to be in a dark, dank tunnel.

Their footsteps echoed as they followed Reggie deeper into the darkness.

And I'm gonna catch him. She hesitated. *Or whatever.* Motto's never seemed to fit every situation. She made a mental note to talk to her boss about the L.I.P.S. motto. *My internal hard drive's gettin' kinda full with all the stuff I gotta remember.*

"Hey," Happy's voice echoed from behind her, "I think I see a light!"

Sure enough, a faint blue glow grew brighter with each step they took toward it. "Where's this go?" Aloha called out to Jeeves up ahead. The butler held a flaming torch he'd found in a holder on the tunnel wall that he lit with a long wooden match he had in his pocket he carried to light fireplaces.

"I have no idea, Mademoiselle--" The butler spoke in his best upper class English butler tone.

"I'm not a *Mademoiselle*. I'm a professional L.I.P.S. agent, bucko."

"Yes, Agent." Jeeves nodded.

Aloha smirked. *How I love rattling people's chains. They don't call me the queen of interrogation for nothing.*

After walking another ten feet, the passage opened into an oval shaped room made of dirty red brick and tanned sandstone.

She arched her back and twisted back and forth, finally able to stand straight. "*Ooooo!*" Half an hour crouched in a tunnel was half an hour too long. *Shelby's right. I am a too tall tallie.*

Except for Clem, the others groaned softly as they straightened.

"So. Jeeves. Old boy. I'll ask you again. Where in Hades are we?"

"I'm afraid, Miss Aloha, I have no idea."

Aloha frowned. *Not good. It's almost midnight and we're trapped in here.* Her stomach muscles tightened. *My oh-crap radar is on full.*

Twenty Three

MATT GRABBED SHELBY'S HAND to help her off the floor. Once on her feet, Shelby stepped closer to the library door and pressed one hand on the wood. *Hot. Very hot.*

"It's warm," Matt waved one hand to emphasize his point.

Shelby grinned at the zombie. Understatement number ninety-five. "See what happens when you go around touching strange doors."

Matt laughed. Sparkles snorted.

"Is there another way inside?" Reggie stared at her.

Guess not.

Shelby studied the wall and ran one hand over the wood. *My brother is inside and in danger.* She didn't want to think about him being barbecued in the library. *Oh, no, no, no.* Panic gripped her and she fought the urge to pound her fist on the hot door. *We have to find him. He has to be all right.*

"Anyone here ever been on the Universal Studios tour?" Reggie said matter-of-factly.

"Why're you talkin' about amusement parks at a time like this?" Matt looked wide-eyed at Reggie as if the zombie had lost his mind. "What's next, Disneyland?"

Shelby cocked her head at Reggie as panic twisted her guts. *Reggie may be on to something. Reggie saved my life and my feelings for him have grown ever since, I think I trust him.* "Yeah, I have"

"Backdraft. Ever seen it?"

Shelby nodded. At the corner of her vision, she saw Sparkles also nodding. *Clowns go to the movies? I think I would've noticed a guy with a blue face and purple hair.*

149

"Yeah," Matt's tone turned sour as lime juice. "Once."

Where's Reggie headed with this? "Kurt Russell, right? About firefighters?"

Matt face went slack and his gaze dropped to the floor. "Kurt Russell dies at the end."

Yeah, I cried too, big guy.

"At Universal Studios there's a ride that simulates the fires in Backdraft. Ever been on it?" Reggie stopped his hand mid-way from his hair, seemed like an old habit he wanted to quit.

Shelby nodded. *Cool ride.*

Matt shrugged.

Reggie grinned. "Well?"

Shelby smiled. "Oh yeah. I get it. Whoever engineered this created a fake fire to make us think our friends died. "Smart." Shelby narrowed her eyes. "But crafty."

Reggie nodded. "Now all we have to do is find the exit for the escape hatch."

"Wow, that's fantastic." Matt's eyes sparkled and the smile in his eyes reminded her of a child on Christmas morning upon seeing the presents under the tree.

"You two should have your own TV show. Bass and Kincade, Private Eyes, this fall on the World Television Network. Cool, eh?" Matt laughed.

Yeah. She smiled at Reggie's confident expression. *Things may look bad but he sure is cool.*

Reggie slapped his friend on the back. Matt winced. "Yeah, right Matt. C'mon, big guy. I think I might have an idea where the escape tunnel comes out."

They headed for the dining room.

~ * ~

Shelby followed Reggie and Matt into the dining room. The body of their late ghoulish host had disappeared. The chair had been pushed up against the table as if it had been empty all evening. Even the teacup and the silver tea service were gone.

No blood. No body. No mess. No fuss. *Just great.*

"Toulest's gone!" Matt shouted.

"How?" Reggie's brow wrinkled.

Shelby looked at Reggie and frowned. "Why? Then again why not?"

"I don't get it." Reggie said. "The body was here when we left. Who would take a dead body?"

Shelby pulled the chair back from the table. She sniffed the air. *Jasmine?*

Bending down, she searched around the legs of the chair and floor, but didn't see any signs of blood on the carpet.

Reggie walked over and stood beside Matt who had bent over looking underneath another chair. "What're you lookin' for?"

Matt shook his head. "I don't know. I'm just doin' what she's doin.'"

Reggie exchanged a grin with Shelby. "Okay. So how did Aloha and the others get trapped in the library?"

Matt looked sheepish. "Huh. Would you believe, I *don't* know?"

The corner of Reggie's mouth curled. "No. Matt. I don't." His brow pinched and his eyes narrowed. "What I want to know is what *you've* done with the *real* Matt."

Matt's features lost their look of innocence, his eyes hardened with a glint of steel determination. "How did you know?" With each word, his voice got deeper and deeper until he could probably sing *Old Man River* on Broadway.

Shelby crossed her arms and regarded the zombie, her features stern. "You did a credible job, with one exception."

"Which is?" Pseudo Matt seemed genuinely curious, one pale blond eyebrow arched up his gray forehead.

Shelby moved closer to look at the mask Matt wore, a real work of art. His faux skin fit so well it looked as real as if it were his real skin.

"Matt's been on the Universal Studio tour more than any human being on Earth. A record one hundred and two times. He loves the place." Reggie paused. "Just don't ask me why."

Pseudo Matt shrugged and snapped his fingers. "Incomplete research. Hollywood." He sighed. "Always taking short cuts. Producers always expect us to work under these conditions. Short deadlines and far too little prep time--"

"We don't have time for this. Where is my brother?" Shelby uncrossed her arms and her hands formed fists.

Pseudo Matt's eyes widened at Shelby. "I have no idea. But I can show you the tunnel that leads to the dressing room where the extras wait for their cues--"

"You mean there are more of you running around pretending to be us?" Shelby wanted to hit this man. The fear of losing her brothers still raged inside her.

Pseudo Matt nodded. "Yes, of course. Except for one of you midgets."

Shelby glared at the fake zombie. *Now I really don't like you. Midgets?* "Wills didn't have time to recruit enough *little people*, I take it."

Shelby had a sinking suspicion about the identity of the lone little person substituted for Clem. *I'll find out who and why he was doubled. No one can fool me for long.*

She wanted to throttle information out of the actor, but knew violence wouldn't help. They were running out of time and this guy wasn't going to tell them anything. *He's what the movies call the unreliable narrator.*

She looked at her Timex. A quarter after ten. "What happens at midnight?"

Pseudo Matt shrugged his shoulders again.

Shelby's narrowed her eyes as frustration ran through her. "Okay. Let's start at the beginning. How did you get this job?" Shelby let her impatience surface in her voice.

Pseudo Matt reached behind his head and pulled off his rubber mask accompanied by the odor of sour sweat. "This thing's too hot."

He tossed the mask to the floor then ran his thick fingers through his shoulder length chestnut brown hair. He tossed his hair like a shampoo model to loosen the damp curls so they cascaded around his strong, lean face, and chiseled chin that bore a dimple reminiscent of Michael Douglas. His arrogant smile made her smile. *He's cute.* Her eyes narrowed. *Too cute.*

"Sorry." The actor crossed his arms over his muscular chest and his sky blue eyes crinkled at the corners while a half smile curled on one side of his wide mouth.

I'll bait the guy with flirtation then reel him in.

"Names Alpha, Alpha Rucksack." The blue-eyed rogue acted like his nose was glued to the ceiling. *Stuck up is such an unattractive trait.*

He held out his hand. "I needed a job as an out-of-work-actor-sometime-bartender," he offered a sly smile one side of his mouth curled slightly as his eyes narrowed to slits. "I'm pleased to make your acquaintance."

She took his calloused hand in hers. Odd to have such rough hands as a self-described sometime bartender. She glanced at Reggie.

His scowl spoke volumes. *Do I detect jealousy? Very cool.*

She turned her attention back to the actor. "Yes. Nice to meet you, too. My name's Shelby Bass."

His eyebrows arched in surprise. "Really? Cool. I've never met one of the Family Bass in person."

"Whoa, there, bucko. You know me?"

Pseudo Matt smirked. "I heard you people were sensitive."

Shelby growled, "What--?"

He held up one hand. "Please don't be offended. I didn't mean anything by it. I've been following your act for years. I used to be a high wire man myself before I became an actor and--" He stopped and winced like an elephant had stepped on his foot. If he hadn't been such a handsome specimen of manhood that respected her family's circus work, she would've slapped him into next week.

"I must be getting soft in my old age, but I'm gonna cut you some slack, dude. We have to get out of here before midnight. I've a feeling something bad's gonna happen." *It's as if we're mice in a maze. Every time we get close to discovering something important, we're stopped by a new disaster. The window closing, the electrified door handle, Toulest is murdered then her body disappears, a fire, and now a doppelganger zombie.*

I don't think Zero's goal is to kill us. He could have done that any time. No, there's something else going on.

"The danger is escalating. We have to be extra careful."

Reggie grunted his agreement.

Shelby didn't understand his silence.

She sighed inwardly. Now she had no idea what's real and who the enemy was really who they say they are.

She eyed Rucksack. *He proves anyone of us could be a spy.*

She wiggled her index finger at Reggie indicating he should come closer. She cupped his left ear with her hand and whispered, "We need some alone time."

His eyes had a lustful look in them. *Oops! Wrong choice of words.* "That's *not* what I meant."

Geez, why are guys always thinking about sex? Then again, we girls aren't much better.

~ * ~

The house contained more secret passages than a castle made of Swiss cheese. *I saw a castle made of cheese once in the Louvre in Paris, Wisconsin.* The red brick room held nothing, and Jeeves had led the team down another dark, damp tunnel.

Jeeves handed Aloha the flaming torch, obviously not wanting to be in the lead anymore.

Aloha hadn't seen a single spider since they entered the tunnel. *Good thing too. I don't really like spiders much. Apparently, our little hairy friends don't like crackling flames.*

Finally, Aloha walked to the end of the tunnel with the group behind her. A solid orange red brick wall was in front of her. A handwritten note was taped to one of the grey stone bricks.

It read, *Press here.*

Aloha scowled. *This breadcrumb bit is getting tiresome.* Sneaking around in dank tunnels was no way to investigate. *I'm the woman from L.I.P.S. I kick butts for a living.* She shook her head.

Someone bumped into her from behind and she inhaled sharply. A hand stayed on her bottom. "Hey! Watch it, pal!"

She glanced over her shoulder to see Clem behind her. Her eyes narrowed and she nodded at his hand.

"Huh, sorry, Agent Armstrong." Clem's eyes widened, and he removed his hand from her bottom. His cheeks were red as a fire engine.

Little people. She rolled her eyes. *He's as horny as his sister.* Turning around, she pressed one hand flat on the cool bricks.

The stone wall rumbled and scraped as it moved inward. She stepped back as the ground beneath her feet shook. She pressed a hand against the wall to brace herself and keep from falling. Whoa! *I did that? What do ya know, I guess that note was right.*

When the floor stopped moving, Aloha looked at her hands, winced then ran her dirty palms down her leg. *These pants are sooo gonna be washed when I get outta here.*

She held up the flaming torch in order to peer inside another dark room beyond the new doorway.

"What is it?" Reggie's voice echoed off the tunnel walls.

She backed up. Bright light from the room beyond the doorway made her squint and blink. She shielded her eyes with one hand until her vision cleared.

In the room were brilliant red and yellow flames coming from oil lamps that had crackled to life to chase the darkness into the corners of the room when the entrance opened.

From over her shoulder, Sparkles said excitedly, "Hey. It's an office. And it looks just like mine back home."

Weathered wooden planks covered the floor. The walls reminded her of cheap pine paneling.

Office? It's a double for my uncle's rec room. How can Sparkles' office look the same?

In the center of the room was a cigarette-scarred tan pine desk near one of the oil lamps that cast very little light. Beside the desk was a small pine side table. Behind the desk sat a tall backed executive chair. Two matching pine Captain's chairs were in front of the desk.

Aloha led the way into the room. Looking over her shoulder, she could see the rest of the group walk in. Books, books, and more books lined bookshelves on three of the walls. *Again with the books?*

The desk's faded, chipped surface had nothing on it. Not a pen, a notepad, nothing, not even a paperclip.

What did I expect to find, Dr. Frankenstein's book explaining how he did it?

Aloha sat down heavily on the wine-colored leatherette chair behind the desk. There were two drawers on one side of the desk and a pedestal on the opposite side. With a drawer in the middle.

Ah, a place to keep those paperclips, or maybe those two pennies that come standard issue with every desk._

Aloha slid open the middle drawer. Sure enough in the change tray were two shiny copper pennies. A large brass key ring with several keys lay in the drawer. One key looked like it belonged to a safety deposit box. *Interesting.*

Jeeves sat stiff backed in one of the Captain's chairs. *Is he even human?*

Happy went to one of the bare walls and ran the flat of his hands over it.

"Looking for another exit?" Aloha asked.

He grunted and tiptoed as high on the wall as he was able to reach with his hands down to where the wall met the floor.

Aloha plucked one of the pennies out of the tray. The sparkling penny had the year nineteen forty-six. *Odd. It looks pressed yesterday, though Lincoln looks younger than I remember him.*

Shrugging she placed the coin next its cousin in the tray.

Reggie had walked over to stand beside her and gazed into the drawer. Now that he was closer, she could smell his after-shave. The pungent odor made her nose wrinkle. *Who wears Old Spice anymore?*

She glanced at him.

He nodded and gave a tight smile.

She looked back into the drawer at the keys. *Reggie seems different. Is his head bigger? Hmmmm. I know. It's the way he's carrying himself. His posture is like Jeeves' all of a sudden. Strange. More strange than normal for him, though I've no idea what's normal when it concerns zombies.*

"Nothing. I'm still looking--" Happy explained.

"For what?" Sparkles crossed his arms and erupted with a mad laugh.

Aloha frowned at the clown. What's wrong with him?

Suddenly a smell like strawberries filled her senses. Immediately black spots blurred her vision.

What's happening? She inhaled deeply trying to get air into her lungs. *I'm gonna pass out. The air.* Her nose wrinkled. *Gas!*

Her body sagged in the chair and collapsed face down on the desk. In the few seconds before she passed out, she managed to turn her head to the side. Through bleary eyes, she saw her companions stumble about like drunken sailors after a night on the town. Then, like puppets whose string had been cut, each in turn collapsed to their butts and began to giggle like children. *Giggling? What the...?*

Her thoughts jumbled together, but her professional agent training told her if they didn't find a way out of here quickly, they were in real trouble.

Oh, crap. She snorted and giggled. *I feel silly.*

Twenty Four

ALOHA, PUSHED HERSELF UP FROM the desk. She covered her mouth with one hand to stifle a last giggle.

She ran her tongue around her lips and closed her mouth. She smacked her lips and winced. *Yuk. Morning breath tastes awful.*

She didn't know how long she had been out. She stood and scooped the keys from the change tray then, on trembling legs, stumbled to the left wall of bookcases. She pressed her hands flat on the books to hold herself up and blinked repeatedly to try and clear her mind. Through blurry vision, she could make out a few of the titles. Deep in the back of her gas-addled memory, she remembered something--something that might save them from this gas.

She recognized one of the titles. She'd slapped Rocky's face extra hard when he gave her the book for her birthday. Her ex-boyfriend's swollen face was purple and black for two days. Too bad, he hadn't told me he had an engagement ring in his pocket. The book had seemed like a joke. *Yeah. Right. Real funny.*

The book, *The Power of A Loving Man: 13 Keys to Setting Your Heart Free* by Jeff Jernigan.

She looked down at the keys resting in the palm of her hand, which seemed to double in number then triple as her vision alternately blurred, cleared, then blurred again.

How many keys are there? With her other hand, she grabbed at one key and only found air.

Unable to focus, she shook her head to clear the cobwebs from her mind. The room spun around her.

She pressed one hand flat against the books to steady herself, but it only made the bookcase seem to move with her as if she were at sea. Her stomach protested as she swayed side to side.

There has to be thirteen keys. Thirteen. Yeah. A frown marred her forehead. *Thirteen is the unlucky number. Not a good sign.*

Aloha's strength retreated as her body sagged against the wall. The keys fell from her fingers to land with a clatter and skitter across the floor. In desperation, she reached out and managed to yank the Jeff Jernigan book from the shelf. It landed with a *thump* on the floor.

Aloha winced as she opened her eyes too quickly. She closed them tightly as her head swam. Moaning, she didn't move. *My head hurts.*

Calling on her inner reserves, she reached out until her fingertips touched the books. She rolled onto her side with a grunt then struggled to her knees and crawled closer to the bookcase. She used a shelf for leverage to pull herself up with a groan.

She sniffed the air. *No odor of strawberries. Good. The gas must have dissipated.* She shook her head. *Mind clearing.*

She blinked again. Happy and Clem, Jeeves, and Reggie lay on the floor scattered about like bowling pins. Moans, groans and movement signaled they too were waking.

How dare they gas me! I'm a federal agent. She looked around at the others again. *At least we're not dead. But why gas? And where did the gas come from?*

"What kind of gas is that?" Happy pulled out a white and red polka dot handkerchief from his back pocket and blew his nose. "It sure smells yummy."

"Hey." Clem rubbed the top of his head. "Someone hit me."

At his feet lay a book.

"Wrong, guy." Aloha pointed at the offending book at his feet.

Clem nodded and glared at the offending book.

"Owww." His tone suggested his pride was hurt more than his head.

"This isn't what I signed on for. *He* could've killed us--" Clem began.

"Shut up!" blurted Happy.

Aloha eyed them suspiciously. *What's going on? Who's "he?"*

Clem had just revealed something that he didn't want them to know. *Maybe these two are in a secret alliance in this silly show.* She turned up her finely honed L.I.P.S. crap detector to full strength to analyze every clown word.

Time for the interrogation queen to do her thing. She opened her mouth to speak.

"Who are you two arguing about?" Reggie stood and interrupted before she could say anything.

Ah, the direct approach. Not bad, zombie boy.

"Nothing." Happy scowled at Clem.

If looks could kill.

"Never mind him." Happy's frown deepened as he stared at Clem, whose shoulders slumped sheepishly. "He's an idiot."

These two aren't going anywhere. They'll slip up again. It's not like I can use a rubber hose on them, even though they're pissing me off.

"Right now our priority is finding our way out of here." Aloha looked down at the Jernigan book at her feet. "A key is gonna to get us outta here."

Dropping to her haunches, she scooped the key ring off the floor where she'd dropped it.

"What do you mean?" Reggie sat in one of the Captain's chairs.

"Well, this key ring," she held it up, "contains thirteen keys--"

Oops. Only five keys? Searching her memory, she could not recall the exact number of keys on the ring before she lost consciousness. But there were more than five. All eyes were on her, waiting for her to speak. *As the only L.I.P.S. agent here, I have to say something, or at least sound like I know what I'm doing. Thirteen sounds right.*

"Well, at least there used to be thirteen."

"How do you know for sure?" Happy frowned and arched an eyebrow.

Clem nodded.

"I--"

Before she could form a plausible answer to the clown's question, Clem continued. "She's right. I think there were thirteen keys just as she says. Someone came in here when we were out cold and took the other eight."

She nodded. "Makes sense, Clem."

She shuddered. *But how would they get in here?*

Sparkles crossed his arms over his chest and frowned. "But why would someone do that?"

"Maybe whoever owns the keys?" suggested Clem.

Aloha smiled.

"One of these books must hold the key." Then again not much about a reality show is meant to make sense so why not? "We have to find a book with the word key in the title."

She nodded. *I must be off my nut.* Books with the word key in the title? *The side effects of the gas must be stupiditis.*

She turned to scan the titles of the books on the shelf. These were written by Jacqueline Suzanne. But they had nothing to do with keys. She studied the back wall of the shelf after she'd removed the first Suzanne novel. Using her fingers, she probed the back wall until her fingers grazed a smooth, cold metal catch. *Interesting.*

Aloha grasped the catch between her fingers and pulled it hard. Looking around, she heard a soft scraping sound reminiscent of sandpaper on wood. A puff of cinnamon tinged the air as the wall in front of her pivoted into the room forcing her to step back. *Uh, oh. Now what have I done?*

Jeeves, Clem and Happy stood frozen in front of the walls they had been searching and watched her silently.

Reggie snorted, his lips twisted in a wry smile.

"Yeah, I know." *Great. Another tunnel. And a tunnel for little people given how low it is the ground.* "Place has more secrets than my hairdresser." Aloha blew at a strand of hair that had fallen across her eyes. *My do is coming undone.*

She bent forward at the waist, careful to keep her lower body in the office in case the door closed quickly and stuck her head inside. Then she'd get out of the way fast if something happened. *Don't want to be trapped.*

Bright glowing lamps shaped like old-fashioned torches, with clear glass bulbs at the ends that encased a natural gas blue and yellow flame, ran along both walls. About halfway up the wall, the gas torches were set into black steel sleeves that reminded her of flower bouquets. The square-shaped tunnel had rust-red bricks, with chalk-white grout where the floor and the walls met. *Now this is my kind of tunnel.*

Aloha's nose twitched. The smell of cinnamon grew stronger with each step.

"Anyone got gum?" Clem quipped.

~ * ~

The swinging door *swooshed* closed behind them as Shelby and Reggie entered the kitchen. They'd left Sparkles in the dining room to keep watch over Pseudo Matt. He wasn't going anywhere. *He has to finish the job to get paid doesn't he?*

Aloha entered through the swinging door after them. Her curvy body looked like sin in tight jeans and her red hair hung loose about her shoulders.

Where did she come from? Wasn't she in the library? She doesn't look like she's been in a fire.

Aloha stopped short and a single eyebrow arched as she stared at them.

"Where have you been?" Shelby crossed her arms and moved to stand closer to Reggie, "weren't you in the library with the others?"

Aloha shook her head and moved to sit on a stool. "Nope. I checked the garage for open doors and windows. No luck I'm afraid. At least not a door that isn't booby trapped."

Shelby looked at Reggie--not sure she was the real Aloha. *She could be an impostor like Rucksack meant to fool us. Aloha and I agree the danger is getting worse. If this Aloha is an impostor, she could be dangerous.*

Reggie's eyes narrowed as he, too, crossed his arms.

He gets it. We're on the same wavelength.

Shelby took a step closer to Aloha. "So what are we going to do?" She frowned and used her finger to signal to Reggie to come closer. He took a step closer.

"Say, Aloha why don't you look for hidden passages in here?"

Aloha shrugged gazing around the kitchen. "I thought we already looked in here?"

Shelby forced a thin smile to her lips. "Yeah, but you are the professional agent. You may find something we missed."

Aloha grunted, turned away, and ran her hands over the smooth wood paneling.

Reggie walked over to Shelby and bent down. She cupped his ear with her hand and whispered, "I wonder if..." She didn't want to believe there was a mole working for Wills but there had to be. Having a spy among them made perfect sense. Every time they found a clue, something happened to stop them. Someone had to be feeding inside information about their activities to Wills. "What if some of us on the inside were recruited by Wills to keep an eye on the rest of us? Maybe not everyone, but there has to be someone on the inside."

Reggie blinked at her.

"Think about it. Every time we find a way to escape, one of us has a crisis."

Reggie nodded. "Yeah. So, if we assume you're right, then one of the team members is working for Wills against the rest of the teams--excluding, of course, you and I and Aloha here." Shelby let her arms fall to her sides, moved to the counter an apple from the fruit bowl sitting there. She rubbed it on her shirt. "I think the mole is going to steal the prize if we find it." Shelby grinned and took a bite of the apple.

Reggie smiled briefly at Aloha. "Makes sense to me." He cocked one eyebrow. "Don't you think so, Aloha?"

Aloha grimaced but nodded slowly.

Good thing she doesn't play poker. Her poker face is awful. I can read her like a book. I'm ninety-nine percent sure she's not our Aloha. The real Aloha comes up with way crazier scenarios than moles and stolen prizes. I still doubtful there even is a prize. But I know there is a diamond.

She chewed the apple and wiped away the juice that ran down her chin. *I can't let the mole take the diamond when we find it. I need to make her think she's one of the good guys and keep her thinking we believe her.*

"We three are safe, as they say on the reality shows." She indicated Aloha with a slight tip of her head. "Even you, Agent Armstrong."

Reggie nodded. "I agree Aloha's on the trail of Arnold Zero. But what about that actor, Rucksack? He wore a disguise. And if he wore a disguise, and isn't really *my* Matt, then where's *my* Matt?"

Reggie's eyes were bright, and his hands waved about like he was conducting an unseen orchestra. "And maybe Sparky and Happy aren't who they appear to be either. And maybe Jeeves and Toulest aren't who they say they are." He patted his chest with both hands. "And maybe I'm a fake, too."

Aloha's forehead wrinkled and she growled. "This is just stupid. What a waste of time."

Shelby let a brief smile played across her lips. *Good, she thinks her disguise is working.* "She's right." She looked at Reggie. She set the half-eaten apple on the counter. "We're being paranoid." Her gazed locked on Aloha's body so she could gage if she would notice a difference--her ample breasts visible under her tight white shirt to try and discern if they were the same size as before. She quickly gave up. *What do I know about tallie cup sizes?*

How am I supposed to know if she's changed?

Reggie shrugged. "Okay. But we should keep our eyes and ears open."

"L.I.P.S. agents *always* have their eyes wide open." Shelby nodded.

"So what now?" Reggie scanned the kitchen with its shiny steel appliances and tiled floor.

"Are you two *sure* you're done with the twenty questions?" Aloha's tone heavy with sarcasm. "I know you think I'm the mole. Which I'm not."

Shelby's face grew warm. *I guess my poker face needs work, too.* She looked away from Aloha's chest to Reggie's blue eyes. "Let's go back and talk to Pseudo Matt. He offered to show us to the dressing rooms. Maybe he'll lead us to a tunnel or a secret passage and we'll find the rest of the gang. There have to be hidden tunnels. How else could the actors playing our doubles appear where and whenever?"

Reggie's brow creased. "Yeah, you're right--we make a heck of a team don't we?"

She smiled and nodded. "Let's go, *my lord.*"

He bowed at the waist and waved one arm in a sweeping motion, "After you, my princess."

Ignoring the possibly fake L.I.P.S. agent, Shelby laughed and walked through swinging door to the dining room where they'd left pseudo-Matt. Reggie followed, then Aloha.

Just as she expected, the fake Matt sat at the dining room table sipping red wine from a crystal glass. For some reason, he had put on his Matt disguise again. Over the brim of the cut crystal glass in his hand, his eyes followed them when she, Reggie, Aloha entered.

"Having a party without us, buckaroo?"

He set the glass on the table, then dropped his hands onto his lap.

"You're going to lead us to the dressing room. We think that's where we'll find our missing friends." Shelby approached the table and scowled at the actor.

Rucksack's blond eyebrows arched. "Really?" He lifted the glass to his lips as his eyes narrowed. He took a sip then again placed the glass on the table. "How do you know?"

A shadow of a smile spread across Shelby's features. *We'll find the real Matt soon. At least I hope so.* "Elementary, my friend. Elementary."

"You have bigger problems." Rucksack shook his head.

Shelby frowned. *I don't trust a fake zombie.* It suddenly dawned on her she hadn't believed there were zombies until a few days ago. *What am I thinking? Fake zombies. Real zombies. Trusting the undead is just strange.*

"Do you know where the dressing rooms are?" Rucksack snorted.

Twenty Five

After the narrow escape from an office filled with strawberry giggle gas, this very clean, very dry, and very well lit tunnel was a welcome change. Aloha whistled softly as she led the group through the tunnel.

Happy, Reggie, Clem, and Jeeves followed her. *Girl guide training does come in handy when you don't know where you are.* Jeeves' features bore his servant-patented expression free zone. *It seems like we've been in here forever.* "What time is it?"

Clem stopped and studied the face of the Captain Kirk watch on his right wrist. "It's eleven oh two."

Happy and Sparkles laughed nervously they're eyes flitting to each other as they left the office. *I knew it. They're scared.*

Not that I blame them. She stepped carefully over the cobble floor. *I'm getting a little worried myself.*

Clem seemed to be doing well. That blow on the head earlier, certainly hadn't slowed him down any, given he easily kept step with the others.

The tunnel curved out of view to the left. Aloha moved at a slow pace, as the darkness swallowed the light and only about ten feet were visible ahead.

I'm not taking any chances this time.

For all she knew, the floor could open up and swallow them, or they'd trip over the prize and it would be a bomb that would blow up in their faces.

Girl, your imagination is really getting a workout.

The curve ended when they came to a junction where the passageway connected to several openings. The oval junction had a ceiling lined with lights that were on. When she approached the center, she could see there were five tunnels leading off the junction each going in a different direction. Which way now?

Aloha stood trying to figure out what would be the best tunnel to get them out of there, when the ground began to tremble. "Did you feel that?" she gazed at Reggie who now stood beside her.

He shrugged.

Behind them the wall next the tunnel they'd just left suddenly collapsed with a loud *thunk* sending up a choking cloud of dust. Reggie, Jeeves, and Clem scattered like pins at the bowling alley to escape the falling bricks.

Aloha coughed and waved away the dust with the back of her hand. She blinked repeatedly to clear her vision.

Reggie and the others were busy wiping the dust off their clothes and shaking their heads to get the dust out of their hair.

"No worries. There are four other tunnels." She brushed her pant legs with the flat of her hands. *Only which one is the right one? Place is like a maze and I've a sense if we choose the wrong one the situation will get worse.* "We only need to choose the right one."

Aloha glanced over at Jeeves, his eyes were crinkled at the corners. *Now that's out of character. He has no sense of humor.*

"Com'on let's take one of these tunnels."

"Which one?" Reggie shook the last of the brick dust from his hair.

"Does it matter?" Aloha stepped toward the group.

Reggie nodded and stepped beside her. "Let's follow Aloha, everyone. Okay?"

Everyone nodded in unison.

Good that settles it. Aloha looked at each tunnel in turn. They were pretty much identical. All made of the same bricks as the one that had just collapsed. Dirt floors. Gas lamps affixed to the walls. *How do I choose?*

She stuck her index finger in her mouth then held her finger up testing for a breeze that would indicate an exit at the end. After testing only the second tunnel entrance, she felt a breeze.

She smiled. "This is the one."

She hoped this was the tunnel that ended where she'd find Arnold Zero.

Her boss had told her to drop the case of the theft of formula from the top-secret if-I-tell-ya-I-gotta-kill-ya government laboratory or she'd be fired. But she knew in her gut Zero was behind the theft. The formula had to be here somewhere.

But L.I.P.S. hadn't been able to prove any connection between the reclusive billionaire and the stolen top-secret formula. She had known better. She'd followed Zero's henchmen all over the country and she knew his MO. He stole industrial secrets all the time.

The rumor was the secret formula involved zombies so it had to be worth money. A *lot* of money. Zero would never have passed on the chance to corner the zombie market. And knowing Zero, his plans included taking over the world with a zombie army.

Her boss disagreed. *And there's the rub. I'm lucky to still have a job, even a suspended job is better than no job. But if I solve the case, I'll be reinstated, and then who knows I could be running the L.I.P.S. some day.*

The connection had to be this reality show and Wills, especially when she'd seen that zombies were involved. A surveillance report she'd seen a few days ago confirmed Zero had paid Wills in cash, and he'd used his personal ATM card to get the money. *Mistake number one.* She'd illegally hacked his bank accounts.

Of course, if her boss found out she'd hacked Zero's ATM card, she'd be fired for sure. But like her father always said, an Armstrong never gives up even in the face of great personal sacrifice. *Like getting fired.*

L.I.P.S. agents always get their man or woman or clown, or zombie, or midget--sorry, Shelby--correction, or little people.

When Aloha glanced at Clem, his eyes were wide. "What's the matter with you, guy?"

"Nuthin'," he took a step away from her, "you're scarin' the crap outta us is all."

She looked down and saw she'd made a fist and was punching the flat of her other hand. Her hand was red.

Oops! Bad idea She shook her hand to try and shake out the pain. *This never works but that smarts.* Her face grew warm. *You're way too serious, girl. These people are civilians, not cops.* Aloha faced the others. "Sorry, everyone. I can be a little…intense. Sorry."

She knelt and rested on her haunches then drew a circle and four random lines in a ray pattern off the circle in the dust with her index finger.

Reggie and Happy squatted next to her while Sparkles, Jeeves and Clem stood. Jeeves wore his standard issue non-committal expression. *I guess butlers don't squat.*

"There are four tunnels to choose from. Any one of which may lead to the house above or maybe even outside. We're going to split into teams and explore different tunnels."

Clem paled and his body trembled.

"I don't think that's such a hot idea." Happy stood and dusted himself off.

"And why not?" Aloha stared at Happy.

"Well, for one thing we could get cut off from each other and there's strength in numbers. And for another, *L.I.P.S. Agent Armstrong* if we split up who's going to protect Jeeves and Sparkles?" Happy looked at her with his lips pursed in a thin line.

Aloha snorted. "What about you, Reggie and Clem? Don't you guys need protection?"

"I can take care of myself. Reggie and Clem are resourceful. They don't need you or anyone else." Happy crossed his arms.

Really? She eyed Sparkles. *The way his feet are shuffling it's like he's gonna to pee his pants any second.*

Aloha arched an eyebrow. "I hoped you'd say that."

She pointed to one of the lines she'd scratched into the dust. "Jeeves you take this tunnel. And Sparky you go with Clem," Aloha pointed to another line. "Reggie, you come with me down that one. And since you're so brave, Happy you take the last one. By yourself."

She looked at her watch. "We'll meet back in here in ten minutes. Okay?" Aloha frowned. "We need to know where these tunnels lead. Any objections?"

Happy scowled at her.

Aloha waited with Reggie until each team disappeared into their assigned tunnels. The tunnels were lit by the same lamps as the first tunnel so at least there would be enough light.

Aloha smiled to herself. "Com'on, Reggie, let's go."

"Huh. Can I ask a question?" Reggie entered the tunnel behind her.

She stopped when they'd gone a few feet into the tunnel entrance.

"Sure, zombie boy. What can I do for you?"

Reggie swallowed hard, his gaze fixed on her ample breasts. "Huh. Why did we split up? Really, I mean." His gazed shifted away from her chest to look directly into her eyes.

His blue eyes were steady and calm. There was an intelligence behind those passionate eyes. *A man with a rational mind is an awesome thing to behold, even if he is a zombie. I spend far too much time with mad megalomaniacs and crazy dictators. I really gotta get out more.*

"Well, my life-challenged friend, you and I are going to leave the others to their own devices. We're not going back in ten minutes or, with more of the bad luck we've been having on this little adventure, not even in ten years."

"Why?" His gray forehead wrinkled into a scowl. "I'm *not* abandoning my friends."

Aloha sighed heavily. She hoped he was ready for this. Finding out people you trust were being less than honest with you could be quite a shock. *Good thing I'm trained in the art of deception recognition, or I'd have gone crazy a coupla days ago. Their L.I.P.S. intelligence files certainly made interesting reading.*

"Because none of those so-called *friends* of yours are who they say they are--"

"But how? I thought this is just a game--"

"This isn't *just* a game," Aloha snapped. *Take it easy, girl or you're gonna snap like an elastic band. I really need a vacation.*

Her shoulders slumped. "Sorry, Reggie but we need to find Shelby as soon as possible. I suspect she's in danger. And not that Hollywood special effects danger, I mean *real* danger as in Shelby could be about to die."

"Shelby? Shelby who?"

Aloha froze and realized too late that her assumptions had been wrong. A black object about the size of a large cell phone appeared in Reggie's hand. He lunged forward and pressed the object hard against her chest making her stumble. She managed to stay on her feet, but since she was now off balance, she couldn't fight back.

There was a click and her body stiffened as an electric shock seared and burned through her body. Her back arched tensely, pain shot through her shuddering and trembling limbs. Unable to control her legs or arms she sank to the tunnel floor. Every nerve ending assaulted by high voltage electricity. Through blurred vision, she could see Reggie backing off and she lay still.

I don't believe it. A fake Reggie. He tricked me. Me. The woman from L.I.P.S.!

Inky blackness clouded the edges of her vision until the tunnel disappeared.

Oh, crap

~ * ~

Not very funny, fake Matt. Alpha Rucksack had pushed the hidden button that sprung open the secret door.

You'd almost think Rucksack was serious about not knowing where the dressing rooms were until he led them to the hidden entrance, an alcove under the staircase.

Reggie's features were marred by a scowl as deep as the grand canyon. *Poor Reggie.*

Shelby winked at him. *He's cute when he's jealous.*

Reggie followed close behind fake Matt when they entered the dressing room, his brow wrinkled even further.

"Do you believe this?" she whispered.

Reggie grunted, "Don't worry, I can handle this slob."

"Something wrong?" Rucksack's eyebrows pinched.

"Nope. Nothing." Reggie took his gaze from Shelby to look at his friend's double. "Everything's *fine.*"

Shelby stared at the fake Matt who in reality was Alpha Rucksack, actor for hire. *Odd.* His mask fits perfectly now.

You can't tell it is a mask. When I used to help the bearded woman with her makeup, it sure wasn't easy to get everything back in the exact place again before each show. At least by yourself anyway. "Alpha, where did you come from?" The actor looked at her.

She tugged on Reggie's pant leg.

Shelby leaned toward Aloha, who she suspected was also an actor, and motioned with her index finger for the fake agent to come closer.

The L.I.P.S. agent did. Shelby cupped her ear and whispered, "I don't think he's the fake him."

Aloha pulled back and stared into Shelby's eyes then titled her head to look at Reggie. "Think so?"

Shelby nodded as did Reggie.

"What?" Matt opened the door then sat in a makeup chair. .

Reggie and Shelby turned simultaneously to face Matt. *Or is he Rucksack?*

Matt smiled.

Naw, he couldn't be. Could he be? She shrugged. *Weirder things have happened.* "He's him," she said simply.

Reggie's brow wrinkled. "Him? Him who? Matt or Rucksack?"

Reggie's gaze traveled slowly up and down Matt's body, then he broke into a smile. He grabbed Matt by his shoulders and drew him into a bear hug. "You're you!"

"Well, *duh* of course I'm me," Matt's wrinkled brow and narrow eyes displayed his confusion. "Who did you think I was? And who's Rucksack?"

Shelby felt her eyes fill with tears. *What a relief. It's the first good thing that's happened.*

"Did I miss something?" Matt stepped out of Reggie's embrace.

Shelby slapped Matt on the back of his right leg.

"*Owww!* What's matter with you guys? Geez, I came to the kitchen to get a drink of water and you two began acting all strange. Accusing me of being a mole and calling me Rucksack. Who is this Rucksack anyway?"

Reggie released his friend from the hug. His hands still gripped Matt's upper arms. "You disappeared. We. I mean you were gone, and Rucksack pretended to be you. Com'on you know. Right?" Matt rubbed his hands through his hair and shook his head.

"*No*, I don't know. I was asleep until a little while ago." He raised his hands in mock surrender. "That's all, man. Honest." He swiveled his head to scan the row of makeup desks. Mirrors were surrounded by small white light bulbs that were attached to the back of the desks.

"Are you okay," Shelby grinned at the zombie, "really I mean."

"Of course. Why wouldn't I be?"

Shelby shared a smile with Reggie. "He has no idea what's been going on."

"I know. Some guys are just lucky." Reggie released Matt, his arms falling to his sides. "Matt, I'm just glad you're okay."

"Yeah, sure," Matt's puzzled gaze flitted between Reggie, Shelby then at Aloha. The agent averted her gaze and swiveled away in the makeup chair her back to them.

"I like the idea of one of the team members being a mole, though." Matt crossed his arms. "But no one's gonna pry the prize from my cold, undead fingers."

The zombie's eyes narrowed as he studied the line of workstations that ran along the wall. Shelby and Reggie followed his line of sight to the row of makeup desks.

"A guy gets a few extra zzzz's and it's like the whole world goes crazy." Matt spoke slowly as his brow wrinkled in thought.

"How did you know there's a secret door here?"

Matt reached in his jeans pocket and pulled out a folded sheet of yellow paper. "I found this note on my nightstand when I woke up." He unfolded it handed the paper to Shelby. It gave the location of dressing room and the latch to unlock the entrance to the tunnel entrance.

"Over there." She pointed to one corner of the room shrouded in gloom.

Reggie and Matt walked to where the shadows converged about twenty feet from her. Reggie sat on his haunches and began to study the floorboards while Matt tested the wall for openings by pressing the flat of his hand on it.

The eight makeup stations each had a hairpiece dummy covered with a different colored wig. Aloha moved to examine one of the stations more closely, while Shelby stepped up to the one with a purple wig. She ran her fingers through the strands of colorful hair.

Who has purple hair?

At each station, there were plastic trays with compartments, Shelby knew from experience that each contained various shades of theatre makeup. There were also several make-up brushes and trays containing various shades of mascara. Bottles of nail polish lined the space underneath the mirror that looked to contain every shade known to man or woman.

A single leatherette swivel chair--much like those found in hair salons--sat in front of each station. And the air reeked due to an excessive amount of perfume, hair spray, and perm solution. The chemical smells overwhelmed Shelby's senses and she wrinkled her nose.

It smells like a salon for streetwalkers.

Shelby frowned. She eyed Aloha's back. *She may be the double for Aloha, but which others of us have been replaced? And where are my new friends and my brothers? If they're going to all the trouble of planting doubles among us, this prize must be real. Eternal life though?*

"Hey, Matt? Where are the others?" Matt had been replaced by one of them, but the real Matt was back. Maybe he'd seen the others. Or at least the actors.

"I don't know." Matt brow wrinkled. "In fact, I'm having trouble remembering anything before I woke up."

"Useless." Reggie sighed. "Matt's memory has been wiped."

Oh. Shelby frowned. *How does he know Matt's memory is wiped?*

"Yeah. Reggie's right." Matt shook his head. "I don't know anything about anything."

"Hmmmm," a muffled cry interrupted them. The sound came from another corner at the end of the room also deep in shadow.

Shelby squinted into the dim light and spotted the outline of a shadow- shrouded figure lying on its side on the floor in the corner. The figure struggled, and she realized they were small like her. Her heart beat faster. *Could it be?*

She stepped into the gloom and immediately lost any sense of direction. She followed the sound of a muffled mumble that had grown more urgent.

Footsteps came up behind her. She reached out and her fingertips and touched Reggie's muscular arm. "Yeah, it's me," she heard him say.

Zombies can be so comforting.

Finally, they stood over the struggling figure lying at their feet.

Her eyes gradually adjusted until she could make out his face. Her mouth fell open. "Buster!" She dropped to her knees beside her brother.

Her brother struggled against the ropes that held his hands behind his back. His dark hair, matted by sweat, lay flat against his forehead. His eyes pleaded with Shelby to release him.

"Ummm," Buster's mouth was hidden by grey duct tape.

With trembling fingers, Shelby worked to untie the ropes around her brother's wrists.

Reggie knelt at her brother's feet and worked to undo those knots. After the ropes were loosened, Reggie reached up and ripped off the tape across Buster's mouth in one go.

"Owww! That hurt!" Buster winced and rubbed his sore mouth with his fingers. He flexed his lips and moved his jaw back and forth. "You shoulda ripped it off slower, man."

With a wry smile at Shelby, Reggie vigorously rubbed Buster's legs while Shelby did the same to his arms to encourage his blood to circulate. Aloha and Matt stood over them. They looked at each other obviously unsure how to help.

Shelby grinned at them and nodded. "We've got it, guys. Thanks."

This Aloha's definitely not the resourceful girl scout like my Aloha

Buster sighed with relief. "Thank you, thank you, thank you." He rubbed his red wrists. "Man, I didn't think anyone would *ever* come."

Shelby threw her arms around her brother's chest and pressed herself hard into him.

He grinned. "Whoa, don't have to get all mushy on me, sis."

Shelby used the back of one hand to wipe away tears from her cheeks. Her family had never been very demonstrative, except for Shelby and her mother. Her brothers and her father often made fun of them. They teased them that *emotional junk*--as the men of the family called any overt emotional outburst--was for girls. *Real* men were made of sterner stuff.

Of course, there are always exceptions to every absolute. Like the time her brothers watched the Disney movie *Old Yeller*. When the boy shot the sick dog, the men of the house cried like babies. Of course, she'd cried too. *Movies didn't count,* explained Buster. *You'd be nuts not to cry at the movies.*

"Sorry, it's just," she paused, "I missed you."

Buster stiffly patted her shoulder then stood and stretched his arms over his head. "It's okay, sis I'm fine."

"Yeah. I'm glad."

"Me too." Reggie joined in on the family reunion by hugging Shelby.

Nice.

He released her and placed his hands in his pockets.

He let go too soon.

Shelby swallowed hard. "Buster, I have to ask you something." She sniffled. Her doubtful gaze fell over Reggie who gave her a barely perceptible nod of encouragement.

I have to be sure. Don't wanta waste tears. "Are you the *real* Buster?"

"What kinda stupid question is that?" Buster's brow creased into a frown.

Shelby face grew warm. "It's a long story. I'm sorry, but I need to know."

"Do you think I tied *myself* up?"

Shelby shook her head and grinned. "No, of course not. That would be silly, bro..." She walked over and opened a makeup drawer. Sure enough, she found a bottle of water. She took it and handed it to her brother. *I read in TV Guide once actors kept bottle water in their makeup drawers. I never imagined it'd be true.*

He took it from her, unscrewed the cap, and tipped it back. He drained the contents in two long swallows.

"*Burp!*" he smiled, "thanks I needed that." He tapped his chest with his fist eliciting a softer *burp*. "As I was about to say, what's silly?"

"Huh. Perhaps I can explain." Reggie stood his hands hung at his sides.

Saved by my zombie. Sweet.

Shelby nodded--she didn't know what Reggie was to her just yet. *A boyfriend? A lover? A fiancée? Nope, he isn't any of those things--at least not yet. Her friend. Yeah, but more than that. Hopefully much more. Boyfriend?* She shook her head. *I wish I knew. I'm so confused about him right now. I hope I figure it out soon.*

"Buster, let Reggie explain," she spoke softly to her brother, "please."

Buster stood and crossed his arms as his brown eyes studied the zombie with the let's-get-on-with-it-pal look. Coupled with this-better-be-good was certainly intimidating.

Shelby rose to her feet last. Reggie cleared his throat. "You see. Huh. It's like this, Toulest is dead--murdered, actually--and her body's missing. And then you were missing, Herbie's still missing. Then the fire and--the others were separated from us--the L.I.P.S. agent Aloha--"

"Aloha?" Buster's voice was clearly skeptical, yet his eyes twinkled.

Shelby hoped this made some sense to her brother because it sounded pretty silly even to her, and she'd lived it.

"Then this fake zombie, who is really an actor--" Reggie ignored Buster's rhetorical question.

"Don't tell me," Buster erupted with a burst of laughter, "his name's Bogus Bob right?"

Reggie's mouth hung open. "*No,* smart guy. As a matter of fact, his name is Rucksack, Alpha Rucksack"

Buster snorted.

Don't let my bro dis you. You go, Reg.

"And he told you this. Right?"

Reggie nodded.

So did Matt.

Buster shook his head. "If this experience has taught us anything, it's that you can't believe anything you see or hear, and especially some nob calling himself Alpha anything."

Shelby nodded. *Makes sense.* Wrapping the fingers of her right hand around Reggie's arm she agreed, "Buster's right, of course."

She stepped closer to her brother. "Buster, I wish we had time to explain everything, but right now we have to rescue the others. It's up to us."

"Why didn't you say so, sis?" He poked at his chest with his thumb. "I'm your man."

Reggie exhaled. The tension in his arm eased.

"I'm in too." Matt grinned and the zombie's normal gray color had returned. *Well at least zombie-normal.*

The good news is this Buster is my Buster. The really good news was we found Reggie's Matt too. The really, really good news was we had allies we could trust. Shelby's eyes narrowed. *Now it's up to me, my zombie bookends, and my bro to save the day.*

And the really, really, really good news is with my brothers back the odds of finding the diamond just improved.

She glanced at the pseudo-Aloha. *Now what to do about her?*

A soft squeak like from a rusty hinge startled Shelby. The sound came from the far end of the dressing room. Leaving the others, Shelby moved cautiously toward the sound squinting into the shadows. Walking past the row of makeup stations Shelby soon spotted an open trap door in the floor. "Hey, guys look what I found."

Aloha came up to stand beside her and together they peered into the dark opening.

"That wasn't there before," Aloha frowned.

"Wow," Buster snorted. "A real trap door. Cool."

Shelby knelt down on her knees so she could stick her head inside. The guys crowded in on her as they stood around the opening. She peered in. Flaming torches were lit at the bottom of the shaft. The steel rungs of a ladder gleamed in the meager light. At the bottom, there appeared to be a dirt floor. It was circular in shape and she could make out several tunnels leading away from the center like spokes on a wheel. "I see six different passageways down there." She pulled her head out of the opening and looked up at Reggie. "This house would make a queen bee a happy home."

Reggie grinned.

Aloha moved to the opening. "Let's check out the tunnels. Surely, it can't be any worse than what we've seen so far?"

Buster snorted then knelt by the trap door and lowered himself down the ladder, quickly disappearing like a rabbit in a hole. *Look at fearless man.*

"After you, sir?" Fake Aloha smiled.

Reggie looked at Shelby nodded then he, too, disappeared down the opening.

The L.I.P.S. agent and Shelby would be last to enter. Aloha looked at Shelby with a half smile on her lips and mischievous twinkle in her eyes. "Spontaneous are we?"

She seems a little too eager, but she has a better sense of humor than the real Aloha.

Shelby laughed. "Let's go." *But just in case, she's going first.* "After you, Miss I'm-the-funny-government-agent."

Fake Aloha chuckled then quickly disappeared down the ladder.

Into the unknown we go. And I have a sinking sense we're going to find more than we bargained for. But no one's gonna stop me now.

~ * ~

Aloha gradually rose from a deep black pit as if she lost in eternity. *Am I flying? It's as if I'm floating on the ocean.* Her eyes fluttered open. *Cinnamon.* The sweet scent of it invaded her nose and mouth. Her brow wrinkled. *The rough curved stonework looked like the ceiling. I'm on the floor. Why?*

Who cares? She closed her eyes again. *My dream is better.* "Cinnamon toast. I'd like to have cinnamon toast for breakfast, Mom," she murmured, as she rolled off her back to lay on her side in a fetal position.

The cold stone floor sent a chill through her body. Images of dirt lying on her bed, gave her a clue that she wasn't in her bedroom in her parents' house. *And I'm sure not twelve anymore.*

She blinked her eyes open and closed. *Owww. Even my eyelashes hurt.*

A groan escaped her lips as she pushed with the flat of her hands on the dirt floor to raise her weak upper body so she could sit. Her arms gave out and she sank back and draped an arm over her eyes. *A fake Reggie.* She pictured her hands around his undead neck. *You're gonna pay for this, buddy.* Aloha's belly tightened and anger swelled from within. *How could I let myself be fooled by an actor? How embarrassing. I'm never going to live this down.*

She rolled onto her back and shook her legs and arms to increase the circulation to her extremities. Then she rolled her neck and gradually the blood began to flow. *Good.* Her surroundings became clearer, and the sleepy fuzziness at the edges of her vision disappeared.

Man, do those things hurt. She flexed her arms and wiggled her fingers. *It's like your nerves are on fire. I'd forgotten the effects of the Taser since we used them on each other in training at the L.I.P.S. Academy.*

Aloha planted her hands flat on either side of her torso and pushed herself into a kneeling position. Her vision blurred as the blood rushed from her head. She sat back on her haunches and took in deep breaths. The muscles in her legs trembled but finally, after what seemed like forever, she managed to stand. Her knees buckled slightly, and she pressed one hand against the brick wall to steady herself. She turned to face the wall, then pressed both hands against the cool bricks. The room rolled like the deck of a ship in the center of a long ocean swell. *I think I'm getting the hang of this Taser after effects thing.* Her stomach heaved and she covered her mouth with one hand. *Or am I?* She closed her eyes again.

Aloha finally opened her eyes as the queasiness passed. She turned around and scanned the room. *I'm still in the tunnel. But I'm alone. Where's that rat bastard fake Reggie and what has he done with the others or are they in this together? It'd be just like Arnold Zero to bribe everyone to get rid of a L.I.P.S. agent.*

Questions without answers are just plain annoying.

"Hello?" She strained to hear a reply. Her voice echoed down the tunnel and finally faded into the distance. Silence.

In the quiet that followed, she heard the sound of hissing from burning torches that lined the ceiling of the passageway. The cinnamon smell in the air seemed to increase with each passing second.

Looking around she saw that fake Reggie had dragged her back into the junction. Again, there were four tunnels to choose from. *But which one did they use? There has to be a trail here somewhere.*

She looked down at the coating of gray dust on the floor of the tunnel and followed the random scattering of footprints to the entrance of each tunnel.

Sneaker prints are everywhere. Her eyes narrowed. *The clowns were here. Big feet. And cowboy boot prints. Normal size. Only Reggie wears cowboy boots.*

Aloha peered into the tunnel where the boot prints disappeared. *They must have gone this way.*

Aloha started down the tunnel, her eyes locked on the floor following fake Reggie's boot prints. She leaned against the cool brick wall to keep from falling her equilibrium still off.

Whoa! I gotta get me one of those Tasers. They really pack a punch. Even better than my Glock. These pants are too tight to carry a gun. She hobbled forward in the tunnel. *If the boss finds out I lost my gun, he's really gonna have me fired, twice. At least twice, maybe more.*

After what seemed like seemed an eternity, but really only about ten minutes later by her watch, she reached another junction with two more tunnels leading off the circle

A sudden loud thud erupted from one of the tunnels. What's that? She sprinted down the tunnel where the noise came from as fast as her weakened legs could carry her until she came to a solid wall of brick. She stumbled and her wrist struck the wall. She looked at her watch and saw the face had cracked. The digital numbers were stopped.

She sighed. *I'm like a rat in a maze.* Her stomach growled. *Without the cheese.* She walked back toward the junction. After a few minutes, she spotted the boot prints in the dirt once again. She smiled to herself.

"You're not gonna get away from me yet, you sneaky fake zombie guy."

She followed the prints retracing her steps down the tunnel until they ended at another floor to ceiling brick wall. *I don't remember this being here.* She frowned. *I thought this tunnel led back to the junction?*

She pressed her hands up and down over the cool, rough bricks, but there didn't seem to be a way to open it nor was there a door. A draft of cold air washed over her legs coming from a seam where the floor met the wall. *Great.* There had to be another secret door here somewhere. Her quarry had escaped. The trail of boot prints ended at the brick wall.

Aloha sat down hard on the dirt floor causing the dust to billow and covering her in a fine brown powder.

I'm trapped. It doesn't look like I'm ever going to escape. She hung her head. *I'm such a failure.*

Anger welled in her. *Crap. It's not fair. This kind of thing never happens to other L.I.P.S. agents.*

~ * ~

Standing at the bottom of the ladder beneath the trap door, Reggie offered his hand to help Buster and Matt, then Aloha, and Shelby down from the ladder. Shelby saw the end of the ladder was two feet above the floor. Matt yelped when he landed hard on his butt.

Buster and Shelby glanced at each other then in a perfectly timed move let go of the ladder rungs, did matching flips in the air, and landed with a dull *thud* on the floor their arms out stretched like wings. *A perfect two-point landing.*

"Wow," Reggie's eyes were wide, "you guys are *really* good."

"Thanks," Buster grinned. "We learned that trick from the Flying Popodoms at the circus. Pretty cool, huh?"

Shelby scanned the room and the six tunnels around them. One had a steep wooden staircase that went upward and looked unsafe with rickety looking handrails that seemed about to collapse. There were boards missing on some steps.

"Don't you think we should test--" Before Reggie could say anything more, Shelby had clambered up the first two steps. They creaked under her weight.

"Orrrr. I guess not." Reggie's brow wrinkled.

This has got to be the way out. At least it goes up.

She looked back and gave her companions a reassuring smile. "You guys wait here. The stairs don't look strong enough to hold all of us. Trust me."

Shelby nodded. *He's right the stairs are in pretty bad shape.* Before taking another step, she tested the boards with the toe of her shoe. She crossed her fingers then took another step. The board squeaked. *Don't break. Please.* Beads of sweat popped out on Shelby's forehead as she carefully made her way up each stair. She stopped and wiped the sweat that dripped in her eyes with the back of her arm.

Her wet fingers gripped the shaky railing. *Man, is this scary.* It wobbled under her touch. The stairs beneath her creaked and snapped with each step. She gazed upward at the stairs that snaked to disappear into the gloom above her. *There must be ninety-nine steps to go.* She glanced over her shoulder behind her. *And I've already climbed ninety-nine.*

When she looked down, she saw four, tiny pale faces gazing up at her from a sea of darkness. She gulped then looked up into the inky blackness above again. *More darkness.* With a snap the step below the one she stood on fell away to be lost in the dark. *Great.* One way trip. *No choice.* She swallowed hard. *Gotta keep goin' if I'm gonna find us a way out of here.* She steeled herself, held her breath, and took another step. The stairs wobbled slightly then settled beneath her. She let out the breath. *When a Bass says you can trust them we mean it.*

Finally, after what seemed like an hour, she arrived at the top step. Breathing hard she found a little people –sized door with a burnished copper-colored doorknob.

Testing the doorknob with her fingertips to make sure it wasn't booby-trapped, Shelby twisted it in her hand. A sharp *click* echoed in the enclosed space. *That's way too easy*

"You okay up there?" Reggie's voice echoed from below.

The thick, musty air made it hard to breathe, but her breathing slowed. She blinked away the stinging sweat that dripped off her forehead into her eyes and cupped her mouth with one hand, "I'm okay. I found a door."

She took in a deep breath, held it, then using her fingers she gently pushed the door open. It opened easily but squealed on rusty hinges.

Shelby winced in the fierce sunlight that assaulted her. She shut her eyes tight. *Where am I?*

After several minutes of blinking and wiping tears until her vision cleared... *My bedroom? What the...how?*

She stuck her head out the door into the shaft. "Hey, guys come on up!" her voice echoed down the shaft.

Reggie soon crawled through the open door on his hands and knees, then Buster walked in, then Matt crawled in and finally, Aloha crawled in.

"There were missing steps," Reggie gasped. "I think most of the ones below us fell off."

Once inside they stood and gaped at Shelby with her arms thrown wide. "Welcome to my room," she chuckled, "we're back where *I* started." Sure enough, everything was just as she left it including the cheesy gray, red and navy wool quilt on the bed. The same room where she'd lay on the bed with Reggie.

Shelby let her hands drop to her sides. "This explains the cinnamon."

"What?" Reggie blinked in confusion. He walked across the room and looked out her bedroom window.

"Oh. Yeah. Sorry, Reggie. I guess I didn't mention it earlier. The scent didn't seem important at the time, but when I woke up after the first night, my room smelled of cinnamon. Frankly, I prefer rosewater myself. That's why I'd love to have a bedsp--"

"You know what this means, don't you?" Buster's brow wrinkled and he looked at his sister. "You don't you get it, huh?"

Shelby grimaced and shook her head. *He's finally fallen off his skateboard.*

"Someone came into your room while you were sleeping, sis."

Someone had been following them wherever they went. This someone used the secret passageways as if it is their own personal Route 66, and they had the only up-to-date roadmap. She sighed. "Yeah. They could have hurt me or worse." Her stomach tightened as it dawned on her she could have been violated while she slept.

"I agree," piped up Reggie, "and if he or she had, I would've--"

"What? What would you have done? Exactly?" Buster gave the zombie a withering stare and folded his arms across his chest.

Reggie moved to stand by the bed. "Well, I don't know. Exactly. But I would have done *something.*"

Reggie really cares about me. Cool. Cupid's arrow had finally hit her bulls eye.

First, he saves me then he shows he cares about me. I think I've fallen in love with a zombie.

Reggie's puppy eyes locked with hers. Her face grew warm.

She averted her gaze and her eyes narrowed. *Too bad, I can't tell him anything about me. I've blown any chance with him.*

184

She turned away and walked to gaze out the window at the deserted sound stage. *But he and his fellow zombies did steal radium, after all. That means he's a thief, too. Maybe he'll forgive me when we find the diamond? You never know. He might go along with us. Then again, maybe not, given that the Gnotborst jewel is apparently his family's diamond. This situation sucks. Why couldn't we have met somewhere else?*

Maybe if Buster and I find the diamond and I give it to him, Reggie'll understand. "Reggie, you wait here. Buster, and I have do something," she gripped her brothers arm, "unless Buster and I--"

Buster glowered at her but before he could tell her to let go he fell silent and his cheeks lost their color.

He placed a finger over his lips, "Shhhh." He cocked his head to one side like a dog who just heard a dog whistle. He listened intently for several seconds his brow furrowed in concentration. "Do you hear that?" Buster whispered.

Shelby listened intently until, at the edge of her hearing, she heard a voice. A woman's voice spoke softly.

Buster yanked his arm free of Shelby's grip and ran to a dark stained four-drawer rosewood dresser shoved against the wall. "It's louder here."

Shelby glanced at Aloha and took a step back. *Whoa, is she scary looking. The scowl, the penetrating stare at nothing, the vein in her neck throbbing.* Shelby cringed. "You thinkin' what I'm thinkin' agent lady?"

"No."

Boy, she seems pissed about something. So what? There's someone crying on the other side of that wall? There's no need to get mad. Shelby tapped her brother on the shoulder.

"Help me move this," she indicated the dresser.

Buster nodded then moved to one side of the dresser beside her.

Matt went to the other side of the dresser and gripped the ornate molding. After counting to three together, they moved the dresser away from the wall.

Once it was a few inches away from the wall, Shelby managed to squeeze herself into the gap between the wall and the dresser.

"It's. A. Tight. Fit," she breathed. *Man, is it hot in here or is it just me?* A breath of heated air blew across her legs. *Aha!* A breeze of heated air came out of a crack where the wall and the floor met.

There has to be another of those secret tunnels behind this wall. But where's the trigger mechanism that'll open it?

"This is pointless." Aloha perched on the edge of the bed watching.

"Yeah. Thanks for the support." *Fake LIPS agents are sooo annoying.* "Reggie, open the drawers to the dresser." One by one, she could hear Reggie opening and closing drawers. The wall did not budge. "Try opening them together." He did as instructed. Still nothing.

Shelby glanced above her head and saw the wall sconce. She stood and tapped at the metal looking plate of the sconce and heard a plastic *ping*. *Fake?* She snapped her fingers.

"What is it?" Reggie stood back as she squeezed out from behind the dresser.

"Reggie, open all of the dresser drawers. Buster, get a chair. Matt you help him." She stepped in front of the dresser. "When Reggie has all the drawers open use the chair on the side of the dresser to reach the lamp. Then when I give you the signal, pull the bracket toward you."

"Won't it just break?"

"No. I'm thinking it's a hidden key."

Buster frowned but nodded.

Matt shrugged.

Reggie grinned.

At least he gets it.

She squeezed back behind the dresser. She heard the chair legs drag the fibers as Buster moved it across the carpet.

"You know, dear brother you are not the only one with deductive reasoning capabilities." Her voice echoed in the confined space.

Buster chuckled.

Looking up she saw his tiny fingers grip the ornate bracket at the base of the lamp waiting for her signal. *Here goes nothing.* "Okay, Buster." She squeezed her eyes shut.

She heard a loud *snap and* opened her eyes to look up. *Uh, oh. I'm wrong!*

Buster held the broken bracket in his hand as he stood on the chair. "What did I do?"

"Told ya," Aloha said sardonically.

Shelby edged out of the space. *I don't get it. I was so sure.* Just as she cleared the back of the dresser, a trap door in the rug opened directly in front of Buster, who had came toward her to offer his hand to help her stand.

One foot hung suspended over the open trap door and his arms waved wildly in the air, his body swayed back and forth like a willow tree in a high wind. His eyes were wide and frantic. His swaying stopped, his arms still straight out from his sides like a high wire artist until he managed to stop himself from falling in. Without any noise, the trap door closed. "Whoa," Buster tip-toed backwards and until he sat in an empty leather chair. He wiped his brow with the sleeve of his shirt. "That's too close for comfort."

Shelby stared at where the open trap door had been. *That's something you don't see every day.*

"Call 911. We almost lost another one," Aloha's smirked, "Or is it the same one almost twice?"

Shelby scowled at Aloha then knelt on the floor and ran her hands across the carpet. She found nothing indicating there had ever been a trap door. *How is this possible?* The fibers were tight, there were no broken threads, and she couldn't see any signs of a break in the carpet. *But it certainly explains how some of us are disappearing.*

"That's just wrong." Reggie nodded and leaned against the wall nearest him bedside the dresser. There was a sharp *clicking* sound and a section of wall behind the dresser swung away creaking on steel hinges.

"Okay. *Now* it opens." Shelby shook her head.

A scent of cinnamon filled the room. And the sound of a woman crying was louder now. That voice was familiar. *Aloha?* Shelby's eyes narrowed. *We got you now fake Aloha.* Shelby looked back to the bed and saw the Aloha double had disappeared. *Where did she go?*

We'll catch up with her later. Right now, I have to rescue our Aloha. Shelby peeked around the dresser into the tunnel. Inside she saw the soft glow that came from oil lamps that hung off rust-red brick walls. The dusty floorboards were made of wooden planks. Shelby squeezed into the opening and walked through into the tunnel. Sure enough, the red-headed L.I.P.S. agent sat on the floor, her face buried in her arms, and her knees hugged to her chest crying softly. "You okay?" Aloha looked up her red-rimmed eyes made Shelby's heart break. *She's in bad shape. I better call for help.*

When Aloha didn't respond Shelby yelled, "Aloha's in the tunnel!"

"Say what? How?" Reggie rushed to the door and stuck his head in.

"Do you know where the other Aloha went?" she asked the zombie.

"She told me she had to go to the bathroom. She'll be right back."

Shelby nodded. "Sure. Of course she will."

I knew it. The fake woman from L.I.P.S. has escaped.

Her eyes narrowed. *We'll meet again, whoever you are.*

Shelby knelt next to Aloha and placed an arm across her shoulders. Aloha responded by burying her head against Shelby's arm.

But right now, I have to comfort a friend.

Twenty Six

Shelby had never been so glad at any time in her life as when she saw Aloha alive and well. The real Aloha had been alone with her back against the wall when they had found her. She seemed none the worse for wear except for the crying.

"What time is it?" Shelby had a growing sense of unease. Toulest told them midnight was the critical hour and something very bad was going to happen.

"What's the matter with *your* watch?" grumbled Buster.

"I broke it back in the tunnel."

"Eleven thirty-one," offered Reggie.

"Thank you," Shelby was pleased when he grinned. *He's the best.*

Reggie, Matt and Buster managed to squeeze into the tunnel behind her before the entrance closed once again trapping them.

Upon seeing Reggie, Aloha's eyes went wide and she pointed at Matt. "Is he real?"

Shelby assured her this was the real Reggie. "And you were faked as well. But your double got away."

Aloha got up and patted the dust off her legs. She explained that after separating her from Happy, Clem and Jeeves, the fake Reggie zapped her with a Taser, and she got lost in a maze of tunnels and dead ends.

Reggie stood on one side of Aloha, Shelby on the other, as they walked further into the tunnel. Matt and Buster had moved ahead testing the bricks along the way by pressing on them for signs secret doors.

"Where're we goin'?" called out Buster.

"We have to get the fake Aloha and make her lead us to Wills." *And find the diamond then get out of here. I hope.*

Aloha's clothes, hair, face, and hands were covered in layer of gray dust. *But, she's back. At least this looks like the real Aloha.*

My gut is telling me the fake Aloha is the key to end this game.

"I'm the *worst* L.I.P.S. agent ever," Aloha moaned, the bitterness thick in her voice. *Yup, she's the real Aloha all right.*

Shelby glanced at Reggie. "You okay?"

Reggie averted his eyes. Shelby smiled to herself. *He's so cute when he's uncomfortable.*

Shelby turned her attention to the stricken agent. "Is there anything we can do?" *Boy, is she in a bad way.*

"Fresh air and a soft bed will do you a lot of good right now," Shelby added softly. "What happened back there? And where are the others?"

Aloha sniffled. "Jeeves, Clem and I escaped the fire through a hidden door."

Relief washed over Shelby. *My brother is okay and so is Jeeves.*

"That fake Reggie attacked me!" Aloha scowled at Reggie. "Are you sure you're the *real* Reggie?"

Reggie shot a sardonic look at Shelby. "Yeah. It's the *real* me."

"Did we kiss?"

His ears reddened. "Yes, we did."

Shelby smiled. "You're real. Too bad. I so wanted to kick your butt." He took a step away from her.

"No. No. Not you. I mean the fake you."

"Oh." Reggie glanced at Shelby. "Good."

Shelby sighed and patted her friend's arm. "It's okay, we're all real here. We'll find that faker together. Okay?"

Aloha nodded.

Finally, they found the door to Shelby's bedroom. They entered and the door closed behind them with a *thud.*

Aloha groaned as she fell backward onto the tattered white-knit bedspread. The bed's springs squeaked in protest. She rolled on her side facing the wall.

Reggie opened a window and immediately a soft breeze flowed over them from the open window.

"Good idea thanks, Reggie." Shelby sat on the bed next to Aloha and stroked the agent's long red curls. "You'll be okay." She froze and her gaze shot to the open window. A frown creased her brow and her eyes narrowed. She looked at Reggie. "How did you do that?"

"Do what?" Reggie had moved to an empty chair and sat down.

She pointed at the window. "How did you open the window?"

Reggie's blue eyes flitted to the open window then back at her. "I don't know."

Reggie rushed to the open window and grasped the window frame with both hands.

I'm not letting him take this on alone.

Shelby moved to stand beside Reggie and gripped the bottom of the window frame with him. After she touched the outside of the frame, just like the one before, it moved downward and started to close by itself. *Oops! Bad idea.*

They let go of the window frame simultaneously and looked at each other. Shelby was relieved when their fingers didn't stick. "Darn things close all by themselves." Reggie grinned.

Shelby laughed and headed for the bathroom. "Yeah, this time we're not falling for the old window-closes-on-your-hands-trick."

Once she was alone in the bathroom, she stood in front of the mirror looking at the dark circles under her eyes and the traces of soot on her cheeks and chin. Carefully she washed her face hand and hands with a worn powder blue face cloth and a bar of white soap.

I'm in love with Reggie and I'm scared. If the prize is really eternal life, what do I do? My brothers will want to steal it, and my dad will want to sell it to the highest bidder. But it could save Reggie and his friends from certain doom. And then there's Aloha.

The L.I.P.S. agent could be a real help finding the diamond and the prize before midnight. I don't know what's going to happen, but it can't be good.

"You should tell Aloha that you and your brothers are crooks." She spoke to her image. *It sounds like an even worse idea when I say it out loud, but I'm sure she knows anyway. Like she so often says, the L.I.P.S. have files on all of us.*

Setting the washcloth on the edge of the sink, she gazed at her freshly scrubbed features then twisted her lips in a sardonic grin.

"So what you gonna do, lady?"

Without answering her own question, Shelby left the bathroom.

"It took you long enough," complained Buster before he disappeared into the bathroom slamming the door behind him.

Aloha smiled, took Shelby's hand in hers, and led her to the bed where they sat down beside each other.

"What's wrong, Shelby?" She placed a comforting arm around Shelby's shoulder.

Shelby avoided looking at Aloha. "I like you, ya know."

Aloha patted the back of Shelby's hand. "And I like you, too. You were very nice to me back in the tunnel. So tell me what's wrong?"

Finally, Shelby turned to look at Aloha. *I have to tell her the truth about me and my brothers. How're we gonna be BFF's if we have secrets between us?* "We're professional thieves. My brothers and I," she blurted suddenly.

Aloha's features sagged, but she didn't say anything.

"We're thieves," Shelby repeated. "But I'm sure you knew that," Shelby chuckled, "like you always say L.I.P.S. agents know everything about everyone."

Aloha's cheeks flushed crimson and she averted her eyes. "I didn't know *that*," she whispered.

Twenty Seven

OH, CRAP.

Aloha sat next to Shelby on the flowery bedspread, her arm still around her shoulders. The agent's normally full lips formed a thin line, and her eyebrows formed a scowl. "You don't seriously think we're just circus performers did you?"

I don't get it. The L.I.P.S. "knows everything." I thought she knew. This is bad.

"You're a crook?" Matt's eyes were wide as saucers. "Cool."

Shelby cast the zombie a disparaging look.

Aloha grunted. "Well, yes, as a matter of fact, I did think you and your brothers were actually circus performers. I've been undercover with the clowns for the past three months and those guys seem to be doing quite well--"

"Did you see your paycheck?" Shelby rolled her eyes at the obvious.

Aloha shook her head. "Nope. It's policy that undercover operatives have their pay direct deposited to an offshore account the Service has for paychecks in the line of duty. If we take the paycheck we call it double dipping."

"But I thought you were suspended?" Reggie came and sat next to Shelby. He took her hand in his and gave it a gentle squeeze. She looked at him and smiled. *He's so sweet.*

"I thought double dipping only applied to chips and dip," Matt suggested.

Oh, brother. Is she kidding about double dipping?

193

Aloha ignored Reggie's question. Instead, she slapped her forehead the palm of her free hand. "How could I be so stupid? I really am the worst federal agent ever."

Buster exited the bathroom emitting a satisfied sigh. Matt immediately went into the bathroom closing the door once again.

"We need to talk about this," Aloha frowned and stood. "Alone."

Shelby swallowed hard. *Time to backpedal. Fast. Me and my big mouth. Why did I think I could tell Aloha anything about my life as a thief? She's a cop.* Her shoulders slumped. *The one time I trust someone outside the family, and I get burned. Serves me right if I spend the rest of my days behind bars. I'll never get to Hawaii now.*

Her face grew warm. "Yes, we are circus performers, but we moonlight as professional thieves." *Man, give me a shovel and I'll dig a hole to China.*

"Listen, Shelby, why don't we leave it there for now. We'll get this thief stuff cleared up after the show." Aloha shrugged. "I'm sure we can work something out." She smiled. "We're still pals. Okay?"

Maybe we're gonna be BFF's after all. Shelby said, "I want to ask you about the prize. You said something that made me think the prize will save Reggie--" Aloha's eyes shifted to Reggie, whose eyes were wide.

He opened his mouth to speak when a sudden sharp rap on the bedroom door made them go silent.

Who's that?

Aloha placed her right index finger over her lips. She stood lay her hands flat on the wall behind her and edged along the wall toward the door.

Aloha moved slowly to the left side of the closed door her hands pressed flat against the wall at her sides She nodded for Shelby to move. "Stand on the other side," she whispered. "When I open the door, be prepared to jump them." Aloha looked Shelby up then down. "Maybe just grab the guy around his knees."

"What about them?" Shelby indicated Reggie who still sat on the bed and Buster standing by the dresser.

"Back up."

"Oh." She tilted her head to indicate the bedroom door. "But how do you know it's a bad *guy*?"

"L.I.P.S. agents have built in load-of-crap detectors, with optional bad guy sensors. It's a bad guy all right. Trust me."

Those sensors of hers don't work all the time. That didn't help her with the fake Reggie. Awww, but who cares? The woman from L.I.P.S. is back! "Cool." She gave Aloha the thumbs up sign.

Aloha crouched slightly. She raised her arms, her hands held out in front of her ready to spring like a cat when the bad guy entered. Shelby stood on the opposite side of the doorway also ready to pounce. *I'm like a little tiger.*

Shelby reached for the doorknob, twisted, pulled hard and the door popped open. Shelby abruptly dropped on all fours across the threshold. A heavy body hit her ribs hard and tripped over her to land face down on the carpet. Like a pro wrestler, Aloha fell on the intruders legs and pinned them and part of the upper body to the carpeted floor.

Shelby collapsed underneath the intruder with Aloha on top of the pile.

"Mademoiselles! Release me!"

Jeeves? I'm getting squished.

"Aloha, a little help here," Shelby grunted as she struggled to untangle herself from Jeeves' legs and push Aloha off her. Her nose was pressed into the carpet, and it smelled of stale smoke and dust. *Ewww. Gross.*

Aloha rolled off Jeeves' back and stood up beside her.

"Huh. Sorry, Jeeves." Shelby pulled her legs free and stood.

The butler grunted and stood up pulling at the sides of his suit jacket with his hands. "Ohhhh," he groaned. His wispy hair looked like it had been combed with an electric hand mixer.

The perfectly pressed butler is a real mess--he's crumpled and dusty.

Shelby brushed off her jeans muttering, "Why do I let her talk me into these things?" She froze when her eyes locked on the silver handle of a knife sticking out of the middle of Jeeves' back.

He groaned again softly, sagged to his knees, then collapsed face down on the stinking carpet and lay still. Reggie dropped to his knees beside the stricken butler's side.

Shelby shivered, though she wasn't cold. "Ahhh. Aloha?"

"I noticed." Aloha knelt next to the injured butler.

"In the movies isn't it always the butler who did it, not someone *did* the butler." Shelby frowned. "I hope he's okay. He's not such a bad guy, ya know."

"Yeah," agreed Buster.

"Yeah, well, murderers don't care much if you're a nice guy or what kind of work you do," murmured Aloha, her forehead creased.

Reggie looked up, sighed, and sat back on his haunches. "It's not good. His pulse is weak."

Abruptly he shuffled backward. "Help me roll him on his side. Now! He's still alive," he added in a more urgent tone.

Shelby dropped to her knees and helped Reggie roll Jeeves on his side.

Jeeves gasped and his eyes fluttered open. His usually placid features were twisted in obviously excruciating pain.

Shelby winced. *That must really hurt. Then again, a knife in the back isn't exactly a mosquito bite is it?*

"I'll take over the questioning. After all I am a professional."

Reggie and Shelby stood and stepped back to let the L.I.P.S. agent get closer.

"Easy, buddy. Try to breathe." Aloha bent over the butler and leaned closer to whisper in his ear, "Who did this to you?"

Jeeves gasped for air from between clenched teeth, his pale face bathed in sweat.

"The kil...ler...is...is...zer..." he strained to speak, his words separated by gasps for air.

He held up one hand and formed an O shape with his thumb and index fingers.

A long moan escaped between his lips. Jeeves' body tensed as the pain seemed to increase then his gaze became unfocused. His hand dropped limply to the floor with a soft *thump*. Coughing, air rushed from his lungs as his body gradually relaxed like a leaky balloon. He shuddered once and lay still. His eyes were open, unseeing.

"Wow," Buster sat on the bed and his hands trembled. "I've never seen anyone die before."

Buster stared at Shelby who shuddered. "I have, bro. It's awful." *Now I'm really thankful we weren't there when Mom died.*

Aloha pressed her fingers once again to the butler's neck, then paused and glanced at Shelby and shook her head. Her eyes brimmed with tears. Aloha placed her hands over his eyes and gently lowered his eyelids.

"Is he dead for real?" Buster didn't move from the bed as if he were frozen, unwilling to approach death.

Shelby nodded, her eyes also brimmed with tears. "Hard to believe I know, big guy, but Jeeves is dead and he ain't coming back. Horrible."

"What's that last thing he said? I couldn't make it out." Reggie moved to stand beside Aloha and placed a hand on her shoulder.

Aloha glanced at the little man then blinked several times and cleared her throat. Her lips formed a grim line. "He told us the name of his killer."

Gotta keep it together. Shelby nodded and her brow creased. "Yeah. I've heard the name Zero somewhere before. Hey, didn't I see a movie about a Zero on the late, late show?"

Buster nodded. "Yeah. Zero is the alien leader in Attack Spies From The Fifth Dimension."

Aloha cast the Buster a disparaging look. "This is no time for jokes."

Buster smiled weakly. "Sorry, but I'm not joking."

This is going from bad to really, really bad.

"Hi, guys. What's happening?" Matt had returned from the bathroom.

Matt was stopped by the sight of Jeeves lying on the floor. The other too fell silent. He drew in a sharp breath and his eyes went wide. "Hey! Why does Jeeves have a knife in his back?"

~ * ~

Shelby gripped Reggie's warm hand in hers after they sat on the bed next to Buster and stroked his cheek gently. "Someone murdered Jeeves," Reggie murmured.

Aloha stood beside the bed her arms folded across her chest. "Aren't we being a bit premature? We need an investigation and an autopsy to determine murder."

Shelby reluctantly released Reggie's hand and stood. "So he fell on the knife?"

"Yeah, Shelby. He's dead." Matt shook his head then sat on a chair. Buster sniffed.

"Thanks, Matt. How can you tell?" Shelby pasted a tight smile on her lips. She shifted her gaze to Aloha and scowled.

Aloha ignored Matt and Shelby. "You might be right, Reggie." She crossed her arms and began to pace the room. She stopped at the window and studied the window frame. "I didn't mean to suggest his death is an accident."

"Then what do you mean?" Reggie stood.

Aloha turned and frowned. "I think Jeeves and Madame Toulest's deaths may be the work of a genius so cunning that all of our lives could be sacrificed. Secret tunnels. Doubles pretending to be us to infiltrate us. People going missing then reappearing." She nodded, her mouth a grim line. "There's more going on here than some reality show."

"And what pray tell, *exactly,* is going on that's worth killing us for?" A single eyebrow rose on Shelby's forehead.

Aloha blinked at Shelby and Reggie. The look on her face clearly indicated that the answer was as obvious as her hair was red. *It's really beginning to get on my nerves when she does that. It may be obvious to her.*

"Why, eternal life, of course." Aloha made it sound like eternal life was the most normal thing in the world.

As if!

Shelby and Reggie looked at each other.

"Do you get it?" she whispered.

Reggie shook his head. "Nope."

Aloha grunted. "C'mon people. The prize. The Bachelorette: After the Prize, right?"

Shelby scanned the room, everyone stared at Aloha uncomprehendingly. "The prize is eternal life. Remember?" asked Shelby.

Reggie chuckled grimly. "Are you kidding? I'm a scientist. I don't believe in fairytales."

I knew it. He doesn't believe it either. We have a lot in common.

198

"More likely the real prize is some top-top-top secret Whammo Bomb, or the map to Blackbeard's treasure, or the cure for the common cold…" Reggie's brow furrowed. "…or do you really think Wills is telling the truth?"

Shelby grimaced. *Oh, well. What do I know anyway? When in Hollywood.* "Yeah, I think you're both right. Wills is telling the truth." She crossed her arms over her chest. "Maybe for once," she murmured. Her gaze flitted between Reggie and Aloha.

Aloha's features broke into a wide grin. "Of course, I'm right. I'm the woman from L.I.P.S. We're always right."

Oh, brother.

"The secret of eternal life is the most valuable prize since the invention of the paperclip."

Paperclip? Where does she get this stuff?

"So what do we do next?" Shelby stuffed her hands in the pockets of her blue jeans.

A smile played across Aloha's lips. "I thought you'd never ask. We find the killer and solve the mystery."

Twenty-Eight

SHELBY WALKED INTO THE EMPTY kitchen on the tips of her sneakers trying not to make any noise. Looking around, she let her shoulders relax. *Good. No ghosts, no dead bodies, and no one hog-tied.*

And no Herbie, no Clem, no Sparky, and no Happy.

I hope they're okay. Wherever they are. We've only been here three days, but it feels like an eternity. She shook her head a walked across the kitchen. Reggie, fully mobile again, Aloha, Matt and Buster followed her.

Buster walked to the fridge and opened the door. Matt joined him.

She grinned. *The guys love their food.*

I don't know if we have time to eat. Alpha Rucksack told us we only had until midnight and I'm sure that's not too long from now. Her brow wrinkled. *I wonder what he meant by something bad happening?*

She watched Aloha open and close cupboards. *I should buy her a magnifying glass like the one Sherlock Holmes used.* She sighed. *Maybe Rucksack's lying, how much worse can this get?*

Reggie walked to the gas stove and turned on two burners.

Matt and Buster raided the fridge and came back with a flat of eggs and a loaf of wheat bread. "Do ya like scrambled eggs?" Buster pulled an egg from the tray and tossed it in the air. He missed catching it by an inch, and it smashed on the floor. *Yuk!*

Matt laughed. "I'm not gonna clean it up. Shelby cleaned it up yesterday--"

"I did what?" Shelby sputtered.

"Ya know. When Reggie and you made breakfast." Matt stared at her as a frown formed on his brow.

"Whoever that was, it wasn't me." She looked at her brother. "Buster, you know domestic chores and I don't mix." *If anything, I'm the domestic anti-goddess. What use are men who don't keep the place tidy so I don't have to?*

Reggie's brow furrowed, his eyes narrowed. "You mean? We were replaced too?"

Matt cracked three eggs into a ceramic bowl. "C'mon, stop kiddin' around. You two were *really, really* friendly." He wiggled his eyebrows suggestively. "If you know what I mean."

Aloha had found a loaf of brown bread, dropped two slices in the toaster, and slapped the lever down. She opened more drawers.

Shelby glared at Reggie, who had placed a non-stick fry pan on the burner, "*What* did you do?"

"Nothing," he held up his hands in surrender, "it must've been my double." She moved closer. "Honest." His eyes pleaded for mercy.

"I otta smack you." She grinned and playfully tapped his leg.

He stepped back to the stove, as Matt poured the scrambled egg mixture in the frying pan.

"You wanta double latte, skinny, with a twist?" Buster stood by the espresso machine near the large steel fridge.

"Yes. I'd *love* one." Shelby's brow furrowed.

"Is something wrong?" Reggie looked up from the eggs he was stirring with a wooden spoon.

"Just missing and dead people." She winced. *I really didn't need to see dead people.*

Reggie nodded. "I know what you mean. But I think we need to eat something or we'll never have the strength for whatever lies ahead."

He was right of course, but Clem could be hurt. She worried about him.

Buster seemed genuinely pleased to make coffee. He ground the espresso beans in the coffee grinder, placed them in the portal filter, then affixed the handle to the machine. It didn't take long before the machine-generated steam and the aroma of fresh espresso mingled with the smells of eggs, butter, and toast.

Shelby's stomach growled. *How long has it been since I ate? So much has happened it's hard to remember.*

If everyone has a double running around the house, then who was real? She glanced at Reggie. *And who isn't? Oh well, at least it'll keep the audience guessing. This Reggie seems to be the real Reggie but how do I know? There has to be a way to figure this out.*

Shelby walked over, sat at the kitchen island, and ate the breakfast Reggie, Matt and Aloha had made for them all.

Her gaze flitted from Reggie to Aloha who sat opposite her around the island. Aloha had a plate of food in front of her, but picked at her eggs with a fork. *Is she on a diet? Or is it something else?*

Shelby frowned as her gaze fell upon Buster and Matt. Matt had a large white dinner napkin stuffed into the collar of his shirt, and Buster looked all puffed up with pride. *They're obviously enjoying their status as chefs du jour. But what if?*

Aloha sipped on a steaming latte, "Ya know I've been thinking about this double business. If one of us is a double then it should be obvious."

Shelby nodded and shifted her gaze to her brother and his zombie pal. "Say, Buster, Matt. I'm wondering if you know where Clem and the others are?"

Buster shrugged while Matt had the look of pure-blond-surfer-bum vacantness on his gray face. *How Reggie became friends with a pair of party animals like Matt and Herbie she'd never know. They don't seem his type.*

"What do you mean, Agent Armstrong?" Matt kept his eyes focused on the frying pan.

Aloha took another sip from her mug then shrugged. "The real people would know certain facts that no one else would know. Normally our files at L.I.P.S. would contain everything," she paused and eyed Shelby, "but it seems our files are incomplete."

Shelby's face grew warm. *Oops. My thief persona is coming back to bite me.*

Aloha's eyes narrowed over the rim of the mug as she took another sip. "A few choice questions might be *very* revealing."

"Good idea. Twenty questions might reveal a lot." Shelby nodded.

We make a great team. Too bad we're on opposite sides of the law. "I'll start." Aloha smirked and nodded. "Buster, what's Dad's first name?"

Buster looked at her quizzically. "Why?"

She sighed. "There are so many doppelgangers running around this place that I have to know who's who. And you might not be the real Buster Bass."

Buster nodded. "I'm wondering the same thing about you, Shel until you asked that question."

"What's an apple ganger?" Matt brow wrinkled.

Reggie laughed. "That's Matt all right."

Shelby smiled tolerantly. "He's really not the sharpest pencil in the set is he?"

Reggie grinned. "I help him at exam time." He held up one finger. "Watch this." He faced Matt. "Hey, Matt what play did you make in the big game against Purdue?"

Matt smiled coyly. "I threw a hitch pass and Kominsky ran it for a touchdown." He smiled and his chest swelled. "I won the game single handed."

Reggie eyed Shelby. "He may not be modest, but it's certainly Matt. He's one heck of an athlete."

Shelby grinned at Matt then explained, "Not apple ganger, Matt. It's *doppelganger,*" she explained. "It means double, twin, or mirror-image, as in there are copies of each of us running around this house. I've been tricked by imposter's a couple of times. In fact, we all have at one time or another."

Pausing to let her words sink in, she watched as Matt's eyes grew wider with each passing second. *Yeah, it is a pretty far-fetched concept, my zombie friend.*

"What I'm concerned about is this Buster, may not be my Buster."

Reggie's brow furrowed. "And since we know who *we* are, *we* want to make sure this isn't a trap."

Buster shook his head slowly and walked across the kitchen to the espresso machine where he refilled his cup. "Uhhh. Sis. Me and Matt have been in the kitchen together. We're definitely real." Matt nodded.

Before Shelby could continue, there was a loud *bang*. Shelby turned to stare at the door in time to see the swinging door fly off its hinges with an earsplitting *crack,* then across the kitchen to slam hard against the wall opposite them.

"Incoming!" shouted Reggie. He wrapped his arms around her waist dragged her under the stainless steel counter.

Flaming bits of chairs, dining room table, and rug filled the air and rained down around the counter. Shelby pulled her legs in tight against her body.

"What's happening?" Buster screamed over the sound of the explosion.

Aloha dropped under the steel counter beside Reggie and Shelby, her hands covering her ears. A coffee mug shattered like artillery fire as the cups hit the tile floor.

Matt drop to his stomach to her left and used his hands to cover his head. Buster yanked the door to the walk in freezer open to use as a shield and stepped behind it with his eyes squeezed shut.

Shelby cupped her ears.

Aloha's features were pinched and her eyes were squeezed tight.

Shelby cringed waiting for another blast. After what seemed like an eternity, and there were no more explosions, she removed her hands from her ears.

The sound of crackling fire echoed off the walls. Choking smoke filled the air making seeing difficult. Coughing, she touched Reggie's hand. "You okay?"

Reggie's eyes were wide. "Fire!" Holding Shelby's hand tightly in his together they scrambled from under the counter.

Shelby swiveled her head and squinted into the gray smoke only to see the back of Matt's shirt was on fire.

"Hey, Aloha!"

Aloha scrambled out from under the counter and ran over to help Reggie pat out the flames on Matt's back.

"No, guys. Wait!" cried Shelby. "There's going to be another bomb!"

Shelby reached out from under the counter to grab at Reggie and Aloha. Another explosion rocked the room throwing Aloha and Reggie off their feet as if they were rag dolls.

Reggie looked up at her. "How did you know?" He coughed. "Bombs always come in more than one."

"Huh?"

"Movies."

Reggie blinked. "Oh."

Shelby hid her head with her arms as a second explosion ripped through the room. She blinked away dust as she watched Aloha being slammed hard against the counter. Aloha groaned, her features twisted in agony, before she sank to the floor. Blood dripped down her cheeks hitting her shirt from an angry gash on her forehead.

Shelby rushed from under the protection of the counter to her friend's side. *What do I do? I gotta do something.*

She stared at the bleeding gash on Aloha's head then at her shirt. *Bandage. I'll use my shirt.*

She tore several strips of cloth off the arms of her shirt and wrapped them around Aloha's head. She then went to the sink to grab a damp cloth that she pressed against the makeshift bandage.

"I saw this in a movie," she assured Reggie. "It'll stem the bleeding."

He grinned at her. "It's just a bump." He touched the spot on his head where he'd been hit by flying debris. "I'm okay. It's a good thing you love movies."

Yeah, right. It was a guess, big guy. I just guessed right. I don't see Buster. I hope he's okay. Matt had managed to stand, but his legs wobbled and he looked as woozy as a sailor on a weekend pass. But there were no signs of visible injury, except for the burned shirt.

"Wow!" Shelby glanced at the shattered door to the hallway as Wills walked through.

The unlit cigar between his teeth drooped at the sight of Aloha, "Is she okay?"

She nailed the producer with a glare. "Wills! Of course, she's not okay. And it's your fault. I swear I'm gonna wring your neck, after I save my BFF."

The anger burning deep in the pit of her stomach threatened to boil over. It had been building ever since her father signed the contract for them to appear in this stupid reality show.

A ridiculously long cigar stuck out from between his thin lips.

Wearing a bleached white suit, his hair slicked back like some greasy gangster, Wills reeked of cheap hair gel. *He gives little people everywhere a bad name.*

With slow deliberation, Shelby rose to her feet, her fists clenched at her sides, her mouth in a snarl. Her fingers were clenched so tightly her nails threatened to draw blood.

Reggie rose to his feet from the floor and moved to stand next to her. She glanced at him and saw his tight scowl. *Yes, Reggie, you're right Wills is behind this mess. He's played us all along.*

Her gaze drifted to her injured friend who sat slumped over against the counter. Aloha's chest rose and fell. *Thank God, she's still alive.* Her gaze shifted to Wills. "What do you want, Wills?"

Shelby planted her fists on her hips in a heroic pose. "It's time for the world to say, little people, and zombies of the world unite against tyranny!"

Wills gaped at her then his eyes traveled over Matt and Reggie to finally stop on Aloha. "You people have gone mad."

A thin smile crossed Shelby's lips.

Wills eyes widened and his mouth chewed on the end of unlit cigar. Then he rolled it in his mouth between trembling fingers.

He just realized he's outnumbered. Shelby stood and glared at the producer. *I'm gonna make him tell us everything*

"Chipper!" Wills shouted backing up, his hands in front of him like a shield.

A mountain-sized man entered the kitchen. He had to duck to get through the shattered doorway from the dining room. His heavy black boots made the floor creak. *Whoa! He really is a bigun.* He stopped next to the producer who now wore an arrogant smirk. When he rose to his full height, his head seemed to almost touch the ceiling. His hands were the size of Shelby's head.

The giant, Wills called Chipper, wore a navy blue pinstriped suit that looked like it was about to burst at the seams. His Italian shoes were size way-too-large-for-a-normal-human-being.

Wills grinned and pulled a matchbook from his suit vest. He struck a match and lit his cigar. Once he had the tobacco glowing red, he blew a cloud of acrid smoke in their direction.

"Do we have a problem?" He hooked his thumbs on the pockets of his vest.

Wills looks like one of those plantation colonels in a bad remake of *Gone With The Wind.* She eyed the bodyguard. And Chipper was the entire union army all rolled into one.

Giant body guard one, magnificent four zero. *Zero. Didn't Aloha say something about a guy named Zero?* Her eyes narrowed at the smarmy producer. *Wills probably knows him.*

"No. Wills. No problem," Shelby spat from between gritted teeth.

Wills eyebrows arched. "That's *Mr.* Wills.

She glared at him.

Reggie took a step forward.

Shelby placed a hand on his waist.

He stopped and glanced at her.

Shelby saw Chipper's beady eyes watching them all very closely. *He could snap us all in two with one hand tied behind his back.*

Wills chuckled. "Tsk, tsk. Didn't your father teach you manners?"

Shelby glared at him. *I swear I'm gonna boil over any second.* She took one step forward then stopped, when the behemoth grunted and waved her back with one massive hand. *I'm the fly to his swatter.*

Reluctantly, she complied. Her eyes traveled to the slumped form of Aloha Armstrong lying at her feet on the tiled floor. "Since you're here, *Mr.* Wills, can you do anything to help my friend?"

Wills lips curled into a sneer. "Why should I?"

All I need is one minute alone with this guy, "Because it's the right thing to do." She struggled to maintain an even tone.

"Mr. Wills," Reggie nailed Chipper with a glare, "Aloha Armstrong is with the L.I.P.S. It would probably be in your best interest to assist one of their agents. Don't you think?"

Wills eyes narrowed as he studied Reggie. He puffed silently on his cigar, the tip glowing red, the aroma of the liquor soaked tobacco filled the air. After extracting the cigar from between his lips, he rolled it between his fingers.

"I love a good cigar, don't you?"

Reggie's gray features darkened and his knuckles became lighter as the fists at his sides tightened.

He better not pop a seam. Suzie homemaker I'm so not.

"Mr. Wills," Reggie growled, "if you don't help her, how will you ever get more contestants in the future? There have been two deaths already, do you really want a third?" His eyebrow arched. "Surely dead contestants are bad for business. Especially by explosions."

Wills shrugged.

His emotionless eyes sent a shiver down Shelby's spine.

Then, in an instant, his eyes had the look of a bemused troll from one of those dreadful Grimm's fairytales. "Frankly, deaths on this show make it a more interesting and entertaining reality show. I think my employer will be pleased when his profits spike."

Shelby glared at Wills. "Then I'm sure he'll be very pleased indeed with what you've done so far."

She knelt down again and pressed the damp cloth against the gash in her friend's head. *I have to find a way to save Aloha. At the end of the day, she's gonna slap the cuffs on me but I owe her. She saved my life earlier.*

I can't take this crap anymore. He nearly killed us with a fire, an electrified doorknob, windows that close by themselves, and even bombs. Shelby rushed Wills. Before Chipper could react, she was sitting astride Wills chest glaring down at him.

His cigar slipped from his mouth, and his eyes bulged. *A judge would rule it self-defense if I took him out right now.*

Her weight, and the way she sat on his small chest, meant Wills couldn't speak other than to emit a croak and a cough.

Suddenly the giant bodyguard enveloped the top of her head in one massive hand.

Uh, oh.

He lifted her off Wills' chest until her feet dangled in midair.

Chipper looked down at Wills, who coughed and cleared his throat. His face was red as a fire engine.

This isn't the end of me yet. Shelby kicked her legs and swung her fists uselessly struggling to free herself.

With a defiant yell, Reggie sprang forward taking the pose of like a karate black belt. *Wow. He knows karate? Cool.*

Out of the corner of one eye, Shelby saw Matt shaking his head. *Then again maybe he doesn't. Fake karate is not as good as real karate.*

Reggie screamed, "Hi ya!" then kicked Chipper on his shin.

Chipper gave him a disparaging look then swatted him aside with the back of a hand the size of the New York yellow pages.

Reggie *woofed* as he struck the wall hard and slumped to the floor next to the walk in freezer. He gasped for breath. A flap of gray flesh hung off the right side of his face below his chin where Chipper's massive hand had made contact. Matt rushed to his friend's side and held the flap of skin in place.

Chipper tossed Shelby into the air and grabbed her lower leg. *At least now I know what pizza dough feels like. Funny how the world looks different upside down.* Her stomach heaved, and she covered her mouth with her hand. *I don't feel so good.* She burped.

Blood rushed to her head and Chipper's vice-like grip squeezed too tightly on her ankle. *Ouch, does he have to squeeze so hard?* Shelby closed her eyes and pushed the pain from her mind. She took in a deep breath and could only think about Reggie struggling to catch his breath.

Suddenly Buster appeared across the kitchen by himself shuffling his feet like a child who had to pee.

Where did he come from? And why hasn't he lifted a finger to help? I'm upside down, the blood is rushing to my head, I'm dizzy and delusional, and my beloved bro does nothing.

After rolling her eyes, she winced. *Owww! That hurts like a brain freeze. I'm not doing that again.*

Wills sat upright and blinked several times as if he were dazed. Surprisingly, he suddenly laughed.

"You just about made the last mistake of your life, Miss Bass. Chipper will enjoy removing your head. All I have to do is give him the signal." He snapped his fingers and chuckled.

Shelby held her breath and tried to move her feet. *Rats! Nothing. We, who are about to die, salute you.*

Wills wheezed, "Let them go."

Still holding her upside down, Chipper spun Shelby around and around.

Room spinning. Stomach heaving. Not good.

Chipper suddenly flung her into the air flipping her end over end. She flew though the air until finally landing hard on her tailbone. *I'm glad I didn't land on my head. I think.*

The pain of hitting the floor sent shockwaves rippling up her spine. Her vision blurred, black and white spots danced before her eyes. After several seconds, her sight gradually cleared. Flopping on her side, she used one hand to feel her bottom. "My bum hurts."

"Since I'm a compassionate man, I will help you save your friend."

Wills has been manipulating us with doubles and hidden passageways since this show started. Why should I trust him now? He doesn't know we know about this guy, Zero. I wonder if Zero's name could be used for leverage? "Your boss, Arnold Zero, where does he fit in?"

Wills brow wrinkled and his eyebrows arched at the mention of Zero's name.

"Who?"

Wills' gaze shifted to Chipper.

He's knows exactly who I'm talking about, but he's wondering how I know about Zero. At last, a chink in his armor.

Shelby decided to dig further. *Aloha could be right. Wills knows where we'll find Zero, and they're after the prize themselves. But why?* She snapped her fingers. *It has to be because he can't find it without us.* "Zero's after the prize and he needs us to find it for him. And one of us holds the secret." Her eyes flitted to Reggie. He leaned against the counter and grinned at her. He held the loose skin on his face with one hand. *Whew. He's okay.*

Aloha groaned softly, the blood still oozed from her scalp wound. The air smelled of copper, sweat, and floor wax. It was as if Mrs. Brady had stumbled upon Freddie's kitchen nightmares on Elm Street.

Wills grimaced under Shelby's gaze.

That's it! Guy is the lousiest poker player on the planet.

"Miss Bass. What makes you think Mr. Zero needs any of you? I can assure you--"

"Of nothing!" Matt stepped forward. With one hand, he removed a rubber mask that had been hiding his true identity.

Shelby gasped.

"Jeeves!" her voice breathless from surprise, "you're alive! And you're not Matt!" *That's a little obvious, but somebody had to say it.*

210

Twenty Nine

"YES, MISS BASS, IT IS I. I've seen enough of this charlatan and his trickery." *A little corny, but appropriate to the situation.*

Wills face flushed a dark crimson, his brows narrowed and his gaze bored into Jeeves like diamond drills into coal. Wills looked up at Chipper who had tilted his head toward the butler.

Shelby held one hand out. "Jeeves! Be careful!"

Chipper suddenly reached out with his two meaty paws to try and grab Jeeves by his neck. *For a big guy, he's fast. Boy is he fast. Who woulda thought?*

As Chipper's hands closed around Jeeves' scrawny neck, the smaller man put both arms between his attackers arms and pushed away the big man's hands from his throats. Surprise registered on the giant's face as the butler stepped away as fluid as a ballerina, then delivered a roundhouse kick to the middle of Chipper's solar plexus.

The large man's eyes bulged as he doubled over, and his cheeks puffed out as air *whooshed* from his lungs.

From a standing position, Jeeves leapt into the air and kicked Chipper in the Adam's apple with a sharp snap of his foot.

The big man grasped his throat, wheezing, struggling for air, until with as gagging cough he dropped to his knees. His face turned a fiery red, then aquamarine blue, then an interesting shade of purple. He fell face first onto the tiled floor with a *slap*. The floor trembled under the impact.

"Houston, the giant has landed," quipped Reggie.

Shelby nodded at him then shifted to face the producer. "Now, *Mr.* Wills. You will tell these people what's *really* going on."

211

Jeeves maintained his karate stance as he moved ever closer to a sweaty, wide-eyed Wills. *Karate Kid meet the Karate Butler.*

"Say, Jeeves," Buster picked up the discarded mask, "that's some mask. We thought you were dead." He frowned. "How come you're alive?"

Jeeves opened his mouth, "I--"

"There's time for that later." *I'll bet there's less than ten minutes to midnight. And I want to know how you knew stuff only Matt would know.*

"You're quite correct, Miss Bass." Jeeves straightened to his full height.

Wills' fat fingers trembled as they twisted his crushed cigar between his fingers. Jeeves took a step toward Wills and crouched as if he were about to kick the little man.

Wills held up one hand. "All right. There's no need for more violence." His beady eyes flitted to Jeeves. "I thought we had you tied up?"

Shelby snorted. "Yeah, right. Jeeves tied up." She glanced at Jeeves and he nodded. "Oh. Well, he's here now and obviously not dead." A small smile played across her lips and one corner of Jeeves' mouth curled slightly. *I'm actually glad he's okay.* She shifted her gaze back to Wills.

Wills shook his head under her gaze, and his shoulders slumped.

"What about Chipper?" She nodded toward the bodyguard who still clutched his throat, the skin on his face the color purple irises. He had rolled to his haunches and wheezed for air.

"Okay. Okay." Wills' features paled and his eyebrows rose. "I'll tell you anything you want to know. Just don't hurt my boy again."

Reggie's eyes opened wide. "This behemoth is your son?"

Wills nodded and fidgeted with the fat cigar between his lips. "Slight throwback in the gene pool."

"Slight?" Shelby grinned. "I'd say back to the Cretaceous."

Wills eyes narrowed. "Very funny. Now what do you want to know?" He gazed up at the ceiling. "Sorry, Mr. Z."

Reggie, Shelby, Jeeves, and Aloha headed for the basement of the old house. Shelby had her doubts about anything Wills told them, but she had no choice but to try and find that secret entrance.

212

It was the only hope she had of finding the diamond and the prize. The bonus would be finding Herbie and Clem, and now Matt. Her stomach tightened. *I hope they're okay.*

Somewhere in the basement was the location to secret entrance of a hidden chamber where Wills claimed the prize would be found.

Buster stayed behind to keep watch over a hog-tied Wills and Chipper.

Glancing at her watch, she realized there were six minutes left until the deadline. *My gut is telling me Alpha Rucksack told us the truth. We're running out of time. Something bad is gonna happen.*

"Reggie? Do you think we should have left Buster with Wills?" she whispered, as she made her way carefully down the creaking wooden steps that led to the dark, dank, basement. The single bare bulb hanging from a single wire over the stairs did little to cut the gloom. *Who uses a twenty-five watt bulb anymore?*

Reggie had found a kerosene lamp, which helped.

"Whoops." She grabbed the railing when her foot missed a step. *He should have gone first.*

"Yeah. Sure." Reggie used the kerosene lamp in his right hand to help see the four remaining steps. The yellowish light cast eerie shadows over the mold-covered brick walls of the basement, but it couldn't pierce more than a few feet into the inky blackness.

Shelby managed to make out two steps at a time with Reggie following close behind ever deeper into the darkness. Jeeves and Aloha were a ways back acting as the rear guard out of range of hearing what Reggie and Shelby were saying.

"But what about Wills? Do you think he's telling the truth? About this secret passageway, I mean."

"Naw. Probably not." Reggie shook his head.

"How can you be so sure?" The plank beneath her creaked loudly.

"You okay?" Reggie's tone told her he was concerned about her.

"Yup. I'm fine."

"Buster will keep an eye on our host. There'll be no funny business while my brother's on duty." Reggie nodded in the semi-darkness. "Let's keep going."

The step beneath her foot squeaked loudly startling her until, with her next step, she stood on a rough unfinished cement floor. *Man, terra firma is so not over-rated.* She let out a breath.

She heard footsteps coming up from behind. Jeeves and Aloha had caught up.

"What is it?" Reggie, his voice anxious, placed a hand on her shoulder, "Sorry. I guess you can't hear my thoughts. I'm fine."

"Hey, watch it," Aloha grunted, "You stepped on my foot."

"Sorry," Reggie whispered. "It's *so* dark in here."

"Yes, Mr. Reggie and you just stepped on my foot as well," Jeeves said.

I can barely see my hand in front of me.

Reggie leaned toward Shelby, but at an odd angle, due the uneven floor. He wrapped one arm around her shoulders and pulled her to him.

He set the lamp on the floor. Rats ran away from the circle of light to disappear in the shadows.

His eyes widened in what she assumed to be surprise. "Well. I thought," he moved the arm around her shoulder to his side, "I mean. I..." He gazed at the floor, avoiding her inquisitive stare. His gray face flushed taking on a reddish hue.

He's embarrassed. How sweet. I so love this man. She smiled gently, cupped his chin in her palm, and gazed directly into his eyes. "It's okay, Reggie. I think you're too cute."

He smiled weakly.

Shelby grinned.

A soft, sexy smile crossed his lips and his eyes sparkled.

"Now I know what Buster means about you two," Aloha said dryly.

Reggie squinted at the L.I.P.S. agent standing at the edge of the circle of light with her hands buried in the pockets of his jeans. "Is there a problem, Aloha?"

"You two *really* need to get a room."

Shelby gazed back at Reggie and released his chin. For several seconds they gazed at each other saying nothing, then they burst into laughter.

After the laughter subsided Reggie stood, "We've got work to do, remember?"

"I guess the first thing we should do is find the light switch. There definitely isn't enough light in here, and there isn't one at the top of the staircase, but there has to be a light switch down here somewhere." Shelby walked a couple of feet leaving the circle of kerosene lamp light to move toward the wall to her left. "Anyone see a dangling string?"

"I'll look over there." Aloha disappeared into the shadows

The sounds of tiny feet scurrying across the cement made her freeze. *Ewww! Rats. Uggg.* A small furry body with a long tail ran through one edge of the circle of light. She stepped back into the light, her gaze flitting from side to side looking for more rats.

"Uh, oh." She tensed as something brushed her ankle. "I felt that!"

"You okay?" Reggie called to her anxiously from the other side of the room. He'd left the lamp on the floor and followed Jeeves into the darkness looking for a light switch.

"Oh. Nothing." She turned and ran toward Reggie's voice. From all around, her came the sound tiny feet scrambling to get out of her way, she stopped. Shivers ran down her spine. "Oh, crap."

She broke into a run and bumped into Reggie's butt. "Hey, watch it."

"Sorry." She backed up a step and scanned the darkness at her feet for more rodents

Crap. Crap. Rat. Rat. She held one hand out ahead of them in the darkness.

Finally, her fingertips contacted a wooden post. She removed her hand from Reggie's butt and wrapped her arms around the post. *I like wood. I really, really do.* With her eyes closed, she hugged the wood to her chest. *My island of pine.* She lifted her feet off the floor. Beneath her, she heard the sound of rat toenails against cement.

Reggie held the lantern up to the column she hung from. The glow illuminated a black switch plate with a single switch affixed to another wood post three feet to their right.

"There's the light switch." Shelby held out one arm, pointed at it, then quickly grabbed the post before she fell.

Reggie approached the second post stepping lightly to avoid trapping any rats underfoot. Just as he reached for the switch, the scratching all over the room reached a crescendo as vermin scurried for cover. *Smart rats. Who woulda thought?*

Reggie's hand stopped, his finger frozen over the switch. "What's that?" He glanced at Jeeves, who stood on the bottom step of the stairs watching.

"Nothing to worry about, sir." Jeeves features twisted in disgust. "Vermin prefer darkness."

Shelby scanned the dank basement as the light came on. There were still shadows but now she could at least see the corners.

Funny. Aloha's gone. Now where did she get to? She was right here a second ago.

"Have you been paying any attention to what's been going on around here?" Shelby let go of the post and dropped to the floor. "Aloha's disappeared."

Reggie looked around the basement. "She's right. Every time we seem about to achieve something bad stuff happens."

Stuff?

"But, sir and mademoiselle what other options do we have?" Jeeves stepped off the stairs.

Affixed to another post was another switch identical to the first one. Without waiting, Reggie moved to it and flipped the switch on just like the other one, but this time nothing happened.

Then, from somewhere overhead, a humming noise began that reminded her of a really bad version of the Vienna Boys Choir. The high-pitched hum grew louder and louder, increasing in intensity with each passing second. Shelby covered her ears as the sound hit a painful pitch. *Off key or what?*

"What did you do?" she yelled at Reggie.

He had his ears covered with his hands, and his features were scrunched like he'd sucked on a lemon.

The room suddenly exploded with pure white light far brighter than from the lantern and blinded them. Shelby screamed and shut her eyes. "Owww!" The light still shone through, she covered eyes with her hands. Tears ran down her cheeks due to the glare. "Turn it out! Turn it out! Please!"

She gradually opened one eye. *Inky darkness? Oh, crap. The rats!* "Someone turn a light on! Please!"

A sudden light burst to life only this time it came from the bottom of Reggie's shirt. *Oh, no! He's on fire!*

I've got to save him. I care about him too much. Ignoring the heat and flame, Shelby gripped the fabric of his t-shirt as tightly as she could and yanked him backward.

Losing his balance, he stumbled and knocked her off balance as well. He fell on top of her, knocking both of them to the floor in a tangle of arms and legs.

She managed to kneel and roll Reggie over and over until the flames were snuffed out.

He's out. Now what about me?

She patted down her blue jeans, relieved not to feel the heat of flames. Once the flames disappeared, the basement returned to darkness and quiet. Even the rats were silent.

"Hello?" She listened intently to figure out where the rest of the group was in the dark. No reply. Nothing. No movement.

It startled her when Reggie groaned, and she heard his raspy breathing. A shiver ran down her back and the hairs on her neck rose. *Oh, crap! This is so not good. He's burned. He might die. I don't care about the diamond or the stupid prize anymore. All I want is Reggie.*

"Someone help me!" cried a weak voice she couldn't readily identify.

Is that Reggie or Jeeves? She coughed from the acrid smoke that had invaded her mouth and nose. Fingers grasped her ankle, and she jerked her leg away.

"Hey! Shelby is that you?"

She sighed with relief. *Reggie.* "Yes. Are you okay?"

"Yeah."

"Aloha?" Shelby called. Silence. *Where did she go?*

"Well, I don't think Jeeves is okay. I heard his yell for help and I thought it was you, Reggie."

"Can you see anything?"

"Not much." Shelby blinked several times, but couldn't keep her eyes open because of eye-burning smoke in the air.

If I only had a double set of eyelids like Mr. Spock on Star Trek. Then I'd be able to see if Jeeves is okay, and maybe even help him.

A blood-curdling scream made her freeze. Ignoring the sting of the smoke she opened her eyes. Her pulse raced. *I have to do something, fast.*

The screams echo died. Suddenly the crackling sound of florescent tubes coming on filled the room with white light.

Shelby squeezed her eyes shut again. *Ouch. Too bright. Too fast.* The rough cement hurt her hands and knees, but she crawled slowly forward with her eyes closed in the direction of the screams. *Jeeves needs help.*

"I'm coming!" Her voice echoed off the walls. "Reggie. Where are you?"

"I'm right behind you," he coughed between words, "I think."

She heard his jeans scuffing over the cement from behind her as he crawled.

She crawled forward slowly, gingerly testing the cement for cracks and rats.

The powerful stench of burnt flesh grew stronger. She suppressed a gag. *Oh, no. Could it be Jeeves?*

Revulsion gripped her as she reached out to find hot, crunchy material. His clothing burnt and a pile of soft ash. This must be what was left of him. "EWWW!" She inhaled deeply, suppressing a sob.

Jeeves is dead, times two. No! It's not fair! She choked back a sob at the image of the poor butler burned to death.

Reggie bumped into her leg in the darkness. "Sorry. Well? How is he?"

"Not good. He's dead." Her voice caught and a tear tickled down her cheek.

"Oh," his voice dropped to a whisper. "What do we do now?"

That was a good question, and one she didn't have an answer for.

"I--" Tiny rat feet scuffed around her causing her freeze in mid-sentence.

"That's just great!" Her angry voice echoed off the walls. "Can't we ever get a break?"

"I'll try to find the stairs and get help." She heard Reggie crawl away.

"I might as well come with you." She crawled toward where she had last heard him. But she didn't find him. She sighed and reached out with her hands in the darkness and found only empty air.

"Reggie! Where are you?"

Silence. "This isn't funny, big guy. Where are you? Really." Listening intently, she heard the sound of tiny feet scratching over the cement floor but no reply from Reggie.. *He's gone. I'm alone.*

Her face grew warm. *This sucks. I'm just plain old pissed off!* "If you're listening, Zero, you better bring him back. Now!"

The only response was the scratching sounds of rat toenails on concrete. *Pooh, craaap.*

I'm probably the only warm body in here. Rats love warm bodies.

Shelby stood, swallowed hard, then took a tentative step toward where she hoped the stairs were. Her hands were out in front of her like an ant's feelers. One rodent squealed as she stepped on its tail. She stepped forward uncertain of which direction to go. Footsteps sounded on the wooden staircase somewhere in the darkness in front of her. The footfalls stopped when she stopped moving. *Is someone coming down or going up?*

Her heart beat hard in her ears and a mass of goose bumps ran across her arms. *Why am I blessed with such good hearing?*

"Who're you?"

"It's me." *Aloha? Maybe.*

"Me who?" Shelby grunted.

"You know, me!"

"Aloha? Is that you?"

"Yeah, of course it's me. Who did you think it is, the Ghost of Christmas past?" The L.I.P.S. agent's voice came from in front of her and above her head. *She must be on the stairs. Good, now I know the direction to go to get out of here.*

Before she could take a single step, there was a *click* and a bright light flooded the stairs. Shelby covered her eyes with both hands. "Hey!"

"Sorry."

Shelby blinked until she could make out the shape of Aloha standing in the middle of the staircase. *Am I glad to see her. Even if she's a fake Aloha, it's is better than being eaten by rats.*

Shelby stood at the bottom of the stairs looking up at Aloha. "Did you see Reggie? Do you have a flashlight?"

"Yup. Right here." Aloha held up the silver aluminum flashlight and when it came on she directed the blinding white beam into Shelby's eyes.

Shelby used her hands as a shield. "Hey! Watch it!"

"Oops. Sorry," the light went out with a *click*.

Aloha--or her double--stomped down the steps until she stood towering over her. Her nose wrinkled as the L.I.P.S. agent came closer, her boots stomping down the stairs. *Cinnamon. Yuk. I'm sooo sick of--*

Cinnamon! A memory surfaced at the back of her mind. The first morning--unconscious in her room--the smell of cinnamon. *Maybe Aloha isn't a government agent? Is Aloha Armstrong a renegade agent or a criminal mastermind? Naw. What a stupid idea. Aloha Armstrong is a loyal L.I.P.S. agent.* Her eyes narrowed. *Or maybe not!*

"Where's Reggie, and Matt and Buster?"

"They're fine." Aloha finally stepped off the bottom of the creaky stairs. "How 'bout you?"

Shelby looked at the L.I.P.S. agent through watery eyes. "I'm still in one piece, but the smoke in here is awful."

Shelby noticed the bandage tied around Aloha's head. There were dark brown stains on the bandage. "What about you?" Shelby pointed at the bandage.

The federal agent shrugged. "Flesh wound."

Yeah, right.

Aloha used the flashlight as a pointer to scan the room. White puffs like dandelion seedlings floated through the pale yellow beam of light. Reflections of glowing eyes flashed as rodents scurried to escape the swath of light.

Aloha wore a grimace on her face. She placed one hand casually on her right hip. "Kinda stinks in here doesn't it?"

The flashlights beam rested on a shiny black line of paint running along the cement floor. A deep frown creased her brow and she bent forward at the waist as she used the beam from the flashlight to follow the line of tape. It suddenly jigged to the right until it disappeared beneath a dark stained wood door with a worn brass doorknob.

"Oh, ho. What do we have here?" Aloha crossed the room in two quick strides.

Shelby scrambled to keep up. *I don't remember seeing that before. Not that I can see much between being blinded one second, then being plunged into total darkness the next.*

As they approached the door, Aloha used the flashlight to examine the edges where the frame and the door met.

Another secret door? Puh-leease.

Shelby used her thumb to wipe off the smoke blackened face of her watch. *Oh, man, we've only got four minutes.* "C'mon what're you waiting for?" Shelby moved a step closer to the door. "Why don't ya just open the darn thing?"

Aloha shushed her with an index finger over her lips. "Please. Be patient," she whispered as she waved Shelby back away from her.

Shelby stepped back.

Aloha pushed the door inward with the end of the flashlight to find two pairs of eyes blinking back at them. Their hands and ankles were tied to chairs and their mouths were stuffed with gags and covered by gray duct tape.

"Hummmpppfrrr," they mumbled in unison.

"Jeeves and Clem!"

Aloha handed the flashlight to Shelby, then knelt to untie Clem's ropes first. Shelby went to peel the tape off Clem's gag. It came off with a tearing sound.

"Ouch!" Clem croaked, "it's about time." He stretched his mouth.

"Yeah," chimed in Jeeves after Aloha removed his bonds, "and get that light outta my eyes."

Shelby wanted to shout for joy. *They're alive.* The smile disappeared from her lips. *But what about Reggie?*

"Have you seen Reggie?" she whispered.

"Are you kidding?" Clem shrugged off the loosened ropes from around his legs. "We've been literally in the dark since we were dragged in here and tied to these chairs."

"How long do you think you've been in here?" Aloha had just removed the last of the ropes from Jeeves' legs. Alternating between them, Aloha rubbed the Jeeves and Clem's legs vigorously to help them regain their circulation.

Clem shook his head. "I don't know exactly."

"But, Clem you and he," Shelby pointed at Jeeves, "And you, Aloha. You…" Shelby's stomach twisted in knots.

"Jeeves, you went missing only a few minutes ago," Aloha finished for her.

Jeeves shook his head. "No, Mademoiselle. Mr. Clem and I have been in this closet longer than an Egyptian mummy."

Shelby chuckled. *I think my bro's sense of humor is wearing on this guy.*

Clems' eyebrows rose. "A mummy? Where?" He looked around the room.

Oh, brother.

Aloha laughed. "You guys must be the real deal."

Clem frowned and faced Shelby. "What's she talkin' 'bout?"

Aloha walked away and started up the stairs. The boards creaked loudly with each step. "Follow me, I believe we're victims of the old switcheroo. These guys are real for sure. Definitely. Why and who is behind this whole affair is subject to debate. If my agency is correct, then Arnold Zero is the who. Why is a more complex issue. It may be a simple matter of ratings." Aloha shook her head. "I'm certain no one died in any fires. It's all special effects."

The L.I.P.S. agent led the way using the flashlight on the steps. The others followed single file with Shelby coming up last. She glanced over her shoulder at the dim basement. Her brow furrowed. *This is a dead end in more ways than one. The diamond sure isn't here and now we've lost Reggie and who knows who else. We better find the diamond and the prize soon.* She looked at her watch. Two minutes to midnight. Time was almost out.

"Ratings?" Jeeves rubbed his right wrist, which was red and bruised from the rope.

"Yes, the real players, us, may not have been providing enough drama or romance," Aloha paused on the stairs and looked over her shoulder at Shelby, "so Zero provided actors in disguise. Ya know to add excitement."

Shelby's face grew warm. The twenty-five watt bulb over the stairs picked this moment to burn out. *Figures.*

The flashlight's beam of white light cut a swath through the gloom. She shrugged. "After the kidnapping of a few players didn't add enough pizzazz, he needed something to add even more excitement and thrills."

"Like video games?" suggested Clem.

Aloha smiled. "Exactly."

The sound of footfalls behind her made Shelby pause and listen, but she was afraid to look over her shoulder. *Who's moving? Those footsteps sound like big uns, and they're too big to be a rat, that's for sure.*

"Hello. Who's there?" Shelby glanced at Aloha who turned the flashlight on the basement below them. She panned back and forth, but Shelby couldn't see the owner of the footsteps.

A familiar throaty chuckle could be heard behind her. "Well, it's about time you got here."

Her mind reeled. *That voice. It seems familiar yet different somehow.*

"Dad? Is that you?"

"No, Miss, but he knows yer here." A tall red haired man wearing a black leather jacket stepped out of the shadows.

Thirty

REGGIE'S EYES FLUTTERED OPEN. He blinked and looked down to see both arms tied to the arms of a chair with rope. Oddly, the arms of the chair were cushioned with purple velvet. *Huh? What's happening? Who tied me up?* The chair rocked loudly as he struggled against the ropes.

He frowned. *I remember a fire, running for the stairs, then falling through the floor. Then nothing.*

Reggie blinked a few more times to clear his vision. *This really sucks.*

When his sight finally cleared, the room came into focus. A bare light bulb in a steel accordion-like lamp sat on a plain wood table in front of him. A mirror covered the upper half of the wall opposite him and ran the length of the wall. This looked like an interrogation room used in every TV cop show--cliché.

What's going on? Where're Shelby and the others? His brow furrowed. *This better not be a joke.* He pulled his arms and twisted his upper body in vain against the ropes. *It's not funny.*

"I'm a prince," he shouted, "release me at once."

He caught a flash of movement from the corner of his right eye. *I'm wa-a-ayy jumpy.* Reggie craned his neck to look around the bare room. *And I'm alone.*

A deep male voice cleared his throat, startling him. From his right, a quick spark of light lit up the outline of a man striking a match. The yellow flame lit the tip of a cigar and a puff of smoke rose into the air.

Reggie coughed.

The man's features were hidden by shadow.

"What's the matter, boyo?" The voice spoke with a Scottish lilt. "Feelin' a wee bit sorry for yerself are ya?"

Reggie nodded. "Yes." *No point in lying.*

The man stepped into the light. The man had worn blue jeans, a new looking jean shirt, and a waist length black leather jacket.

Reggie closed his eyes and tensed his body waiting for the guy to hit him in the face. Instead, the man stepped back. He puffed on his cigar as his intense emerald eyes studied his captive, his other hand stuffed inside his pants pocket.

"Do ya know why yer here?"

"A reality show of course."

The man smiled grimly then glanced over his left shoulder at the mirror.

Reggie's eyes widened. It must be a two-way mirror. Someone must be watching from the other side. *Am I in a real police interrogation room? But that can't be right. I didn't do anything.*

"No, we aren't the coppers." *Weird. It's as if the guy can read my mind.* "Name's Shamus MacFee."

MacFee pulled out a black wallet from his back pocket. He flipped it open to reveal a picture of himself in a plasticized window. The identification card had the royal crest of Gnotborst on it. MacFee's picture, and the words *Gnotborst Security Service Inc., (1973 Ltd)*, were printed in black letters beneath the royal crest.

Shamus MacFee must work for Dad. But what about Shelby? Is she around here somewhere?

MacFee's blond crew cut and ruddy cheeks suggested a young double-o-seven. "MI6?"

"Special Air Service, actually." Shamus smiled grimly his lips pursed.

"Why am I tied up? As a Prince of Gnotborst, I demand you release me immediately." Somehow, he suspected he wouldn't like the security agent's response. Reggie frowned. "And where are my friends?"

Shamus shook his head. "Sorry, lad, but me boss wants me ta ask you some questions first. I'm sure me and you are gonna be good pals, don't ya think?"

The leprechaun-like twinkle in his eyes contrasted with the thin smile on his cruel lips. Stepping out of the light back into the shadow, MacFee walked back hefting a chair in one obviously strong hand. His chair was identical right down the purple armrests.

Shamus reached under the seat. Reggie heard a click. The agent sat as his mouth curled at the corners and his eyes twinkled. The chair arms on either side of him folded under the seat cushion. *Neat trick double-o-nine.*

Reggie gazed down at the armrests of his chair. *I hope these don't fold up with me still tied to them.*

"We don't have much time," Reggie paused, "Shamus, is it?" His desperation, edged by growing anger, twisted his gut into knots.

There were rumors of what these guys were capable of, and the rumors weren't kind.

Nodding, Shamus turned the chair around and straddled it, his arms resting on the chair back, his wry smile fixed on Reggie.

"Never mind the time. Now, me boyo, what do ya think I want ta know?"

"Who's behind the mirror?" Reggie paused then blurted. "Is Shelby okay?"

The mischievous twinkle disappeared from his Shamus' green eyes. "I'll be asking the questions, lad...yer Daddy sent me."

~ * ~

"Who are you?" Shelby trembled and stared at the man who helped them to get out of the dark basement. They stood in the foyer of the house. Clem and Jeeves were studying the front door for booby-traps while Aloha stood beside her.

I've never been so happy to get out of a basement ever.

The man's calm emerald eyes studied her. "Sorry, Miss, but I'm not at liberty ta tell ya much."

At that moment something inside Shelby snapped. *Whoever he is, he's gonna get both barrels.*

"This show is *horrible!*" Shelby heaved a sigh of relief between sobs. *It feels so good to say the words out loud.*

Shelby wiped her left cheek with the back of her soot-covered arm.

His calm eyes gazed at her. "It'll be okay, Shelby."

She frowned. "You know me?" Gazing beyond him, she wondered where he had come from.

Clem turned away from the front door and stepped between his sister and the man. He glared at the stranger. "My sister asked you a question, mister."

The man regarded Clem and, his pale lips formed a wry smile. "Name's MacFee. I came here ta bring yur sister home."

Shelby touched her brother's arm. He glanced at her. She nodded and mouthed she'd be okay. Reluctantly he stepped aside. "But how? We haven't found the…you know, the prize yet. The game isn't over. Clem, Sparkles, Happy and--"

"Are fine," interrupted MacFee. "And the show doesn't matter--at least not anymore." His eyes narrowed.

"But the diamond? The prize."

"The diamond," blurted Clem his eyes wide. "In all the excitement, I forgot about diamond."

Shelby opened her mouth to scold her brother but before she could do so MacFee continued, "We've made other arrangements. You and your brothers don't need to steal anymore. In fact, ya won't need to work in circuses or freak shows either."

"And what arrangements would that be, Mr. MacFee?" The woman from L.I.P.S. stepped to stand beside Shelby. Jeeves and Clem stood behind MacFee, watching him silently.

MacFee sighed and ran one hand through his red hair. "Aloha Armstrong isn't it?"

Aloha crossed her arms over her chest and arched an eyebrow. "Do we know each other, sir?"

"No, not exactly, but yor boss told me all about you and why you're here." Aloha's eyes widened and both eyebrows arched.

"But, I don't understand." Shelby stepped around Aloha.

MacFee shook his head. "It doesn't matter. We've taken care of everything."

His eyes shifted to Aloha. "That includes you, Miss Armstrong."

A knot formed deep in the pit of Shelby's stomach and tightened. *No. Not this time.*

My father must have hired this MacFee guy to "save" me. Then he can control my life, like he has always tried to. But this time I'm going to run away to Hawaii and be a surfer babe and live in a little grass shack with Sir Reginald Kincade the zombie-lord-in-exile of Gnotborst and no one, not even this man or my father, is going to stop me.

Her shoulders slumped. *Crap. Who am I kidding? I've seen far too many movies, and read too many fairytales.*

MacFee had been standing watching her, his eyes and his demeanor patient.

She drew back her shoulders. *But I have to try.* "No, MacFee. No. I'm leaving with Reggie Kincade. We're going to Hawaii."

He shook his head. "Huh? I don't think so, Miss Bass. I've discussed this with Reggie's father and we've agreed--"

"Reggie's father? What's he got to do with this?" Shelby crossed her arms and scowled. "Nothing! Are you blind? People are dead, or at the very least badly injured--I was nearly electrocuted--and now Reggie's missing--" She spun away from MacFee her back now to him.

MacFee grunted. "A bit melodramatic don't you think?" He tsk-tsked. "Just like he told me, she's full of fantastic dreams, heart on her sleeve--"

Shelby turned back around and fixed her steely gaze on MacFee, silencing him.

"I've had enough of this," she muttered. "It's like you've been talking to my father about me."

MacFee nodded and stuffed his hands into his jacket pockets. "He said since you were a child you dreamed of unicorns and fairytale princes and princesses."

Her nose wrinkled. *Cinnamon. Why? What's cinnamon have to do with all this?* Silence sat heavy between them as they all stared into each other's eyes. *I'm worried. I don't think this is over.* A knot formed in her stomach. *Now we have to find Reggie, and we all have to get out of here. But before I leave, I have to know who's behind this, Zero, Wills, my father, or Reggie's father, or maybe all of them. MacFee is gonna answer a few questions.*

Shelby's skepticism faded. "All right, Mr. MacFee, tell me what's been going on. And tell me about Reggie's father."

"Hey, sis." Shelby looked at Clem. "What time is it?"

She looked at her watch and realized it was ten minutes after midnight and nothing bad had happened.

Shelby's brow wrinkled. *It proves Rucksack lied. And it proves never trust an actor disguised as a zombie. The manipulation continues.*

~ * ~

Reggie could barely swallow, his throat dry, his lips swollen and chapped from thirst. The ropes tying him to the chair burned his wrists with their rough weave. He didn't flinch from the intense stare of Shamus MacFee.

Shamus sat with his arms folded on top of each other staring intently at Reggie. *This is like a staring contest with a cat.*

And Reggie wouldn't give in to this guy. Nervousness made Reggie prattle on about the events that culminated with him being tied up here. *Wherever here is.*

Shamus listened passively showing no signs of being bored, mad, sad or affected in the least by Reggie's story. In fact, his placid features didn't register any emotions at all.

Guy must be one heck of a poker player.

Reggie explained about the murders, the doppelgangers, and how they discovered the many hidden passageways and tunnels. About the gas and the fire in the library. About various members of their party being knocked out and then revived.

As he explained, it dawned on him that they had survived a lot. *I have no idea how we made it this far.* Those other reality show contestants were wimps compared to what they'd survived.

Reggie finally paused as his story got to the part about the basement lights going out and him being kidnapped.

"I could really use a glass of water."

Shamus sat expressionless.

"Please?"

Finally, Shamus offered a lopsided grin, nodded, then stood and waved his hand over the wall next to the mirror. A hidden door slid aside noiselessly. He stepped through and the section of wall slid back into place.

Now that MacFee was gone, Reggie studied the room for any avenue of escape. Plain walls. A door with a doorknob. A mirror and a few sticks of furniture. *Nothing useful. No way out.* Near the ceiling, in the shadows, he spotted a red light. It must be a surveillance camera. *Probably for the show.*

As unbelievable as it seemed, especially after all that had happened, the show was still going on. Murders, kidnapping, missing persons--no matter, the show must go on. *Stupid show.*

"Hello?" Reggie squinted into the mirror. "Whoever you are, release me. I'm a prince." Reggie's voice echoed in the quiet. "I have rights."

Moving his head and gazing in different directions, he checked the mirror for any sign of an action or shadows. *Nothing.* Using his body weight to move the chair, he managed to shift the chair backward. It scraped loudly across the yellow tiles.

Reggie smiled at the surveillance camera, "For all you viewers at home. Watch this."

He grunted as he stood still tied to the chair struggling against the weight of the chair. He lowered one shoulder and braced himself for an abrupt ending as he ran toward the mirror. He closed his eyes as he picked up speed and winced.

This is definitely gonna hurt me more than the mirror.

But instead of contact with an immovable object, he kept going. *What the...?* He stumbled back and forth under the weight of the chair but managed to stay on his feet. He realized he now stood on the porch of the house looking out over the soundstage and behind him was the outside wall of the house. The twisted shape of the house cast its eerie shadow across the stage.

The lights were low and long shadows ran across the floor away for the black house.

How did I get out here? A molecular transporter? Naw. Too Star Trekkie.

Reggie nearly tripped as he stepped down the two wooden steps to the soundstage floor. The weight of the chair on his back still made him tilt back and forth. He was slightly off balance. *Could be an illusion though. I read something about this in Technology Monthly. The interrogation room could be a hologram. Cool if it is part of the show. It would certainly explain how the actors could move around so freely. I could go back and test it, but no way am I going back in there.*

MacFee told me Dad is involved in this, but where is he? I have to find the guys first, he paused and his stomach muscles tightened, *and Shelby.* His eyes narrowed. *And no holographic security agent is gonna stop me.*

Reggie studied the post that supported the roof of the porch. The ceiling looked solid. He turned to one side and grunted as he slammed the chair against the post. He heard a crack, but the chair didn't break. One more should do it. He braced his feet then slammed his back with the chair as hard as he could against the post. The chair fell to pieces to land with a *clatter* on the steps.

I'm free.

Pushing off the rope, his gaze shot to front door of the house with its gargoyle doorknocker. *I have to go back. For Shelby's sake.*

Reggie walked up the creaking steps to the door and studied the knob carefully. *It looks normal.* He licked his dry lips, held his breath, then stabbed at the door knob with his index finger. He let his breath out when nothing happened. *I'm creeped out, but not shocked. Good.*

His fingers trembled as he slowly reached out for the knob. After closing his eyes, muscles tense, he held his breath again. *Here goes nothing.*

Guess I'm good. He relaxed his shoulders then turned the doorknob and pulled hard. It came off in his hand with a *snap. Great. Now what?*

Bending down he peered into hole where the doorknob used to be and saw only blackness as if the hole was clogged or covered by something on the other side. "Great. I broke it." *Now what am I gonna do?*

Reggie stood and raised one leg and like a cop breaking down a perp's door, and kicked hard. It didn't move.

Reggie winced and grasped his knee with both hands. "Owww!" A throbbing pain shot through his foot into his knee. He doubled over and gasped. *Not smart, dude.*

He leaned on his undamaged foot and braced himself against the wall beside the door. A creak from the hinges surprised him, then the door swung inward. *Yeah, right. Just my luck. I'm such an idiot.* He winced as he hobbled toward the doorway one hand on his throbbing knee.

He hobbled into the foyer. From somewhere in the darkness, he heard the thumping rush of someone running. He turned toward the sound and squinted into the gloom. He started when he saw an outline of someone coming toward him. His eyes widened. *What the heck? He's gonna run me over.* Glancing down at his sore knee, a rising sense of panic came over him. *Uh, oh. I gotta get outta here.*

He turned and hobbled toward the door to the house. "Owww. Owww." A wall of steel bars came down around him like a cage with a *clang.*

He turned around in the cage staring at the steel bars. Trapped. *Oh, crap. There is no way I can kick out steel bars.* He winced as his knee pain reminded him of his bad decision about trying to kick in doors. *Not that I'm good with that karate stuff anyway.* He winced when the knee throbbed. *Man that hurts. I should have listened to my Sensei and quit that class.*

"Hey there, big guy, what seems to be the trouble?" came a disembodied voice from behind.

I know that voice. He must be a she.

Thirty One

SHELBY GLARED AT THE SPOT on the worn carpet where MacFee had been standing. He left them saying he had an issue to deal with. Aloha, being a federal agent, offered to accompany him, but he insisted he had to go alone. He assured Shelby everything would be okay. *But he didn't answer my questions.*

She lowered her head and stared at the dirty rug. *MacFee knows the King of Gnotborst? I don't think so. At least he hasn't told me anything I don't already know.* She sighed. *Zero wins.*

What do we do now? The deadline has passed and we still haven't found the diamond, or the prize. Her shoulders tensed. *But the show doesn't seem to have ended so what does Zero have planned next?*

She looked at Clem, Jeeves, and Aloha sitting with their legs crossed on the carpet whispering urgently to each other. *At least we found Clem and Jeeves isn't dead.*

Aloha paused occasionally to glance at her and offer an encouraging smile.

Shelby nodded each time and offered a small smile.

A two inch round bright red button affixed to a wall at the bottom of the stairs leading to the bedrooms above caught her attention. Her eyebrows rose. Beneath the button hung a small white sign with the words *In case of emergency* in red letters. *I've never seen that button in the foyer before. I wonder if it means something?*

She stood and walked to the button to examine it more closely. Written along the bottom of the sign were tiny black block letters that were almost too small to read.

"The fine print," she muttered. *Figures.*

Leaning her hand against the wall, she moved closer to the sign and bent forward in order to peer at the small words. Squinting, she made out the first word of the tiny sentence. *I really gotta start carrying a magnifying glass.*

"Aloha? Do have a magnifying glass by any chance?"

"Nope, sorry. They're not standard issue for L.I.P.S. agents." Aloha still sat on the floor.

Figures. "What about you, bro?"

"I do." Clem stuck his hand in his pocket and pulled out a two inch round plastic disc with a glass center. "I found the prize in my caramel corn."

Shelby grinned. He handed to toy magnifying glass to her.

Pressing the small toy magnifying glass against the sign, she managed to make out some of the words. *What do ya know? The button just might work.*

The first word was, *Warning.* The next word was longer. She spelled it out loud, "...E...m...e...r...g...ahhh, emergency--or is it emergencies?" Shelby snorted in frustration.

Given the length of the tiny print that ran the along the perimeter of the sign, it would take forever to decipher the full text.

Aloha, her brothers, three zombies, two clowns and even a heroic butler were depending on their ability to work together to find a way out of here before something bad happened. Shelby glanced at her watch again. *If, as I suspect, there is a new deadline. A hidden timetable. It's the only thing that makes sense. I gotta find Reggie.*

"What are you doing?" Aloha moved to stand over her shoulder.

"Finding a way out of here before whatever disaster is going to happen next actually happens."

Clem snorted. "Yeah, sis. Disaster. Someone's pulling both your legs." He stood and walked away. "I'm going to the kitchen to get something to eat. Anyone want anything?"

Aloha bent down and peered at the sign. "What does it say?"

"Something about emergency and, I hope, a way out of here." Truth was she had no idea what would happen if she pushed it. But there was only one way to find out for sure if the button was connected to anything. She knew she had to press it. *I'm gonna press the button.*

Her fingers trembled. *I could set off the Whammo super bomb and Nevada will disappear off the map, on the other hand, I could release a big cardboard sign with the word BANG written on it.*

Her fingers hovered over the button for several seconds as various scenarios came to mind. The most terrible was a mushroom cloud filled with fire and death by radiation.

She swallowed hard but her mouth had dried, and her breathing was shallow. She decided to throw caution to the wind. *Here goes nothing.* She closed her eyes and pressed the button. There was a *click* followed by silence.

After several seconds when nothing happened, she opened one eye. *Another dead end.* She eyed the button with contempt. *A button to nowhere. Attached to nothing.*

Shelby stepped back and frowned. "I can hardly wait until I get the heck outta here," she muttered.

"I wish you hadn't done that." A woman's voice whispered behind her.

Shelby stiffened and the hair on the nape of her neck rose. *Aloha, Jeeves and Clem are supposed to be covering my back.*

But it's okay because I know that voice. The tension left her body as she relaxed her shoulders. Shelby turned slowly to face the owner of the voice. "I was wondering when you were going to make your dramatic re-appearance."

Madame Toulest, dressed in her trademark floor length gown, with her gray-streaked hair now piled high atop her narrow head, had appeared from the shadows. *I love being right. I feel so Nancy Drewsy.*

"How did you--?" Madame touched her hair as if she wasn't used to it being put up.

"Know you weren't dead?" Shelby finished.

Toulest nodded, her bloodless lips a thin line.

Shelby chuckled and glanced at Aloha who stood and moved behind Toulest to prevent an escape. "Everything we've seen since we've been here has been faked--"

"Miss Bass, you may have just cooked everyone's goose. You should *not* have pushed that button."

Clem hurried back to hide behind Aloha his normally ruddy complexion had paled.

She grinned at her brother.

Clem stuck his head out from behind Aloha. "I'll be back your backup." The L.I.P.S. agent grinned and nodded. Shelby smiled. *Now this is more like it. Backups backing backups. Cool.*

The smile faded from Shelby's face. "But, I thought the button is for emergencies?"

"Did you read the fine print?"

"Huh...no, there isn't time." Shelby frowned. "I mean I'm trying to save everyone before any other bad stuff happens." She cringed inside. *Bad stuff? That's the best I can come up with?*

Toulest sneered. "You? You're a kid, and a midget. You can't save anyone--"

"Watch it, Madame." Jeeves took a step toward the late night horror hostess. "We don't respond well to slurs."

Before Jeeves could say anything more, the floor shifted under their feet, and he stumbled to the wall and held his hands up to stop himself from falling.

Whoa! Earthquake?

Toulest stumbled around like a drunk as the floor shifted beneath them even more violently.

Shelby held her arms away from her body like wings, just managing to stay on her feet and then shifted her weight to the balls of her feet. *Who woulda thought the stuff they taught in high wire class would come in handy? And I used to think high-wire class was as useful as algebra was to a lion.*

The floor bucked wildly, as if it had become the ocean and they were surfers hanging ten.

Aloha, Jeeves and Clem finally fell flat on their bellies. Their screams and yells overlapped making it impossible to discern one voice from the other as they were tossed about like rag dolls. Panic ensured and everyone yelled at once.

"Hey!"

"What's happening!"

"Mommy!"

Good thing I don't know who said that last one.

"Yikes!" Her arms were straight out from her body, but still she stumbled back and forth on the undulating floor.

A pale-faced Toulest finally slammed into the hallway wall using her hands and body pressed against it top stay standing. "What's happening?"

"Did you ever see Carrie?" Toulest yelled.

Shelby nodded. Once a late night horror movie hostess, always a late night horror movie hostess. "Yeah. Stephen King. The guy from Pulp Fiction, John Travolta. Young girl with telekinetic powers kills her high school senior class at the prom. Babe had issues. What about it?"

The floor shifted violently beneath her feet, slamming Shelby into the wall causing her to stumble. She end up pinned by the force of gravity against the wall next to the button.

Toulest's wide eyes reflected raw fear.

You've seen wa-a-ayy too many of those B-grade scary movies, lady, thought Shelby.

"Do you remember the end when the house is sucked into the earth?"

Shelby nodded as she dodged a section of plaster from the ceiling that fell next to her. "Yeah. So?"

"We--the house and everyone in it---are going to be sucked into the Earth just like in the movie Carrie. It's going to be the big dramatic finish to the show. No one wins. And no one gets the prize," Toulest yelled. "You've killed us all!" A loud crack sounded above her, and Toulest jumped to her right when a wooden railing from the staircase above them slammed into the floor just missing her. "That isn't the plan."

"And how do you know? And why should I believe you?" *She's lying. Zero wants us dead. He always wanted us dead. Destroy the evidence. And keep the prize for himself.* "You've been part of this big lie from the beginning."

Toulest fell to the floor on her butt with a *smack* as the floor shuddered and enormous cracking sounds rendered the air. "No! I'm just an actor."

Chalky dust floated through the air, filling Shelby's nose and mouth. She coughed and pushed herself away from the wall as a large crack started from the top and tore down the wall at an angle and a section came loose and hit the floor.

Oops! She could be right. But when someone other than me is right it's just wrong. She spat dust from her mouth. *Yuk! House doesn't taste so good.*

Cracks snaked up the walls, and across the ceiling, and floor. *Yup, Madame Toulest was right. We're doomed. I've killed us all.* In an attempt to be heard over the sounds of the house coming apart Shelby shouted, "All right, I believe you! What can we do to stop this?!"

Toulest shouted back, "48-27-15-16-57." Looking over her shoulder from the floor, the old woman's face paled, and she screamed as a crack opened up beneath her. Her screams echoed as she dropped out of sight through the gaping wound in the floor.

Numbers? But what do the numbers mean? Shelby moved back toward the red *in-case-of-emergency* button. Something Toulest said niggled at her. The answer had to be there somewhere in the fine print.

She quickly scanned the floor and patted down her pockets. *I lost the magnifying glass.* Squinting, she studied the long line of fine of black printing along the edge of the sign. She braced her feet far enough apart to keep maintain her balance against the constant undulating floor. She coughed. *Can't breathe.* Tears filled her eyes from the dust as she blinked several times. *Must concentrate.*

The screams echoed over the sounds of cracking timber and falling debris. The staircase creaked accompanied by the sounds of wood rendering. Shelby cringed. *Ouch, that hurts my ears.* She peered closer at the button., *There!* Near the end of the string of tiny characters were a few words she could just make out. *If pressed in error, the reset code must be entered within five minutes.*

Reset code? That's it! Numbers were the key. But where do I enter the numbers? She quickly scanned the wall for sign of a hidden panel or keypad of some kind. *Nothing. No keypad. Nuts!*

If I'm right, we're one minute from doomsday. Besides, it says so in the fine print.

Suddenly the floor shifted and a gap opened in the floor beneath her. She grabbed the button and hung off it to keep from falling through.

This is so not good.

Thirty-Two

"48-27-15-16-57! 48-27-15-16-57!" Shelby hung from the red button, her feet hovering above the gap in the floor, her eyes closed, yelling the numbers repeatedly as loud as she could hoping something, anything, would happen.

Suddenly the shaking, undulating floors stopped. From overhead, she heard creaking as the house settled. In the distance something heavy crashed. It sounded like an elephant tripping. *And I know that sound.*

Hope the others are okay.

A rushing sound made her look up, and she saw a board falling toward her from above. *It's going to hit me.* She looked down and saw the jagged hole beneath her. *And that won't be good.* She swung her legs back and forth then, held her breath and swung away from the button for the last time, she closed her eyes and let go. She flew through the air and landed on her back just as the board whizzed by where she'd been seconds ago. She lay still breathing deeply.

The board made repeated bangs as it struck the walls that echoed from the gap in the floor.

Opening her eyes, which stung from sweat that had dripped down her face, she wrinkled her nose. Shattered wood, heavy beams, dust from plaster stretched across the foyer blocking the doors to the dining room and the library. Cracked floorboards and partially collapsed interior walls lay about her in piles as high as her waist. The dining room, the library and the kitchen were now buried in rubble. The debris also blocked the front door. *I can't go that way.*

239

But a large tear about three feet high and two feet wide had opened in the outside wall.

I hope the others are okay.

She tried to move, but something heavy across her legs and waist stopped her. Looking down, she saw a two by four rested across her body. Grunting with effort, she used both of her hands to heave the piece of wood off her. Rolling over she pushed herself up. She winced as she stood, and a stabbing pain shot up her right leg. *Crap that hurts! Hope I didn't break a bone.* She took two steps, stopped and winced. *I think I'm okay. I have to be.* She ran a hand down her leg and felt dampness. *But I'm bleeding.*

Thankfully, the hole in the outside wall is large enough for me to squeeze through.

"I'm *so* outta here," she muttered. "I don't care where it leads just as long as it's out of here." A darkened room was visible through the hole in the wall. *I'll look for the others once I'm outside. At least I hope this leads to the outside. I wish I knew where I was going.* She looked around at the shattered hallway and the heaps of rubble. *But what choice do I have?*

She limped to the small opening, her hand clasping her wounded leg. *I'm walkin' like a movie-zombie. Can you say irony?*

I'll live. But did it have to be my favorite jeans?

After stumbling through the rip in the wall, she found the other side lit up from a dropped flashlight. Four people, two tall and two small, lay on their backs on the floor side by side. The room she had just walked into was the basement? *Oh, man, why does it have to be the basement? I'm never going into a basement again. Ever.*

She retrieved the flashlight and used it to see their faces. *Aloha, Clem and Jeeves. Thank God.* They were breathing, but unconscious. She placed their hands over their bodies. They were dirty, but not bleeding. Aloha had lost her head bandages somewhere along the way.

How am I gonna get them out of here?

She swung to flashlight over the fourth figure. Her heart beat harder. *Buster?* "Hey, Shelby!" *He's awake!* "Keep that thing outta my eyes will ya."

Shelby wiped at her eyes with her sleeve and she realized she'd found her brother *alive!* She swallowed a laugh. "Buster!"

"Me, too," Clem stirred.

"Me, three," added Aloha standing up.

"And me, as well, mademoiselle." *And Jeeves.*

"What happened to you guys?" Shelby reached out and hugged Buster. "I'm so glad you're all safe."

"When the ground shook, we hit the floor, and then we were fallin'. Has there been an earthquake or sumthin?" asked Buster. His question buzzed like bees in Shelby's brain. *Operation overload.*

"Where's Wills?" Shelby looked around but there was no else.

Buster shrugged. "We got separated when the floor collapsed."

Shelby sighed and released her brother. "To answer your question, no it wasn't an earthquake. As far as I can tell, I pushed a doomsday button." She grinned sheepishly. "I almost Carrie'd our butts before I figured out how to stop the end of the world."

"Can we get outta here?" Aloha's tone dripped with sarcasm.

"Sure." Shelby looked at the staircase they'd used to get to the basement. *It looks like a heap of broken matchsticks.*

We're so not going that way.

~ * ~

A clown stepped out from a corner of the basement. Shelby recognized him. *Sparkles? Where'd he come from?*

Shelby's face broke into a wide smile and chuckled. *Boy, everyone's coming out of the woodwork.* Her chuckle erupted into full-blown laughter. Her stomach muscles hurt from laughing and tears streamed down her cheeks.

"Hey, guys what did I do?" Sparkles wore a wrinkled frown on his face. His brown eyes were serious. "Did I say sumthin' funny?"

Suddenly, Matt, Madame Toulest, and Herbie stepped from the gloom behind Sparkles.

Oh, my. I must be dreaming. How can this be? So Stargate. Cool. She sighed. *Whatever. I'm just glad to see they're all okay.*

She looked at Aloha, Clem, Buster and Jeeves who joined her, and her eyes brimmed with tears from happiness.

"You okay, sis?" Buster grinned. "You're sure laughing."

"Yeah. Better than ever, bro." *But I wonder where Reggie is?*

Matt had a white strip of cloth tied around his head like a bandanna.

This is the weirdest group I've ever seen. The Weirdsville gang formed a horseshoe shaped semicircle around her in the confined basement. Their eyes flitted between her and each other.

Shelby began to laugh uncontrollably.

"What's wrong?" Aloha moved closer, her movements uncertain.

Shelby waved her away still unable to speak through her choking laughter.

Buster shrugged. "Is there a doctor in the house?"

Clem frowned. "What kinda stupid question is that?"

Buster shrugged. "I don't know. I thought that's what you say at a time like this. At least that's what they say in the movies and on TV."

"Well, we gotta do sumthin." Buster sounded determined to act.

"Now that's more like it." Shelby stopped laughing. "There's nothing wrong with me. I'm just so relieved."

Suddenly there was a deep rumble, followed by an entire wall of the basement swinging aside to reveal the dimly lit sound stage and a startled Reggie.

Thirty Three

SHELBY SAT ON A CHAIR on the soundstage, her body weary with fatigue. One arm lay across Buster's shoulders as he sat in the chair next to her. He grinned at her. Aloha sat on the steps of the old house, her arms rested limply on her thighs, her face smudged with dirt, her red hair askew. The clowns and the zombies lay around the stage floor in a loose circle comparing notes on what they'd seen and heard.

Aloha glanced at her and offered a thin-lipped smile. Shelby nodded at the L.I.P.S. agent. The smile lines at the corners of Aloha's green eyes wrinkled.

The show's over. We can go home. Too bad, there was no prize and, regardless of what that MacFee guy told me and Reggie, we'll never find the diamond. Her eyes traveled over the partially collapsed house. *No one can go in there anymore. It's not safe.*

Suddenly a man appeared form around the side of the house. Best described as a taller than average man, he wore a gray pinstriped Armani suit, black gleaming Italian leather shoes, and a red silk power tie. His short dark curls were peppered with grey.

"Dad?" Reggie stood and his gray flesh paled. "What are you doing here?"

Dad?

The man's blue eyes twinkled.

Whoa! Reggie really is his father's son.

"The King of Gnotborst?" She stood and dusted off her jeans.

He bowed slightly from the waist. "Yes, King Gustav the Third. You have me at a disadvantage, Miss?"

243

"Shelby Bass." Stepping forward, she bowed her head but kept her eyes fixed on his. *Handsome gene pool ya got there, kingy.*

King Gustav bent down and took Shelby's right hand in his. Then he lightly kissed the back of her sooty and dusty hand. "Pleased to meet you, my dear. Your father has told me so much about you."

The king released her hand and stepped back.

Shelby stared at the King of Gnotborst. Her eyes narrowed. *A King and a guy named MacFee know my father? Weird.*

"In fact, it is a pleasure to meet you all."

He waved one hand toward the shadows. "Please come be my guests."

"Where? How? The show's not over and we're under contract." Shelby smiled to herself. *Yeah right. Shows over for me.* She glanced at her brothers' weary eyes. *And I'm, not the only one.*

The King nodded and a ruddy faced man in a tweed blazer appeared from behind him.

"Oh, never mind." Shelby crossed to where Aloha sat and patted the agent on her leg. "What's the worst that can happen?"

"We have a lot to talk about." King Gustav smiled at Reggie, who gaped at his father. "Don't we, Reginald?"

~ * ~

After spending time cleaning up, showering and dressing in fresh clothes the midday desert heat outside the sound stage hit her like a wall. The King explained the studio building was no longer safe. *Duh.* They were to be his guests at a royal reception. *I noticed he left out what the reception was for. I'm worried. Why hasn't Aloha arrested me, and my brothers and I should be in handcuffs not attending a fancy dinner party..*

Reggie gave her a gentle kiss on her cheek and a hug before he left her to go with his father. *Dumping me so soon, eh? I knew it. Back to my old life. Circuses, break and enters. Diamonds that need losing.* She hung her head and a tear ran down her cheek. *It's not fair.*

Shuffling her feet, she walked around the corner of the building to see an elaborate red, white, and blue striped tent, much like the ones the circus used, set up in the middle of the studio parking lot. In its heyday, the lot must have been able to easily handle a thousand cars. The tent covered at least half the parking lot.

She shielded her eyes from the bright sunlight then fell in line with her brothers, the clowns, and the zombies. and they shuffled across the cracked pavement toward the massive tent. *Now the dirty, tired group looked like zombies. Great. Off to jail we go.* Aloha appeared from the tent. She was smiling. She came up beside Shelby.

"Everything okay?"

"Yeah, sure. Why?"

"Nothing. Never mind." *I guess she's not going to arrest us.*

MacFee appeared from the side of the wrecked studio building, looking unscathed. He accompanied the rag tag group to the tent.

Shelby detected a scent. *That smell. Cinnamon?* Craning her neck, she gazed up at MacFee. *It's coming from him? What do ya know, MacFee must have been everywhere in the house.*

The smiling King walked to greet them. He nodded to MacFee as he approached.

Being in the middle of the group, Shelby looked up then down the line. *Our chain gang.*

The King waved MacFee aside speaking to him in low tones, but she could hear the conversation between them. "Is everything ready?" The King spoke softly.

MacFee nodded, his expression grim. "Yes, Highness. Exactly as you instructed." *Why is he always so serious? Does he even have a funny bone in his body like the rest of us?*

The King fixed his eyes on MacFee. "And the others?"

Shamus nodded.

Gustav smiled. "I would expect nothing less."

Shelby frowned as she didn't want to be a pawn anymore. *When am I gonna find out what's going on? MacFee suggested Dad had made a deal with this royal dude. Why? For what? This stupid reality show is my farewell performance with the family Bass, no matter what deal Dad made.*

She marched, head down as she entered the tent. *I'll just slip under the flap and be gone before they know it.* A blast of cooled air washed over her sweaty body. *Man, does that feel good. I can escape later.*

~ * ~

A couple of hours later and major clean up, she walked inside the tent and scanned the room. A sea of men of various ages, were dressed in white ties and tails and women clad in beautiful sequined covered evening gowns representing every rainbow of color mingled and were engrossed in conversation. All eyes shifted toward Shelby and the group.

I'm so wa-a-ayy underdressed for this. I feel like Cinderella at the ball.

She backed up toward the exit. *I'll go get lost in the desert.* "Listen, I think I took a wrong turn somewhere. Sorry. Go on with your party. I'll be running along."

A man with toothpaste-white teeth chuckled as he stepped in her way. He wore a white shirt, ruby red vest with a matching bow tie and shiny black pants. He gently took one of her hands in his. "No, Miss Bass. You and your friends are the guests of honor." The evening gown and trying to walk in heels was much more difficult than she imagined. *Good thing I'm not tall or timberrrr.*

She had agreed to wear the heels after practicing for twenty minutes, but she still wobbled like the Sears tower in a high wind. With her head held high and with renewed confidence, she stepped into the main area of the tent and almost bumped into Reggie.

"Reggie? Is that you?" She scanned him up and down unable to believe he was the same zombie. *He's a vision of masculine prowess.* His once gray zombie skin was hidden behind a makeup artist's skill.

Whoa! Cool! Makeup is a beautiful thing.

She could see the clear desert sky through the tent's opening. An ocean of brilliant twinkling stars dusted across the dark sky.

"Well, look who showed up. Finally, we can eat," Buster grumbled after he sat at the banquet table. The dedicated foodie of the Bass clan had a fork and knife in his hands.

A maroon colored cloth napkin lay draped down the front of his white dress shirt.

She smiled. *He's never looked so handsome.* She gave him a thumbs up. *A tux does wonders for the average guy.*

Her brothers, and her new friends, were all washed, prepped and dressed to the nines just like she and Reggie.

What is dressed to the nines anyway? Why not dressed to the tens?

Reggie took her hand in his. A thrill ran through her. He must have sensed her excitement because his blue eyes looked deep into hers and he mouthed silently, *You okay?*

She nodded and her cheeks grew warm.

Reggie chuckled and nodded in kind.

She wanted to enjoy this moment. *How much longer would he last? Sure, the makeup made him look normal right now, but what about when his skin peeled away? Can I tolerate being married to a rack of bones? Can he remember to watch where he walks so he doesn't run me over? And can he remember not to walk too fast in shopping malls so I don't get left behind? It's been known to happen.*

Sure, these behaviors were simple, little things, but it was usually the simple things that made life so complicated, never mind building lasting relationships. Mixed marriages between tallies and little people could be more difficult and the challenges more to overcome.

But there was time later to think about all this. This night was for celebration. At last, the stupid reality show and game were over.

She looked into Reggie's eyes and got lost in those baby blues. *Let the future take care of itself. Tonight is our night, even if it's our last together.*

King Gustav appeared from behind the tent wall. An elegantly dressed woman with amused grey eyes stood beside him. Sunlight made her steel gray shine highlighting the elegant silver strands . The regal woman wore a diamond-encrusted tiara on her head, and a red sash with a gold coat of arms embossed on the satin fabric. King Gustav wore a matching sash across the chest of his tuxedo. *Whoa. Is this the Queen of Gnotborst? Cool.*

The King held his wife's white gloved hand in his. *They're the royal flush. Cool.*

A man wearing a long tailed red tuxedo adorned with gold buttons and a white wig on his head opened his mouth, "Presenting their Royal Highnesses Queen Helena and King Gustav of Gnotborst."

Shelby leaned toward Reggie and whispered, "I thought you told me your dad was an ambassador? Not a freakin' king."

"Yeah," Reggie winced. "Sorry. My father is a King, but he disowned me when I became a zombie."

Intrigue in the royal court? Interesting. Something else worried her more than politics, ever since the King appeared. *I hope they don't know about the diamond or my butt's in a sling for sure. I hear penitentiaries are really hard to escape from.*

Shelby watched Reggie wait until the Queen and the King were seated then he pulled back her chair and, after she sat, he took his seat. *A real royal gentleman.*

Reggie glanced at Shelby, he grinned then rose and walked to the head of the table. A hush dropped over the room as the murmur of voices disappeared. *Where's he going?*

After bowing deeply, "Mother."

Reggie's so royal, so cool. Who woulda thought?

The King cleared his throat and frowned over at his son.

Reggie obviously caught his father's meaning because he fell silent.

"Pardon me, your Majesty. I have a question." Reggie bowed his head quickly toward his mother.

The King's features were darkened by a frown.

Uh, oh. He's not a happy camper.

"Yes, my son?" His mother spoke with a twinkle in her eyes.

"What's happening here? When I left home--or more correctly, when they kicked me out," his eyes flitted to the King then back at the Queen, "father and you were in Washington--"

His mother silenced him with one gloved finger pressed over his lips. "A lot has changed...your father and I have come to an understanding." Her eyes narrowed. "I am the Queen," she eyed her husband. "I speak for the kingdom now."

The king's rugged features turned crimson.

"But I thought dad was the guy in charge, I mean he's the freakin' King." Reggie scratched his arm.

"Yes, but my darling son *I* am the *freakin'* Queen so I'm now I'm 'calling the shots' as they say in America." She nodded at the King. "I told your father you were to be reinstated as prince and brought back from exile."

The Queen nodded. "But now is not the time for explanations. Now is the time for celebration." She clapped her hands and servers appeared carrying trays of roast chicken, steaming broccoli, cobs of corn, cucumbers, scalloped potatoes, and fresh fruit.

Reggie returned to his seat, his head bent and brow pinched into a frown.

"What's that all about?" whispered Shelby in his ear after he sat.

Reggie leaned over and whispered. "I don't know exactly, but I think I smell a rat."

Now Shelby was worried. Reggie's mother had somehow been *promoted*--if promoted is even the right word--to Queen of the whole enchilada in the old country. And this had somehow allowed their disgraced son back into the family business.

My Spidey senses are so tingly right now.

Just when he was out and on his own, now his parents wanted to drag Reggie back in. What was this, The Godfather Part Four? And if this was the mob movie then who was Al Pacino? She hid a giggle behind her gloved hand.

Reggie cast her a mischievous smile. "This is no time for funny business." He winked. "Funny business comes later."

Her face grew warm. *At least he hasn't lost his sense of humor.*

The King rose to his feet and tapped the crystal glass next to his plate with his fork. "Your Majesty, my son, ladies and gentlemen." The room fell silent and the guests straightened in their seats. The servants stepped back from the table and folded their hands in front of them.

"We are here today to honor the winners of the first season of the reality show *Bachelorette: After the Prize!*" The King paused to pick up a crystal goblet, "I give you Happy, Sparkles, Aloha, Matt, Prince Reginald Kincade, Herbie, and my future daughter-in-law, Shelby Bass."

Everyone at the head table stood. All except Shelby who stared at Reggie, her eyes wide and her cheeks warm.

What? He's kidding. Daughter in law? Who says?

Reggie squirmed under her gaze, but she slowly rose to her feet. Everyone raised their glasses in a toast.

"To these intrepid heroes who have saved us all from certain doom." The King looked to either side of him down the table. The clowns, little people and zombies smiled looked back at him.

He continued. "These heroes have each earned a share in the five million dollar cash prize for winning the show and a small percentage of the profits from a new product about to be released to the world."

Everyone drained their glasses then the King placed his glass on the table and picked up a canister next to his plate. *Flea spray maybe? It certainly isn't what I imagined eternal life would look like. At least I don't think so.* A brown wrapper hid the container's label.

With one swift tug, the King pulled down the wrapper to reveal words.

Shelby straightened in her chair and stared at the can. *I must be seeing things.* She blinked. *I don't believe it!*

Her eyes went wide. "Is that?"

The King grinned. "Yes. It will cure zombies with three easy treatments. Prince Reginald has already had one treatment. A month from now he will receive another, and then another a month after that he will be fully recovered." He winked at Reggie. "Maybe even sooner with half-made zombies."

"But how?" Matt barely contained his excitement.

King Gustav chuckled. "Aren't we the inquisitive one?"

Shelby could feel the heat rush up to her cheeks but kept her eyes focused on the canister. If she looked up at Reggie's healthy skin, she might cry.

The florescent purple label read, *Zombie Away*!

It was the miracle she'd been hoping for. A way to break the Mambo's spell. A way for Reggie and her to be together. *Forever.*

Her eyes narrowed as she held her breath. All during the game just when victory seemed at hand something awful happened. But this time nothing happened. *I'm not taking any chances.*

Letting her breath out, Shelby climbed onto the chair's seat and faced the King. Now at eye level with him, "Your Highness, I mean no disrespect, but given what's happened I'm understandably cautious about declaring total victory."

250

"Shelby," The King's voice was heavy with emotion. "This is real. Your dreams are about to come true. The Queen bought out Zero lock, stock, and production company."

"We hired the best special effects company in the world," he paused and looked at Matt and Sparkles, "and hired some insiders."

Reggie shot Matt an annoyed look.

Matt smiled and shrugged. "Sorry, buddy. He made me an offer I couldn't refuse."

Reggie smiled weakly and sighed. "That's okay, buddy."

"Your Highness," Shelby interrupted, "What has this got to do with me and Reggie?

The edges of King Gustav's mouth curled slightly at the corners. "Miss Bass," he paused and looked at the Queen.

The Queen continued for her husband. "The succession of sons or daughters to the throne in Gnotborst tradition is governed by a test. The heir must prove himself by passing a test that the sitting monarch decides will test his skills to be the future king."

"You mean?" Shelby's eyes widened.

The King nodded. "Yes. This game's a test for Reggie."

"But we could have been--"

"No, Miss Bass. You and the others were never in any danger. And I assure you no one died. My head of security, Shamus MacFee foiled Zero at every turn. In the end, Zero tried to wipe out all the evidence of his deeds, and this destruction included all of you. Zero installed a self destruct mechanism in the house to destroy it." The King nodded at MacFee, who finally smiled. "Fortunately, MacFee had already secured enough evidence to ensure his conviction."

Shelby frowned. "Yes, but what about this *Zombie Away*? I mean how many zombies could there be in the world?"

King Gustav offered a wry smile. "Actually, my dear, there are a lot more zombies in the world than you would imagine."

Shelby's eyes narrowed. *I'm such a doubting Thomasina.*

Finally, Shelby laughed and her shoulders relaxed. "Okay. I'll buy it. Why not? It's no crazier that what we've been through."

The King and Queen laughed, too, which started everyone in the tent laughing. *Is there a laugh sign around here somewhere?*

Reggie held out his hands, which were now pink and healthy. The gray had disappeared completely. "How do you explain me?"

Shelby stared at him uncomprehendingly. Then slowly her features shifted to wonderment. "Arnold Zero has a cure for your affliction?" Her eyes widened as if seeing what should have been obvious for the first time. *Reggie is a prince and he loves me and Zero had the cure all along that would finally bring us together.* She resisted the urge to scream with joy.

"Well, not him exactly, but certainly his research and development department at Big Art Films," the King explained.

"So a low rent Hollywood film production company comes up with the cure of the century and refuses to share the secret?" All of the pieces were finally falling into place. "So, in order to save your only son, and the heir to the throne from a fate worse than death, you bought out Zero. And now you have control of the secret recipe."

The King nodded.

Why not? "Cool!"

"It wasn't as easy as all that. Zero gave us some problems, that's why there were some changes in the script." MacFee shrugged his broad shoulders.

Shelby glanced at Reggie, who smiled at her with a hint of lust in his eyes. "Well in that case, Majesties, I must tell you, I love your son with all my heart."

Reggie gazed at his father. "You called Shelby your future daughter-in-law, Dad. Shelby's a commoner. But I love her, and I'll give up the throne. I'll--"

The Queen held up one hand to silence Reggie, then smiled warmly at Shelby. "As the winners of the contest, we will dub you Lady Shelby and induct you into the royal line of Gnotborst."

"You can do that?" Buster's voice squeaked from down the table.

"My dear, Buster Bass, I am *the* Queen. I can do anything. Our constitution is subject to much interpretation." She smiled mischievously. "Our country is a melting pot from around Europe, Asia, and the Americas, so we try to keep it loose." With the fingers of her right hand, she made the hang loose symbol so popular in Hawaii. Everyone seated around the table chuckled.

Reggie's eyes narrowed. "What about Zero and Wills? What did Zero get? I mean surely he wouldn't sell such a valuable prize cheaply."

Aloha spoke up. "We have Zero in custody."

"For what?" Shelby asked.

Aloha grinned. "For fraud, bribery, making threats, kidnapping, and for spitting on the sidewalk."

You go, girl.

The King's mouth formed a grim line and his eyes hardened. "After Zero sold the studio to us, he wanted to rule the world. And he demanded ransom money by threatening to kill Reggie and the group unless we paid a hefty sum. He then used the secret of the prize as the carrot to attract every megalomaniac in the world who wanted to buy the secret and corner the market for their own devious purposes."

"But he didn't have the rights to anything?" Reggie smiled.

The Queen smiled and her eyes narrowed. "Exactly. He double-crossed us all. Even the despots." She paused. "Once he had everyone's money, and the power of the *Zombie Away,* he intended to build an army of zombies and take over the world. Eventually, he'd be the richest, most influential zombie maker in the world."

Aloha nodded. "Instead, if convicted he'll spend five life sentences in a Federal Penitentiary. We at the L.I.P.S. *really* hate megalomaniacs."

Shelby looked at her new BFF relieved she wouldn't be arrested. "But I thought you were on suspension?"

The L.I.P.S. agent grinned. "I had to make you believe that. Sorry. I was operating undercover. It sure felt good when I slapped the handcuffs around Zero's tiny wrists and they didn't fall off." She leaned closer to Shelby and wiggled her eyebrows. "I had them specially modified just for this arrest." Aloha straightened in her chair. "I made the Super Bowl of arrests. The L.I.P.S. is very proud."

She poked her chest with her thumb. "You're looking at the new senior agent in charge of all paranormal cases for Nevada, Mongolia, and Western Samoa."

"Wow, congratulations," Shelby chuckled, "very cool." *Mongolia?* A small smile played across her lips. *I've definitely changed. I even like clowns now. Who woulda thought?*

"I've been meaning to ask you something, Aloha." The L.I.P.S. agent looked at her expectantly. "You said all those accidents, to my mom, and the clowns mom and dad weren't accidents. How did you know?"

"As I told you before the L.I.P.S. files are very complete about all of you and you'll be pleased to know we've made arrests in all those cases as well. As I said this case is the Super Bowl of arrests."

"Wow. No kidding?"

"I never kid."

And I believe her.

"What about Wills?" Reggie shifted his gaze to his father.

"He's working for us, now," the King explained.

Shelby's features grew warm and her gaze shifted to stare down at the table. The tent hummed with hushed conversation and the *tink* of forks and knifes on fine china as guests ate and talked.

I'm afraid to ask, but I have to know. If I never find out, I'll always think I came here for nothing.

"What about the diamond?" she whispered. *This is the end. I'm a goner. Wedding gown to prison garb all in one week. Not bad, girl.*

Reggie leaned down to whisper in her ear, "How are we supposed to get hitched without a ring?" Her eyes came up to meet his and she smiled.

"That's all the talking we need for now." The Queen took her seat again. "How about we eat this fine dinner our palace chef has prepared for us before it gets cold?"

"Yeah, enough of this jawin'. I'm hungry." Clem grabbed his throat as if he were starving. His stomach growled loudly.

The silent group turned their eyes on Clem then the tent erupted with raucous laughter and wild applause.

Shelby turned her head slightly toward Reggie. *I guess I am the bachelorette, after all.* A small smile formed at the edges of her mouth. *And I won my zombie.*

She turned to face forward. *Boy, this sure doesn't suck.*

About the Author

International selling author, Russ Crossley writes romance under the name Russ Crossley, mystery/suspense under the name R.G. Crossley, and science fiction and fantasy under his own. This year there will be re-issues the romantic comedies, My Zombie Prince and Antique Virgin by 53rd Street Publishing, paranormal romantic comedy, Zomopolis, and a new western romance entitled, The Fire In Their Hearts co-authored with R.S. Meger will be published in 2013 by Champagne Books. Also, look for another Aloha adventure, Bloody Betty Queen of the Pirates, coming later in 2013.

His latest science fiction satire set in the far future, Revenge of the Lushites, is a sequel to Attack of the Lushites released in 2011. The latest title in the series will be released in the fall of 2013. Both titles are available in e-book and trade paperback.

He has sold several short stories that have appeared in anthologies from Pocket Books, St. Martins Press, at Smashwords, Amazon, and other e-retail sites.

With his wife, romance author R.S. Meger, he owns and operates a small press publishing company, 53rd Street Publishing. The company began in April 2011 and now has over one hundred e-book titles and over twenty-five print titles, with more planned in 2013 and 2014.

He is a member of SF Canada and the Greater Vancouver Chapter of Romance Writers of America. He is also an alumni of the Oregon Coast Professional Fiction Writers Master Class taught by award winning author/editors, Kristine Katherine Rusch and Dean Wesley Smith.

To find a complete listing of his work check out his website http://www.rghart.com, http://russstory.blogspot.com.Razor's blog can be found at http://razorandedge.blogspot.com

Feel free to contact him on Facebook or Twitter. He loves to hear from readers

Other books by the Author

Titles as R.G. Crossley

Short Stories

Razor and Edge Mysteries
The Kidnapping of Billy Buttons
String of Pearls
Death by Clown
Beggin' For Murder
Ragged Ice
The Grand Central Mystery
A Strange Case of Undead Murder

Jazz Stiletto Mysteries
A Day Without Sunshine
Skullduggery

Non-Series Mysteries
Mirror Image
Dangerous Waters
Cape Disappointment
Boomerang
The Watcher of Wayburn Street
The Apprentice
Drip!
A Beautiful Friendship and The Parrot of Doom
Robine's Diary
The Christmas Club
Loose Ends
Splatter Pattern
It Takes Two

Anthologies
The Adventures of Razor and Edge:

Five Tales From The Quirky Detective Team

Novels
A Bad Case of Loyalty
The Last Serial Killer
Shear Murder

Titles as Russ Crossley

Novels
Attack of the Lushites
Revenge of the Lushites

Short Stories
Countdown
Shoeless Moe
Round Up At The Burger Bar:
The Story of Trixie Pug, Parts 1, 2, 3, 4, 5, 6, 7
Five Minutes
Blossom Queen, Barbarian
The Secret
The Family Line
End of the Flies
With Death You Get the Eggroll
The Penguin Sleeps With The Fishes
Only The Worthy
Hero For A Day
End of Empire
Strange Bedfellows
Big Business
A Perfect Crime
The Wise Guy and The Pirates
In Search of the Perfect Cup
T.I.N. Men
The Legend of G and the Dragonettes
The Incredible Mr. Fix-It
Lock Stock and Barrel

Divided Loyalties
Cave of Wonders
A Family Empire
Until We Meet Again
Dragon Rising

Presents Anthology Series
Tales of Urban Fantasy
Five Tales of Bizarre Detectives
Tales of Mystery and Suspense
Tales of Weird Fantasy
Spies, Detectives, & Heroes
Tales of Twisted Crime
Tales of The Unexpected
Tales From Space
10 by Russ Crossley
Round Up At The Burger Bar: The Story of Trixie Pug,
Parts 1- 5 The Beginning
Worlds of Science Fiction and Fantasy
More Tales of Mystery and Suspense
Ladies of the Jolly Roger
Justice Served

Titles as Russ Crossley

Short Stories
Tikka's Big Day
"My Partner the Zombie" —
Hungry For Your Love Anthology
(St. Martin's Press)
Big Hairy Deal
One Red Shoe
A Bad Day in Lunden Texas
Hook Island
Grind Manor
Bloody Betty, Queen of the Pirates

Anthologies
Love Stories

Novels
My Zombie Prince
Antique Virgin
The Fire In Their Hearts
with R.S. Meger (coming soon from Champagne Books)
Zomopolis

www.ingramcontent.com/pod-product-compliance
Lightning Source LLC
Chambersburg PA
CBHW032211190626
46810CB00019B/2436